IN THE SILENCE OF DECAY

PINTER P.I. SERIES

BOOK 1

LISA BOYLE

ISBN: 978-1-7366077-7-0 (Ebook)

ISBN: 978-1-7366077-6-3 (Paperback)

Copy Editor/Proofreader: Constance Renfrow

Cover Designer: Rafael Andres

This book is for my parents.

My mom who gave me the writing bug and introduced me to suspense stories. Thank you for always bringing Mary Higgins Clark books to the beach.

And my dad who has encouraged me to put my writing out into the world since I was eight years old. Your bragging on my behalf is no longer embarrassing.

I love you both.

LINDA

LINDA MORRIS LOOKED at herself in the small, rectangular mirror on her car's sun visor. A little bit of lipstick smudged her tooth. She tried to get it off with her tongue, then with a napkin from the glove compartment. This was the expensive stuff. She had picked it up on her last trip to Albuquerque, two years ago now.

The car was turned off, the heat creeping in. In the back seat, Adriel flipped the page of his comic book. She hadn't meant to bring him, but her babysitter canceled, and she still didn't want to talk to Kay for any reason. Linda thought about how lonely she'd been recently. After finding out what she had about her own husband. The man who had held her when she was at her lowest. The man she thought she knew. And then, her sister turned on her, too. Linda wasn't always great at communicating, she knew. She had tried to tell Kay, but by then, Kay was too angry and wouldn't listen.

Linda gazed at Adriel in the mirror. What she wouldn't give to hear him say "I love you" just once. Still, she knew he did love her. Their hearts felt like two sides of the same coin sometimes, alternating beats. She could anticipate his needs by now, knew what he was thinking and feeling. She wondered if that would stop one day. If she would wake up one morning when Adriel was sixteen and no longer know him at all. The thought made her chest ache.

She closed the mirror and snapped the sun visor into place.

"You ready, my little cub? This shouldn't take long."

Adriel nodded without looking up. They both stepped from the car, and he tucked the comic book under his arm so he could hold her hand.

Meeting at a gas station was a little strange, Linda thought, but she guessed it was safe, because it was off the reservation, and of course, the ridiculous teepee building made for an obvious landmark. She scanned the parking lot. Her heart sped up. She didn't know why. This was the right thing to do. She was sure of it. Had already made peace with her decision. Still, her skin crawled, and she thought about pulling Adriel back toward the car. Speeding off along the highway. Forgetting about the whole thing forever. But she didn't. She stepped forward, stood up straighter, and gave Adriel's hand a small squeeze.

MOLLY

MOLLY STARED at her father like he was a stranger. And to her, he was. She couldn't have remembered their first meeting on the tarmac, wrapped in her mother's arms. The way Sergeant Pinter had dropped his bag, buried his face in his hands, and sobbed. That had been thirteen years ago, during the thick of the Vietnam War. Molly had been a baby. She had no memories of this man. Only stories.

He stepped closer. Close enough for her to see his green-brown eyes, the three wrinkles that spread from the corners of each like tree roots, his mouth that twitched a little on each side as if he wanted to smile but didn't quite know how. A few strands of his dark-brown hair fell into his eyes.

Molly scanned the parking lot. She felt so alone here. Isolated. The Texas Panhandle. Where the highway stretched into the sky. It was all one thing. The dusty ground. The sky. Her and her father and his big rig behind him. The flatness could do that to a person. Distort their reality.

"You must be hungry," her father said.

The diner was playing Waylon Jennings, and Molly had never before seen so many men in one place who were different but still the same. She bet they all knew each other. It was hard to be certain, though, since just about no one spoke. They all wore jeans and boots, just like her dad, and stared into their coffee mugs or read the newspaper or pushed scrambled eggs around their plates. One of them was talking to an older waitress. Made her laugh a big, loud laugh that seemed out of place. Other than Waylon, it was the only other sound Molly could hear.

The door swung shut behind them with a ding, getting stuck in the rug. By the time they sat down, that same waitress was already pouring her dad a cup of coffee.

"Mornin', Jimmy," she said. He had introduced himself to Molly as James. Molly's mother had always called him James, but this waitress called him Jimmy. He smiled. The waitress smiled back and then looked at Molly.

"And who's this pretty lady?" she asked. Her nametag said June. She wore fake eyelashes. Molly supposed June was old enough to be her grandmother and so probably too old to know that no one was doing that anymore.

"This is Molly," James said. Just Molly. Not "my daughter, Molly." Just Molly.

Molly smiled at the waitress, who poured her a coffee, too. If June thought it strange that this forty-year-old man—who she probably knew well enough—had brought a fourteen-year-old girl to her diner at 6 a.m., she didn't show it.

"My name's June," the waitress said. "And I take it you'll be needin' a menu?"

"Yes, please," Molly said.

"Same as always for you, Jimmy?"

"And tell Ron even easier on the eggs," James replied.

"Gosh, Jimmy, should he just crack 'em right onto your plate?"

James huffed with a small smile, and Molly wondered if he was trying to laugh.

June's big, droopy breasts moved up and down with the rest of her chest as she laughed at her own joke. She brushed her big, dyed-blond hair from her face and then went to get Molly a menu. She stopped at four tables on her way there and two more on the way back. Molly counted. June winked at her as she handed over the menu.

"Just call for me when you're ready," she said.

Molly ordered a stack of pancakes and a side of home fries and didn't say anything to her dad during the wait. She sipped her sweet, no-pulp orange juice and listened to forks scraping against plates and thought of her mom.

Their last meal together had been Molly's favorite—macaroni and cheese with cut-up hot dogs. Molly knew she was too old for that to be her favorite meal, and she would never ask for it outright. Especially not around her friends. But her mom knew.

Molly should have known right then what her mom was planning. She remembered her mom asking about Molly's best friend, Joan. About algebra class. About majorette practice. Her mom had scraped her fork against the bottom of her bowl, trying to scoop out the last bit of cheese.

She opened her eyes and realized just how long she'd been sitting there with them closed. Her dad, Jimmy—James —was staring at her. But not in a judgmental way. Or even a curious way. Just looking. He was already eating. Molly would have expected him to be nervous. Or awkward, at least. But he didn't seem to be either of those things. And for some reason, that bothered Molly.

"I'm going to the bathroom," she muttered as she tried to slide out of the booth, the sticky red plastic clinging to her legs until finally she peeled herself away. She pulled at her tight orange shorts as she stood, trying to make them longer. She didn't really have to pee. But she could feel herself getting angry at the whole thing. All of it. And she didn't want James to know she cared.

JAMES

HAD anyone asked high school football star Jimmy "Hands" Pinter what his life would look like at forty, he probably would have said a high-paying job, a beautiful wife, a big house full of kids who adored him. Not in a million years would he have said a truck driver and military failure with a dead ex-girlfriend and a daughter who might as well speak Vietnamese for as easily as the two of them communicated. Silence in the truck. Silence here at the diner.

But James had learned how much the world cared about your plans, which was not at all. So, was he surprised? No. Surprised was something he hadn't felt for some time.

He would have married Molly's mother. It was always after the next tour of duty—until it wasn't. Until she was raising a child on her own, one he didn't even know. Didn't seem to care to know. She'd mailed the ring back to him all the way from Dallas to Da Nang with a note that read, *Call me when you want to meet your daughter.*

He'd never called. Now, he shook his head. So much like Dorothy to die and leave him with a teenage girl. She'd had a special knack for being a pain in his ass—and really, his ass only. To everyone else she was warm and accommodating.

Molly finally spoke. "Mom said you were in Vietnam."

Right to it, then. James had never liked small talk much, anyway. He nodded and looked into her eyes. At the anger there. Resentment. She wasn't hiding it.

"Probably killing innocent people. Like the rest of them."

James didn't mean to laugh. It wasn't funny. Nothing about it was funny. Killing innocent people wasn't funny. A child disrespecting their dad wasn't funny. But he did laugh, and Molly looked horrified.

"Your mom ever wash your mouth out with soap for talkin' to her rude like that?"

Molly set her jaw.

"Mine did," he went on. He chuckled again before reaching for his wallet. He took out a crisp ten-dollar bill and two ones and stuck them under his coffee mug. Then he stood. He raised his arm. "Thanks, June, Ron!" he called toward the half-open kitchen.

"See ya when I see ya, Jimmy!" June called back.

The wind outside slammed the diner's door closed. Molly wrapped her arms around herself as a chunk of her light-brown hair was swept from its white clip. She stared at the looming passenger door of his truck's cab. He'd helped her in the first time, and he wondered if she'd try it herself now that she seemed sufficiently angry at him.

She could probably feel him staring and refused to turn around. After a full minute, she grabbed the side handle, climbed onto the step, and pulled at the door handle. The wind was whipping now, pulling dust up into little funnels, whining in fury, pinning Molly to the truck. She couldn't move. She just stood there. Gripping the handles, body pressed against the door.

"You gotta open the door first," James said, coming up behind her. "Then step up."

She didn't say anything, only scooted to the side as he opened the door for her. James took a long sip of the coffee June had poured into a to-go cup for him before checking all eighteen tires and getting into the driver's seat. Molly looked like she was trying to make herself as small as possible. She was scowling, arms crossed over her chest. Well, she would have to get comfortable. They had eleven hours to Phoenix.

James put the tractor into gear and pulled out onto Highway 40. It was his road—felt like it, at least. He'd driven it from Los Angeles to Raleigh many times. Now, he stayed regional. Mostly Oklahoma, Texas, New Mexico, and Arizona. There was plenty enough work right here. And on the weekends, he could sleep in his own bed in his own house.

James had thought driving would take his mind off the things he didn't want it on. And at first, it had. He'd needed to learn how to drive the thing, after all. It was no pickup. The gear shifting, the ability to see miles ahead and slow down long before anyone else had the sense to, the mirrors and the blind spots, the wide and tight turns. It required his full attention.

But soon, his mind started to wander again. Once, during a trip to the VA hospital, he found cassette tapes with books on them. So, he started to order some for himself. Classics. Adventures. Mysteries. Especially Sherlock Holmes. He found it did two things. It satisfied former Detective Pinter's restless brain—always trying to make things into a puzzle even when they weren't—and it kept him busy. When he found himself thinking too much about how realistic a certain investigation technique was, he shut it off and listened to country music.

But now, he sat in silence, wondering what fourteen-year-old girls liked to listen to. What they liked at all. What they talked about, thought about. Fourteen was so long ago. And besides, he had been a boy. He hoped she wasn't the same as he had been at that age.

He could feel her looking at him now. He took another sip of coffee. It was no longer hot.

"So you aren't . . . um . . . mad at me?" she asked. "For what I said?"

What *had* she said? James had already forgotten. Right. The killing innocent people. How could he explain that he wasn't fragile? Teenagers were so raw. Like an open wound. Everything was a slight. Every wrong look, wrong word. Daggers. All of them.

James thought about how his parents would have reacted if he'd made a comment like that. It was unimaginable. Gene and Betty Pinter had been his world. A couple of stand-up adults. They always knew what was right and what was wrong. He respected them. He feared them. And when they were taken away so suddenly, he mourned them deeply.

But who was James? Who did Molly think he was? A deadbeat dad. A killer. She might have even suspected he was a drug user. She knew enough of those. But James was not like her mother. Not in that way and not in most ways.

How did a person demand respect from someone whose life they had left? He had shown up for two birthdays in fourteen years. Stood to the side, arms crossed or hands in his pockets. Ashamed. And jealous. Of all the people there who knew his little girl better than he did.

He sighed. He had no right to demand anything from her.

"No," James said. "No, I'm not mad."

"Do you have, like, a house or something?" she asked. "Is that where we're going?"

"I've got a load." He pointed behind him with his thumb. "We're taking it to Phoenix."

"But . . . it's the middle of the week. Aren't you going to send me to school?"

Truthfully, James hadn't thought past the next few days. He knew he wouldn't have answers. He had loads to deliver.

"School's almost out for the year," he said. "We'll worry about that later."

Molly slouched back in her seat and crossed her arms. Silence again.

[4]
MOLLY

JAMES'S TRUCK smelled like cigarettes and oil and the lemon air freshener hanging from his rearview. The soft bounce of the cab had put Molly to sleep for a while, but now she pulled her knees up to her chest and looked out the window.

Here and there, rocks and cliffs rose up from the flat plains like a giant's angry fist. Where were they? New Mexico? She licked her lips.

"Don't suppose there's a bathroom around here?" she asked.

"We'll find you a bathroom," James said. "You hungry again?"

"Just thirsty."

It was strange to be so high above the regular cars. Kids in back seats strained to look up at her. She could see the ski racks on top of their cars. Molly leaned her head against the window and watched the lines of the road whoosh by below. Her stomach grumbled. Maybe she *was* hungry.

"Rest stop, up here by the teepee," James said. Sure enough, up ahead was a big white teepee. A tourist store.

"We're in Navajo land now, aren't we?" she asked.

"Yup," he said. "The New Mexico part."

The truck rocked from side to side as they pulled off the interstate.

"Might as well gas up, too," James said, driving past the teepee. "There's a place for rigs just ahead."

The road ran parallel to the highway and was dotted with stores and signs and people. Behind them was a big mesa. Molly admired its immensity. It rose up so steep. Almost vertical. She wondered if a person could climb it. The burning red reminded her of a hot stove.

James pulled the truck into a gas station with about four other big rigs. He handed her a five-dollar bill.

Jumping down was much easier than climbing up, and when Molly hit the ground, her chunky-heeled sandals parted a cloud of dust around her.

The bathroom was one of those that stood by itself, separate from the gas station. It felt like it ought to be roofless, but it wasn't. Still, she felt strangely outside.

Molly opened the first stall to find it full of piss and shit. The next one was clean enough. She wiped down the seat with toilet paper, even though she didn't intend to sit. She crouched down overtop as close as she could without touching, trying to avoid the red streak down the outside of the toilet bowl. The path of someone's tampon. Molly wiped quick and flushed with the sole of her sandal, standing as far away as she could from the splashing water.

She could hear the toilet flushing in the men's room as she washed her hands with soap that didn't suds up. No paper towels left, of course. She wiped her hands on her shorts and pushed herself back outside with her shoulder on the door.

The warm wind hit her face as she walked to the vending machine for a Pepsi, but the vending machine was empty. Inside, then, for a cold bottle. The cashier looked to be about a hundred years old, with one long braid that reached down past the counter, but a man. He didn't look at her.

The cold Pepsi started sweating almost as soon as she took it from the refrigerator. The cashier only looked up after he had rung her up and given her the change. His eyes were milky. Cataracts. She had seen them before in her grandmother's eyes.

"Have a blessed day," he said.

"Sure thing," she said as she left.

She stood against the side of the storefront, one foot propped on the wall behind her as she sipped her Pepsi. The wind whipped her hair into her mouth, and she struggled to get it all back behind her ears.

More men that looked a little like James milled about. One with graying hair and crooked teeth winked at her. She didn't smile back but looked at him hard so he would know she got it. She knew what he was trying to do, and it was nothing to be proud of. She turned her gaze away from the men and the trucks and the empty cans tumbling across the parking lot, to the mesas again. Looming, red and brown, and swirling. Chunky looking. The little trees that dotted their bases were spaced out as though they had been planted. The same amount of land between each one.

Then, something caught Molly's eye. Beneath one of the trees. Movement. An animal? A coyote pup? She glanced around for James, who was nowhere to be seen, and walked toward the moving shadow. She knew better than to get right on top of it. Or to move too quickly. She let her Pepsi bottle hang at her side, her fingertips barely gripping its neck.

It was a boy. Curled up with his knees to his chest. Lying on his side.

Shit, Molly thought. She walked faster now but called out when she was still a few yards away.

"Hey!"

His head moved just a bit, and when he saw her, he scrambled onto his butt, pushing away from her, deeper into the shadow.

"I'm not gonna hurt you," she called. Probably about six feet away now, she squatted down to be level with him.

"Whatcha doin' out here?" she asked. Silence. No movement. She crawled a little closer.

"Where are your parents? Your mom? Dad?"

He stared at her, scared, his dark eyes dilated in the shadow of the tree. She reached out her hand.

"I'll help you," she said. "I promise. I'll help you find your people."

Still, no movement. Molly sat her butt down in the dirt.

"My name's Molly," she said. "My dad is James." The word got stuck in her throat for a moment, and she had to pause. "He drives one of those big trucks over there."

The little boy's gaze flickered over her shoulder and then back to her face. His eyes were red and puffy, though he wasn't crying just then. She sipped her Pepsi.

"That your . . . er . . . grandfather in there?" she asked. She was pretty certain the boy was Navajo. He didn't exactly look white to her. Still, he said nothing.

She held up her Pepsi so he could see.

"You like Pepsi? I'll buy you one."

He licked his lips.

"Come on out from there." She scooted just a little closer. He didn't move away. "You hungry?" she asked, much quieter now. He shook his head. Well, that was something.

"This is some land out here. Like that rock over there." She pointed across the highway. "That tall, pointy one. That's got to have a story behind it."

The boy's eyes grew softer, his breathing steadier. Molly knew she should keep talking.

"I'm from Texas," she said. "Dallas. We only have tall buildings there. Nothing like this. But one time, my mom drove me to El Paso. They've got rocks there, too. Hills, I guess you'd call them. She's dead now, though. My mom."

The boy looked up at Molly, then, alert. He grabbed her arm, hard, and stared into her eyes, panicked.

"What is it?" she asked. He pointed at her and then at himself.

"What are you trying to tell me?"

He scrambled to his feet and extended his hand to Molly. She took it and got up.

"You want to show me something?" she asked. He nodded forcefully, but instead of going back the way Molly had come—toward civilization—he took her farther into the rocks, along a maze of walls, pulling her faster and faster. The light didn't quite hit all the corners, and Molly's heart began to beat quicker.

"Hey, bud," she said, trying to slow him down. "Where are we going?" She almost tripped over her sandals.

Abruptly, he stopped. Put his finger over his lips. Now Molly was afraid. The boy pointed around the rock, staring at her. Pleading, really. She looked him over. She guessed him to be about eight. Skinny.

She looked where he pointed, slowly creeping around the rock, heart banging in her chest.

At first, she saw nothing. Just more rocks. More trees. Short, squat pines with long trunks and reaching arms like the one she had found the boy under.

But then she saw the body. She gasped and brought her hand to her mouth.

[5]

JAMES

MOLLY CAME CRASHING into the parking lot, legs covered in dirt, hair spilling from its clip into her face. She looked frantic.

"What were you doin' out there?" James asked. "There's rattlers, you know."

She shook her head as she approached.

"James." Her voice cracked. "There's a little boy out there. He led me to . . ." She swallowed and looked down at her feet. "A dead woman." She looked back up, clearly afraid. "I think it's his mom."

Christ. James had been up and down this highway for how many years now? He'd managed to avoid dead bodies for at least six. One day with his daughter back in his life, and this. It hadn't been that long since Molly had found her own mother dead. He felt the urge to hug her. Instead, he put his hands on her shoulders. She looked for a minute like she could use some comforting, too. But then she said, "Please come. The boy's still out there."

James nodded. "Show me the way."

All the rocks and trees looked very much the same, but Molly had no problem remembering where to go. And soon, there he was. A boy standing up against a rock. Holding himself.

"Hi, I'm James," James said to him.

The boy nodded but wouldn't look him in the eye. He glanced instead at Molly, who grabbed his hand.

"On the other side of this," she told James.

James took a few steps and saw her. On the ground, legs and arms at awkward angles, hair brushed across her face. By her hand, a syringe.

Damn, James thought. Seemed Molly was a bloodhound for discovering overdoses. He shouldn't touch anything. But something was on her arm. Maybe a scar. James crouched next to the needle. He pulled a pen from the pocket of his button-down and poked at her hand until her arm flipped over. He closed his eyes and tried not to let the memories come. *CC* could mean anything. Initials or something. It didn't have to mean to her what it meant to him. He opened his eyes and looked again at her forearm. Carved, too. He shook his head. A coincidence was all it was. Just a coincidence.

He stood up and turned away, hands on his hips. He looked down at the ground. No spoon? No belt? No visible track marks? More likely that she was a mule, he told himself. In deep with the highway runners. Perfectly reasonable explanation. Shame about the boy, though.

James ran his hand through his hair and stepped out from behind the rock. He slowed his breathing. This was not his case. It was not his responsibility.

"You kids want to stay here or come with me?" he asked.

"I'm going to call the police." But as soon as he said it, he knew they shouldn't stay here. They were just kids. Anyone could be out here.

"On second thought, why don't you both come with me. Come on now."

The boy looked at Molly again. She smiled at him.

James said, "I promise we'll come back for your mom. All of us. The police, too."

The boy looked uncertain but grabbed Molly's hand. Her skin turned white where he squeezed.

James had to wait for the pay phone behind a woman trucker. Funny, he rarely saw them. But here was one, in jeans up to her belly button, a hand stuffed in her back pocket, holding the phone to her shoulder with her cheek. She was short, too. James wondered how she reached the pedals.

When she was done, he picked up the phone and dialed 911.

"At the truck stop off exit 16 on I-40," James said into the phone. "My . . . uh . . . daughter here found a dead woman. And a boy. The boy is alive. Could be the woman's son."

Molly's head had snapped up at the word "daughter," like she was surprised to be his daughter. Or maybe just surprised to be called it.

The operator told James she was sending someone out right away, and James thanked her and hung up. He walked over to where the kids were sitting on the curb outside the store.

"State police are on their way," James said.

They looked afraid and lost, and James didn't quite know

what to do for them. He sighed and put his hands in his pockets.

"You kids want some snacks? Twinkies?"

The boy's eyes lit up.

"You stay here," James said. "I'll get some Twinkies."

While he bought the Twinkies, James thought of how much time he was losing. Thought about how he had hoped to never have to see a dead body again. How he wished today could be normal, like every other day. No cops. No kids. He felt bad about that part, because he loved Molly. He did. But maybe this was why he had stayed out of her life for so long. He couldn't contain her. Couldn't control her. Couldn't stop her from wandering off and finding dead bodies. Or finding whatever else. Once she wandered, he would have to follow her. Have to deal with whatever unwelcome thing she encountered. His life was interrupted now. Forever.

The state police came thirty minutes later, long after Molly had licked all the vanilla cream off her fingers and the boy had wiped his all over his pants.

One of the cops was broad-shouldered and a hair taller than James. Probably was strong once. A tight end, maybe. Now he was chubby. The other was Mexican, from the looks of him. Impressive mustache.

James shook their hands. Officers Thorpe and Lopez. They only addressed James. Not his daughter, who had found the woman. Or the boy, who had probably lost his mother.

James took the cops to her, the kids trailing behind.

"Can you tell us about how you found her?" Officer Lopez asked as they walked.

"My daughter did," James said, nudging his hand in Molly's direction. Officer Lopez raised an eyebrow.

"And the boy?" he asked.

"Found him first, I suppose. You'd have to ask her the order of events. Just the three of us in and out of here. I didn't see any prints on arrival."

This time, James noticed flies buzzing around the woman, and the five of them stopped as soon as she came into view. The kids' gazes obstructed by the bodies of the men. Officer Thorpe shook his head.

"Another overdose," he said. "Pretty common around here. Especially on the reservation. Looks like that's where these two came from."

Officer Thorpe leaned down. Put his hands on his knees to talk to the boy. Shout at him, more like. As if his ears had stopped working like his mouth had.

"This your mom here?" he asked. The boy shrank behind Molly.

"You got a name, son?" Officer Thorpe tried again. Nothing. Not a nod or a shake of the boy's head. The cop tried Molly next, and James let her talk.

Officer Lopez was already going through the woman's pockets—looking for identification, James guessed, and trampling all over any evidence in the process.

"This a possible crime scene?" James asked.

Officer Lopez chuckled and pointed to the syringe. "Pretty open and shut," he said.

"What about that on her arm? The carving?" James asked. He couldn't help himself.

Officer Lopez picked up the hand away from the needle. The one that read CC.

He scowled. "These Indians do all sorts of strange things to themselves. Besides, looks like it's healed to me."

James took a deep breath. These so-called professionals didn't know the difference between a healed cut and postmortem one. He opened his mouth to at least point out that a healed wound ought to be pink or red around the scar. This one was yellow and brown. Not normal. But then he remembered he didn't want to be involved. If he said what he wanted to say, they'd want to know who he was. How he knew these things. He didn't have anything on him to prove his identity, and he didn't want to have to. Besides, men like Officers Lopez and Thorpe did not like being told that they didn't know how to do their job. This was not his case, he reminded himself again.

Officer Lopez stood back up, holding an ID.

"Linda Morris," he said.

Officer Thorpe turned from his conversation with Molly. "From where?"

"Sanostee," Officer Lopez said, putting the ID, some coupons, and an ace of spades back into the deceased's front pocket.

"We'll take the boy to the Navajo place up there," Officer Thorpe said. "Can't seem to get a word out of him."

Molly and the boy followed James and the officers back to the troopers' car, where Officer Lopez called the Bureau of Indian Affairs to tell them to come pick up the body.

James looked up at the sky and then down at his watch. Past noon now. He watched Molly talk real nice and calm to the boy, getting him into the back seat of the cruiser. It nearly took the breath from James. It had been a long time since he'd seen Dorothy be gentle and loving like that. But there she was, right there. That was Dorothy, what Molly was doing with that boy. Molly had learned that from her mom. An ache settled over James. He had missed so much. It was easy to miss someone when you didn't see them. But just then, it felt like years of missing Molly were catching up with him. He wished he knew this girl better.

He stood next to her as they watched the cruiser drive off with the boy inside. James finally wrapped his arm around her shoulder. Molly let him.

[6]

MOLLY

MOLLY DIDN'T THINK it was a good sign that she had found two dead women in less than a month, both from drugs. At least she had been prepared for the first. Somewhat. She'd known it was coming, even if not exactly when.

Dorothy had gone over with her what to do when it finally happened. It was just like Molly's mom to be prepared.

"And what will you do when you find me dead one morning?" Dorothy would ask her daughter.

"Call Tricia," Molly would answer.

"Will you call the authorities?"

"No, mom," Molly would say.

"That's a good girl, now," Dorothy would reply, patting Molly's cheek softly.

True to her word, Dorothy did not let Molly suffer. She took matters into her own hands, and on the morning Molly called Tricia and not the cops, Dorothy looked peaceful. Her arms crossed. A full head of blond hair, washed and brushed. Not wasting away on the outside as she was on the inside.

But Molly had not been prepared for what she saw today, and now she sat in James's truck, biting the skin around her fingernails.

James passed her a cigarette. She eyed him suspiciously.

"I'm only fourteen."

"And you've never had a cigarette?"

She had. Plenty of them. She supposed that was the upside to having a dad like hers. One who didn't care much. She took it from him, and he handed her the lighter.

"You've had a tough couple of weeks. First your mom. Now this."

She lit the cigarette and rolled the window down to let out the smell. Habit.

"I'm sorry about your mom," James went on. "I never knew she was into that. She never was when we were together."

This was something Dorothy hadn't discussed with Molly. Who to tell the truth to. Molly hadn't known she would be sitting here with James. Hadn't known James would be involved at all. He never had been before. She'd assumed Tricia would take her in. She'd assumed that was why her mom wanted her to call Tricia. Or perhaps even Molly's grandmother, who she hadn't seen in years. Her grandmother who she never called Grandma or Meemaw or Nana but only ever Rita. Rita the alcoholic. The all-around bad mother, turned born-again, saved by Jesus, Rita.

"I'm sure glad Jesus can forgive her for her sins, because I can't," Molly's mother used to say. Her mother had tried her hardest to keep Molly away from Rita. Molly had thought the very worst-case scenario would be ending up with Rita. But

Tricia called James right away, and Molly somehow felt betrayed.

Molly took a long drag before saying, "It's all right."

"And I'm sorry about this woman. About the boy. It's damn tragic."

"You think she was his mom?" Molly asked.

"Seems like it," James said. Molly pulled up a knee and watched the looming rocks coming at them as if on a conveyer belt.

"He didn't want to be near me. Didn't want anything to do with me until I mentioned my own dead mom. Then he grabbed me and started pointing."

"Wish he would've talked a little," James said.

Molly tapped her cigarette out the open window.

"Why?" she asked. "He showed us. We saw. He didn't need to tell us anything. He must have been scared."

James lit his own cigarette, not bothering to roll down the window.

"I'm sure he's used to it, seeing her laid out like that," James said. "I'm sure you were, too."

No, Molly thought. She was not used to seeing needles and lighters left out on her mother's bedside table.

"And you," Molly said. "I'm sure you're used to it, too. Dead people, that is."

"What'd your mom tell you about me?"

"She said you were in the Army. That you were always gone, even before the war."

"So, what makes you think I'm used to seeing dead people?"

"Because you were in Vietnam."

"Fair enough."

Molly didn't know if she wanted to know more about what James did. She knew about the war. And she knew what the men who fought in it had done. And her father was one of them. That was enough.

She wanted another cigarette but didn't ask. Instead, she rested her head back against the leather seat and fell asleep.

———————

When she woke up, the truck was stopped and her mouth dry and sour from the cigarette. She was thirsty again. James was no longer beside her. She rubbed her eyes and looked around.

The sun was setting, and there were trucks all around. She panicked for a moment before she heard the soft drone of James's voice outside.

She got up on her knees and peeked behind the seat. She had seen him rummaging around back there and hoped she could find a soda. Just trash on the floor, though. But then she realized her elbow was not hitting a solid wall. There was a curtain behind them. She sat up taller and pushed it open.

There was a bed back there. And small cabinets. And Molly's small bag she had given to him that morning. Did James always sleep here? Did he even have a house? She tried to think back to whether he had answered her when she asked. He'd probably avoided it like he did most of her questions.

Molly almost climbed back there to snoop in the cabinets, but just then, James opened his door again. He reached over her to the glove compartment and pulled out some papers.

"Where are we?" she asked.

"Phoenix," James said.

"Are we sleeping here? Like, in the truck?"

"No," James said, stepping back onto the ground. "We'll get a hotel." Then, he shut the door again.

Molly poked around the dash and the center console and James's seat, looking for his cigarettes, but he must have taken them.

She adjusted the rearview so she could see herself, took out her hairclip, and dragged her fingers through each side, trying to get the knots out as best she could. When James climbed back into the truck, he was shaking his head.

"Everything all right?" Molly asked.

"Yeah," he said. "Want a chimichanga for dinner?"

"Sure."

James started the truck back up, waited a minute to check all his mirrors, and pulled out of the spot. He picked up the radio and switched it on just as he pulled onto the street.

"Breaker one-nine for Snoozy Lou," he said.

It took a minute and a crackling of the radio before a gruff voice said, "You got Snoozy Lou, come back."

"Slim Jim here lookin' for that chimichanga place we went to with your road Juliet."

The man on the other end chuckled.

"What's your twenty?" he asked.

"Route 10 headin' east out of Phoenix."

"Keep goin' right into Tempe. Van Buren Street. Past that Howard Johnson 'bout two miles on your right. 4-10?"

"Copy that. Keep it between the ditches."

"Down and out."

James put his radio down. Molly watched the lights flicker on as they passed restaurants and hotels and bars. No one was really out and about . It was too late to be getting off work and too early for late-night activities.

The chimichanga parking lot was full, though—a lit-up sombrero sitting on top of the place. Molly had never thought about parking an eighteen-wheeler in a city and how annoying it was. By the time they sat down, Molly's stomach was grumbling and her mouth felt like she had eaten chalk.

The waitress wore a white blouse and skirt with colorful designs around the borders. Piñatas hung from the ceiling, inches away from the waitress's ear.

Molly didn't speak for a full two minutes after the waitress brought her a lemonade. She sipped and sipped and sipped, her mouth as dry as the desert floor she had sat on that morning with the boy. When she stopped, she made a little "ah" sound without meaning to.

"Tomorrow, I'll have a load ready for Amarillo," James said, plucking a chip from the chip bowl.

"So, you just drive around? Like all the time?" Molly asked.

James cracked a small smile. It surprised her. She hadn't seen him smile much. Something in that smile was familiar. Like looking in a mirror. She looked away, quick.

"I go home on the weekends," he said. "But sure. I'm usually driving."

"Don't you get tired of being in that truck all the time?"

"No," he said. "I don't."

They sat quietly, crunching on chips, looking at the restaurant décor and not each other. Yellow and red lamps hanging from the ceiling. Tiled floors so shiny Molly could see the reflection of her chunky sandal draped over her other leg.

"We'll be making a stop," James finally said.

Molly already wanted her old life back. Resentment began to build in the back of her throat again. She didn't care about any of this trucking stuff.

"At the Navajo reservation," James finished.

She looked at him. "Why?"

He sighed, sat back in his chair, and crossed his arms.

"Something about that woman's death doesn't sit right with me. I'm worried about the kid."

"What do you mean?" Molly asked, her stomach turning over a bit. "The cops said 'open and shut.'"

"Yes, they did. But they're highway cops. Not investigators. This isn't what they do."

Molly frowned. She wanted to tell him that *he* was just a truck driver. Instead, she asked, "Why are you worried?"

"If something suspicious did happen there . . ." James patted his breast pocket and pulled out a cigarette. He turned it in his fingers. ". . . The boy's life could be in danger. If he saw something. If someone saw him see something."

He put the cigarette in his mouth and lit it. Molly's heart began to beat faster. She had liked the boy.

"Why didn't you say something before? We could've turned back!"

James shook his head.

"I'm saying something now. I just want the tribe to know. More'n likely he's just fine. But I won't be able to sleep too well if I don't tell them to look out for him."

Molly bit her lip. "Why do you think you know more than those police officers?"

"Because I do."

Molly hated how sure of himself James seemed then.

Who did he think he was? Making her worry about the boy like that? Maybe she could have forgotten the whole thing before. But now she couldn't.

"And then we're just going to drive away? Hope for the best?"

"The tribe will take care of him."

"What if they don't believe you? I mean, why would they?"

Just then, the waitress set their plates down in front of them. The chimichangas smelled meaty and greasy, and Molly's mouth watered. James leaned forward and put his forearms on the table. One on each side of his plate.

"They'll believe me."

JAMES

THE PRETTY GIRL manning the desk at the Navajo Nation's offices in Sanostee snapped her chewing gum and smiled when James and Molly walked in. The ceiling fan directly above her was on the highest setting—*fwoop, fwoop, fwoop, fwoop.* Her crossed ankles peeked out from under her long blue skirt. She leaned forward on her elbows.

It had been five days since the chimichangas in Tempe. The delivery had been delayed, and Molly spent that time lying beside the hotel pool.

"If you've got a delivery for the trading post, you're in the wrong place," the pretty girl said, though she didn't look too sad about it. She nudged her head toward the window. "Saw your big truck."

She twirled her long hair around her finger. James tried to smile but was a little thrown off by what he presumed to be flirting. This woman was young. Too young for James.

"I'm actually here about the boy that the police brought in the other day."

She leaned back and became rigid.

"How do you know about him?"

"Molly here—" James held his arm out awkwardly, "—found him alone."

The girl's eyes flicked to Molly. She looked anxious now. "And Molly is?" Her eyes narrowed.

"My daughter."

The young woman nodded curtly and stood. She no longer looked like she wanted any part of them.

"What business have you got with the boy?" she asked.

"I just need to speak with someone. His family maybe. About something I saw."

Her eyes grew wide. Just then, creaky, heavy footsteps came from somewhere behind her, and she turned quickly.

A man appeared. A bit older than James and almost as tall. His hair was pulled back in a low ponytail, and a scar below his earlobe ran underneath his chin until it disappeared into his neck. The pocket on his denim button-down had studs in the shape of a star.

He approached James and reached out a hand to shake. "Wayne," he said.

"James."

"What'd you see?" Wayne asked. He stuck his hands in his pockets and rocked back on his heels. "In regards to the boy."

James glanced at the girl, and she quickly hurried off down the hallway Wayne had come from.

"His mom," James said. "Didn't seem like an OD to me. For a few reasons. If there was foul play, I want to make sure the boy is kept safe. He might have seen something."

The corners of Wayne's mouth turned down, and his forehead wrinkled.

"That's not what the state police told us."

"I know," James said. "And I'm sorry they won't look into it further. But those highway cops couldn't wait to hand her over to BIA."

"And you are?" Wayne asked.

"Was. For a long time. Army. CID."

James could feel Molly's cold stare. Wayne's eyebrows went up, and he took a deep breath.

"I'm going to get a coffee," Wayne said. "And then we can take a ride. Would you like one?"

"Yes, please," James said. "Thank you."

Wayne's pickup truck had a back seat, and Molly climbed in.

"Army, huh?" Wayne asked as he drove. "You over in Vietnam?"

James nodded.

"Investigating?" Wayne whistled. "Damn. You must've seen some awful things."

James blew on his hot coffee. "Seen. Heard. The stories I wasn't there for were some of the worst."

"So tell me. What makes you think she didn't overdose?"

"Was she a known drug user?" James asked.

"Can't say I knew her well enough to say. She was known to keep the wrong sort of company, though that was years ago."

James watched the horse corrals out the window. Tan and white horses with their heads in troughs.

"No paraphernalia," James said. "Seemed like the most obvious sign to me. Only a syringe. Nothin' to tie off with.

Would be odd for someone to shoot up enough heroin to kill themselves but put their spoon and lighter away first."

"What else?" Wayne asked.

"Something carved on her arm. It was done after she was dead. I'm sure of it."

Wayne peeled his eyes from the road for a moment to look at James.

"Carved?"

"'CC.' That mean anything to you?"

Wayne didn't answer. Only sipped his coffee. Finally, he spoke. "Can't say it does. The Navajo don't do autopsies. Don't like to be around the dead. Don't like to disturb the dead. Don't even like to speak of the dead," he said. "I'm a little different. But the boy's family won't want you saying her name. We're going to her husband George's house now. The four days where we allow for the dead to cross over to the next world are done. But still. It's respectful to say as little as you need to about her. I know it's difficult in this situation."

James nodded. "I'll try my best."

The trailer they pulled up to was a mint-green color. White roof. White trim. Small white deck.

James watched Molly try to brush the sand off her lips as they waited for someone to open the door. Wayne knocked again. Slowly, the door opened.

"Afternoon, Kay," Wayne said.

"Wayne." Her face was hard and unwelcoming, but she opened the door a bit wider anyway and let the three of them enter.

"This is her sister, Kay," Wayne introduced her. Kay looked alarmed at this. She had high cheekbones and eyes of a strange color. Like a dark gray. She was probably in her early thirties. Slimmer than her sister was.

"Nice to meet you," James said. Kay stared. "I'm James, and this is my daughter, Molly. We called in the . . . incident to the police."

Kay finally nodded, though her face barely softened. James looked down for a moment at the brown rug. The kitchen had a round wooden table with four chairs, hearts painted on them.

"Is George here?" Wayne asked. Kay nodded again.

"Adriel's taking a nap," she said. "George is in the shower. Why don't you all sit down, and I'll get you a drink while we wait."

James tried not to look at his watch. They would still get to Amarillo on time. Kay brought them tea, and they all sipped in silence. Soon, James thought, he'd have to use the toilet. He watched Molly's leg bounce up and down and wondered if she felt the same.

George was still toweling his hair when he walked into the kitchen. He looked surprised to see them but held out a hand.

"George," he said. James stood up and shook it. George was a short man. James felt too intimidating standing and sat back down again.

"James," he said. "And my daughter, Molly."

"James and Molly here found Adriel yesterday," Wayne said.

James wanted to tell him that he was sorry for their loss, but Wayne had said it was more respectful to just keep quiet. Focus on the boy.

Kay stared into her tea mug. George nodded forcefully, eyes glistening, trying not to cry.

James wondered if George would say anything at all about Linda. He gave him another minute in case he wanted to. It felt like he did. James could feel these sort of things, still. He supposed it had come with years of sitting in living rooms, interrogation rooms. Death around him. The Navajo may have had their beliefs, but this man, George, he had something to say.

"I didn't think she'd ever go back to that stuff. Not after what happened."

Kay stared daggers at him, but she didn't interrupt. George's wet hair hung over his shoulders, and he gripped the back of a chair.

"What happened?" James asked, cautiously.

"Car accident. Luckily, Adriel wasn't in the car. But he could've been. Was supposed to be, in fact. She got clean after that."

"That's enough," Kay practically growled. She stood and went to the sink. James could hear cartoons playing in the next room. *Scooby Doo.* He assumed the boy was in there.

"Can I be honest with you, George?" James asked. George nodded, looking into James's eyes. "I don't think it happened the way the police said it did. I think there was something strange about the whole thing. Someone else was there. I'm sure of it. I'm here because I'm worried the boy may have seen something. He could be in danger."

Kay spun around.

"Are you saying she was killed?"

"It's possible," James said.

"James used to investigate for the Army," Wayne jumped in. James was grateful.

"I wouldn't be here if I wasn't fairly sure the cops are wrong about this. I won't go into details. I know you don't want to hear them. But I do need you to take extra precautions with the boy. Is there anywhere you could send him? Just for a little while?"

Kay and George looked at each other. She shook her head at him, as if answering an unspoken question.

"Are you sure that's necessary?" George asked. "Adriel doesn't talk. Never has. Not once. Everyone around here knows that."

James was surprised. He'd thought it was just the shock of most likely witnessing his mother's murder. Her death at the very least.

"Whoever was involved in this might not be from around here. They might not know that."

"If that's the case," Kay said, swallowing hard, "why did they leave Adriel be?"

"Maybe they couldn't do anything more without drawing attention to themselves at the time. Maybe the boy ran. Maybe the person lost his nerve."

The curtains were all drawn. The house dark, except for the lamps in the corners of the kitchen.

"We can take him where he needs to go!" Molly hadn't made a peep since they arrived, and now, she blurted this out without consulting with James at all.

Kay laughed. It was an incredulous, furious laugh.

"You can't be serious," she said. "You are strangers. We aren't giving Adriel over to strangers. We will take him to his cousins in Arizona, and neither of you need to worry about where."

James knew it was time to leave. He would have to teach Molly how to deal with grieving people. Molly looked hurt. And embarrassed.

"I . . . I didn't mean . . ." she stammered.

Kay scoffed. "You people have stolen enough of our children. Now, Adriel is in danger and you—" She stuck a finger at James, and he was glad she was directing her anger at him instead of Molly, "—you are the ones to protect him? How convenient. How righteous of you."

James quickly scribbled his number down on a napkin and pushed it over toward Kay.

"If you need anything," he said. Then, he turned and shook George's hand. "It was nice to meet you both."

Molly stood up, too, and James led her out the door with his hand on her back. Once outside, they could hear Wayne saying his apologies and his goodbyes. He emerged a minute later.

"Kay's a little raw right now," he said. "I'm sure you understand."

"As long as the boy is safe," James said.

[8]
ADRIEL

ADRIEL LAY on the couch with his eyes closed, listening to his aunt clanking teacups around the sink. She was angry. He could hear that.

He could hear all of it. The man and the girl coming in with Officer Tully. The girl's offer to take him where he needed to go.

They thought he wasn't safe here. He breathed in the smell of his new Star Wars blanket. Lavender, like the soap his mom used to wash his clothes. He tried to imagine her hugging him again. The way she would tuck his hair behind his ear. How she would scrunch up her nose when she touched his softly with her finger. Like she could feel just what he felt.

His tears were coming again, and he buried his face in the blanket. He didn't want Aunt Kay to hear him. He didn't want to think about what the man had said. The truck driver, James. But Adriel *did* think about it, because the man was right.

But Adriel would never tell. Because he remembered the

threat. Couldn't forget it. His dad would be next and then his aunt Kay.

He hadn't slept last night, and he hadn't napped, either, like his dad wanted him to. But he pretended he did so they'd feel better.

He wanted to go to Arizona. To Shonto, where his cousins lived. He liked it there. And even though he wasn't worried about his mother's killer coming after him, he was worried about his mother's spirit. Would she understand why he had to stay quiet? Would she be angry with him? It was the bad part of people that stuck around, and though Adriel didn't believe his mom to have any bad parts at all, he would understand if she were angry with him. *He* would be angry with him if he were her. He hadn't protected her. And now he wouldn't tell, either. He loved his dad and his aunt too much.

Still. The thought of being so far away from Diigis Télii, his donkey, made his stomach hurt. He would have to give instructions to his aunt. Don't walk on his right. Let him drink from the puddles. Scratch him under the chin when he does what he's told.

Adriel felt the couch shift. Aunt Kay had sat beside him, softly sniffling. She thought he was asleep. He wanted to touch her. To grab her hand and hold it tight. To be sad and afraid together.

Instead, Adriel slowed his breathing. Squeezed his eyes shut even harder. He heard it anyway. The voice of his mother's killer. *She didn't know to keep quiet. But you will. You'll keep quiet. . . .*

[9]

MOLLY

MOLLY DIDN'T KNOW what she'd expected James's house to look like, but it wasn't this. Big deck. Lots of windows. Too much house for one man. They sat on the deck, Molly sipping some iced tea he had made from a bucket of Lipton instant tea, lemon flavor.

It was dark now, and in the distance, lightning bugs blinked in and out of the trees.

"You didn't tell me you were a detective or something."

"I don't talk about it much."

"Why not?"

James was drinking a Coors. He let it linger on his lips for a moment.

"Not proud of it, I suppose. Those are times I'd rather forget."

"Not proud of it? Why not? Weren't you, like, a cop?"

Molly could see him squinting into the darkness at nothing.

"I was a cop. A criminal investigator," he said. "For the Army."

"Then what's not to be proud of?"

He took another sip.

"I tried, sure. To catch criminals of all sorts. Our criminals, their criminals. Didn't always work out that way, though."

"But you tried."

He sighed.

"Yeah."

Molly uncrossed her legs and leaned forward with her elbows on her knees.

"I don't understand how they could behave that way. The things I read about. That we all had to hear about. How could so many of them do what they did? To innocent people?"

James leaned his head back.

"I think we'd all like to pretend we're heroes. But most of us aren't. Put us in the same situation under the same circumstances and we might do the same thing. Those boys weren't much older than you. Forced to fight a war with no purpose. No enemy. Just an idea. A war they couldn't win."

Molly couldn't believe he was defending them. She shook her head and picked at her cuticles, thinking of what to say to that. But James started talking again.

"Now, lots of what they did I can't understand. But I wasn't a judge. I got the facts. Then the powers that be decided who would pay up. Sometimes, that's all those boys wanted themselves. To pay for their crimes."

He stood abruptly.

"That's enough for tonight. I left a towel on your bed. You're welcome to use the bathroom in the hall. Ain't no one else usin' it."

"Thanks," Molly said, real quiet.

She sat out there a while, listening to the owls and the crickets. She didn't know if she wanted to change her opinion of James. Didn't know what to think of what he'd said, anyway. But something was shifting inside of her, making her uncomfortable. She was starting to feel curious about him. Hungry to know her father. She wanted to ignore it. To go back to resenting him. Wanting to get to know James felt like a betrayal to her dead mother, though she didn't know why.

It was strange not having rules. She kept expecting someone to come outside and tell her it was late and she needed to go to bed. But James had disappeared. She couldn't even hear him moving around inside.

Finally, she started to get nervous. The noises had changed. Everything felt more still, and a chill laced the air. Molly shivered and went inside. She locked the sliding door behind her and wondered if James felt like he was exposed all the time. He hadn't bought curtains for the doors.

She went around the house, checking to make sure all the doors were locked before getting in the shower. Still, she left the bathroom door cracked so she could hear anything strange. James was silent behind his shut bedroom door. Probably asleep. She had never worried like this at her own house, even though it was just her and her mom and they were on the outskirts of the city, where crime was worse than it was out here in the middle of nowhere.

Molly didn't sleep well that night. It was too quiet. Every noise she did hear felt amplified, like a threat. She would drift off only to startle awake to the distant bark of a dog. Or the groan of the floors or the pipes or something inside the house.

At breakfast, she poured herself coffee that James had brewed. She could feel her eyes drooping. Her movements slow.

"How'd you sleep?" he asked.

"Fine," she said. "Don't you ever feel like you're being watched in here? You should get some curtains."

James chuckled. "We can get some in town today."

Molly rolled her eyes. James was so country, referring to Oklahoma City as "town."

He had his back to her, frying eggs.

"Anything else you need?" he asked over his shoulder. "I've got another load going to Albuquerque on Monday."

Molly watched a yellow bird with black wings and a black head perch outside the window. It looked right at her. Molly did not want to spend her summer in James's smelly truck. She missed her friends.

"Do I have to come?" she asked.

She listened to the spatula scraping the pan.

"Yes," James said.

Molly's mom used to leave her for the night by herself sometimes. Though, the neighbors were always right there when she needed something. James was far out here. She thought about the night before and supposed she didn't want to be there by herself, either.

"Probably new clothes," Molly said. "All mine are from last summer. They're getting kind of small."

Plenty of Molly's clothes still fit. But she wanted James to spend money on her. She felt like she had never gotten anything from him. He owed her. Even if it was just a few dresses and some new sneakers. Something.

"And some drawing materials. Pencils and paper. I like to sketch," she added.

"All right," he said. "Clothes and curtains and drawing materials."

[10]

JAMES

JAMES HAD SPENT TOO much on the shopping trip, but Molly was happy. Maybe he was buying her love. But for now, that was fine with him.

They had eaten lunch in town, and now it was almost dinnertime. James was hanging the second curtain above the sliding glass door when his phone rang.

Molly stood a few feet back, head tilted to the side, assessing his work.

"Can you get that?" he asked.

She sauntered into the kitchen and picked the phone up off the wall.

"The residence of James Pinter," she said, her voice chipper.

"Who's calling?" she asked after a moment.

"Oh." Her voice grew quieter. Timid. "Yes, he's here. One moment."

He heard her put the phone on the counter. She returned to the dining room.

"It's Kay. The Navajo lady. The boy's aunt."

Molly's arm was crossed against her body, holding her other elbow.

"Come hold this up," James said. She walked over and grabbed the rod.

"What if my arms get tired?"

"Use the drill, then."

She scowled. James went to pick up the phone.

"Hello?"

"Hi. It's Kay. From the reservation."

"Yes, hi. How can I help you?"

"I've been thinking about what you said. I need you to tell me why you think my sister was killed."

James cleared his throat.

"Someone carved something into her arm. After she was dead."

He heard a quiet gasp on the line. "Why didn't the police tell us that?"

"They thought it was an old wound. Healed. But it wasn't. It was postmortem."

"You can tell?"

"Yes."

"What . . . what was it?" Kay's voice cracked. Desperate.

"The letters 'CC' were cut into her right arm. That mean anything to you?"

The line went silent.

Finally, Kay said, "Yes. Yes, it means something."

James waited. He ducked his head to check on Molly through the wall cutout. She was shifting her weight. Changing arms.

"There's a family here on the reservation. The Codys. Cecil Cody. C.C. They're involved with drugs. Everyone knows they are. I'm pretty sure she used to get hers from them. I don't really know the details."

James breathed a sigh of relief.

"Got it. And these people are known to be dangerous?" he asked. Kay was quiet for a moment. He could hear her breathing softly.

"Let's just say you'd be a fool not to be afraid of Cecil Cody."

"Do you think she got into some trouble?" James asked.

"I don't know," Kay said. "I can't see how she could've. She hadn't hung around those people in years."

"You're sure of that?"

"I think." Her voice was small.

"Well, keep the boy away from them."

"That's already done. But, James?"

He waited for the question he knew was coming.

"Can you help? I want to find out what happened to my sister. I need to."

James had known this might happen the minute he decided to get involved. But he didn't know what to say to Kay now.

"Where can I find the Cody family?"

"At their ranch. It's west of George's. Off 491. Still on the reservation, though."

James sighed again and ran his fingers through his hair.

"Can't say I'll find anything, but Molly and I will be in Albuquerque next week. Can she stay with you while I poke around?"

"Yes, yes, that's fine." Kay sounded relieved. James wished he could assure her that he would find whoever had done this to her sister. But he knew this whole situation could turn into a nightmare. He had no partner. No backup. No one at all to call. He didn't have access to the body. Couldn't determine the true manner of death. He would be flailing around in the dark, putting his own ass on the line while he did so.

"We'll see you next week, then." James hung up the phone.

In the Stables / 56

[11]
KAY

KAY KNEW Molly was just a child. The girl hadn't understood the implications of what she had suggested at their first meeting. Not really. It wasn't like Molly's teachers were telling her what happened to little native kids. Kay was good at starting over with people. She had done it with her ex-husband after his first big mistake and with her sister when Linda decided to get sober.

Kay met Molly outside her squat yellow house. Not quite a trailer but not bigger than one, either. It had been their father's. The house Kay and Linda grew up in.

"Hi," Molly said. She seemed nervous. Kay handed her a bucket.

"Let's go," Kay said.

Molly trailed behind her up the dusty path to the stables. The roof was lopsided, but otherwise, the stables were sturdy. They had been there as long as Kay could remember. Her grandparents had cared for horses out of there and maybe their grandparents had, too. She shook her head at the thought. No, her grandparents' grandparents would have been prisoners at Fort Sumter. The place of suffering, death, and evil.

Kay unlocked the stall in front of them and led Niyol out to the corral. The horse's red-brown coat shone in the morning sun.

Kay could tell Molly hadn't been around horses much by the way she backed up quickly and skittishly.

"You ever ride a horse before?" Kay asked.

"Of course," Molly said. "I'm from Dallas, aren't I?"

Kay snorted.

"They got horses in the big city?"

Molly relaxed her shoulders a bit and smiled. Then, she rolled her eyes and giggled.

"Hang the bucket on the fence over there and come say hello to Niyol."

Molly did as she was told and came back up behind Kay's right shoulder. Kay looked down at the girl's pink suede Vans beside her own scuffed and worn boots.

"Hi Neey-al," Molly said, quietly.

"Nigh-ole" Kay corrected her. "Here." She took Molly's hand and stroked the horse's shoulder with it. "Don't be afraid. Niyol is one of our tamest. She loves the attention."

Kay watched Molly's whole body relax. Horses could do that.

"How is Adriel?" Molly asked.

Kay was surprised she remembered his name. "He's fine. He's safe."

Molly didn't push it. "Is James going to be okay today, too, do you think? Safe, I mean?"

"You call your dad by his first name?" Kay asked.

"Well, we just met a few weeks ago."

"Oh," Kay said. "Did your mom raise you?"

Molly bit her lip and nodded.

"But she died. So, I'm living with James now. Driving around in his truck with him."

Kay bent down, running her hands along Niyol's front left leg. "I'm sorry."

Niyol lifted her hoof when Kay tapped the side of her knee. It needed cleaning. Kay went back to the stable for the hoof pick.

"It's all right," Molly said when she returned. "It wasn't exactly a surprise—my mom dying, I mean."

White people loved to talk about death, Kay thought. She wondered if Molly was haunted by her mother. She didn't seem to be.

"Was she sick?" Kay asked, bending down again.

"Yes," Molly said. "But don't tell James. He thinks she overdosed on drugs. Well, she *did* overdose. But she was sick, too."

Kay lowered the pick and looked up at the girl. "You don't have to tell me about it if you don't want to." She didn't really want to know.

Molly's eyes watered, and she shook her head.

"No one knows," Molly said. "About Mom's cancer. Only me and her and Tricia. I don't know why Mom would rather everyone think she was some junkie." Molly's eyes widened for a moment. "No offense to your sister."

Kay grabbed the pick again and went back to work. "Maybe she didn't want you to suffer," she said after a brief silence.

"Do you think I can tell James now that she's gone? The truth? I hate that he thinks of her that way. Gosh, I'm sorry,"

Molly sputtered again. "I just keep saying the wrong thing. I'm sure your sister was a wonderful woman."

When she finished, Kay stood up. "Your dad doesn't seem to think my sister's death was an overdose at all," she said. "And I believe him. So you can stop apologizing."

She went to hang the hoof pick back up in the stable.

"She was a junkie, though," she went on when she got back to Niyol and Molly. "At one point in her life. But she was also fiercely loyal. And kind. Giving. Generous. She loved too much. She loved me too much."

Molly nodded.

"Me and her were so different. She wanted simple things. But me?" Kay grunted. "I'm never pleased. Still, we were inseparable."

"I'm sorry," Molly said. "My mom and I were close, too. Just being the two of us. Sometimes I feel like maybe the cancer would've gone away. Doctors aren't always right. But Mom didn't give it a chance. Because of me."

She paused and took a deep breath. "Is it normal to feel like this, do you think? Do you feel this way, too? Or am I right and I am to blame?" she asked.

Kay stared at her. *Did* she feel guilty for Linda's death? Every waking moment. But she couldn't tell Molly that. That Kay might really have been the reason Linda died. She could barely admit it to herself. And she certainly couldn't have James knowing. She didn't want him confirming her worst fears. The reality was they might both have been guilty. Kay and Molly.

The two of them stood in the corral together but alone. Afraid. With blood on both their hands.

"You aren't to blame," Kay said, at last.

JAMES

JAMES STEPPED in sheep shit as soon as he got out of his truck. *Damn it*, he thought. He looked up at the sprawling ranch. The house was certainly impressive compared to the rest of the reservation, though it wouldn't hold up against the ranches in Texas. Sheep roamed in every direction as far as he could see, and four young men watched him from the porch. He scraped the sole of his boot against the ground. Only a little came off. He'd deal with it later.

He approached the house.

"You lost?" one of the men called.

"This the home of Cecil Cody?"

"Who are you?" asked a tall, thin man in a rocking chair. He had a mustache and thick eyebrows. Clearly, the men were brothers. Or cousins at least.

"I'm here to ask Mr. Cody some questions," James said.

They stared at him. All four of them.

"You didn't tell us who you are," one said. He was the loudest one. Like he had a built-in microphone.

"James Pinter," James said. "I'm a friend of Linda Morris. Y'all know her?"

He thought at least one of them would cough. Look away. Shift a little. But nothing. Only steely stares.

"You see," James went on, "she was found dead about two weeks ago."

The biggest one pointed at James suddenly.

"Morris! Her boy's the dumb one," he said. "Still doesn't talk and he's, like, fifteen." He laughed, looking to his brothers to join in, but they still stared at James.

"Eight, actually," James said.

"You a cop?" the loud one asked.

"Naw, son," James said. "I ain't a cop."

The one with the mustache stood. "What does this have to do with our father?" he asked.

"I heard she used to come around here sometimes. There were some things found at the scene of her death . . . some questions her family has that I think your father might be able to answer."

Mustache spoke again. "Our father's got nothing to do with whatever happened to Linda Morris. And he's out right now. So, you're gonna have to leave."

James sighed. "I'm not saying he had anything to do with it. But I would like to pick his brain. Her family sure would appreciate it."

None of them spoke this time.

"All right, then," James said. "Well, I come through here from time to time." He pulled a card from his pocket and scribbled his number on it. "In case your father decides he wants to help us out."

James handed the card to Mustache. If he'd flipped it

over, he would have seen the ace of spades, but Mustache just stared at James, and James understood that not only was this family dangerous, they were also good at what they did.

James sat in his truck stopped alongside the road just before the turn to Kay's, taking long, hard drags of his cigarette. Nothing that had happened at the ranch told James anything. He had seen men lie plenty of times, and he wasn't sure those men were lying. Hard to say, of course, since criminals had plenty of things to hide. Still, they didn't seem bothered by the mention of Linda. Or even interested in whatever James had to say about her. They were probably used to lying for their father.

James obviously didn't expect to solve a homicide—if it even was one—after a single conversation. But he still didn't know what to say to Kay. What exactly did she want from him? How hard did she want him to look? He had a job to do, and this wasn't it.

He smoked one more cigarette before driving the rest of the way to Kay's. He found her and Molly at the back of the horse corral. One facing toward the fence, with a boot up, the other facing the horses, arms crossed.

Kay squinted as he approached.

"Talked to the Codys. Left them my number. They'll be calling."

Molly turned to look at him, too. She smiled faintly.

"What'd you think?" Kay asked.

James grabbed the fence post.

"Hard to say after just one conversation."

Kay looked at the ground.

"But nothing about their reaction struck me as particularly telling."

As Kay lifted her head to look at James again, a piece of her hair slipped from her ponytail and into her face. She tucked it behind her ear.

"What'll we do next?"

"Hopefully Cecil will have some answers," James replied.

She took a deep breath.

"I need you to find out what happened. I'll pay you. I don't have a lot, but I'll pay you everything I can. No one else cares about us. The Navajo police can't investigate something that happened off the reservation. You're the only one that will do anything. Please. I need to know."

James gazed out at the reservation. The vastness of it. In the distance, he could see some sheep grazing and, behind them, a jagged, winding plateau.

"I don't know how much more I can do," he said. "I've got no body. No autopsy. One lead that I may or may not have already exhausted."

Kay looked pained.

"I wouldn't ask you to dig her back up. I know how you probably feel about that."

Kay looked up at the sky and then back at him. James noticed how smooth her neck was. The natural arch in her eyebrows that made her look like she was waiting on the rest of the world to catch up.

"Can't you go back to where you found her?" she asked. "Maybe something is there."

"I can." James nodded. "But I can't guarantee that whatever I find will be related to her death. It was a bit out of the way, sure, but not too far. Other people may have walked it since."

"Check anyway," Kay said. "I trust your instincts."

"Why? You don't even know me."

Kay stared into his eyes in a way that made him melt a little. It was such a vulnerable look. So raw. He had to clear his throat and check the sturdiness of his knees.

"I just do," she said. "If I think of anything else, I'll call you."

He nodded. He had to look away.

"Let's go, Molly."

13

KAY

KAY LAY awake in bed that night, staring out the window at the crescent moon. Tears slid down her cheeks, and she didn't try to hide them. She didn't even wipe them away. She was alone, after all. No need to feel ashamed.

She wasn't supposed to talk about Linda. Or cry about her, even. It wasn't the Navajo way. For the first four days she'd done everything right. Didn't cry. Didn't say her name. Didn't talk about her at all. She tried to let her sister's spirit cross over to the next world. She didn't interrupt Linda's journey with selfish displays of pain, even though it felt like she had lost an internal organ.

Still, Linda came to her every night in her dreams. Even during the day, Kay could feel her. Her restlessness. Her anger. It scared Kay, but now that James had shown up, Kay thought she understood. Something awful had happened to her sister. And maybe all of this *wasn't* Kay's fault.

Kay didn't want her sister's spirit around, as angry as it was. She wanted to remember their love for one another. The bond between them that had been so close the neighbors would sometimes mix them up. Even though they hardly looked alike, and they were three years apart in age.

Maybe it was because of this that Kay knew Linda wouldn't leave her until she discovered what had happened. What really happened. There was something important Kay needed to learn.

She would let James pursue the Codys, and she would hope that it was them. That Linda's murder was a simple act of revenge. Or of spite. An emotional death. Or perhaps not emotional at all. A debt repaid. Linda's past coming back to deliver what she was owed.

Kay felt sad that she hoped for that. Guilty, even. But if that were true, then it would be Linda's decisions and Linda's decisions alone that had led to her death.

Kay listened to her own breath. She felt it expand deep in her belly, and then she let it out again. She let that burden lighten only a little. This was how she would repay her sister. For all of Kay's wrongs. For everything she wished she had done differently. Everything she wished hadn't been said. She would make it up to her now, by helping James. She would do anything he asked. Anything.

14

MOLLY

MOLLY HADN'T STOPPED SKETCHING since James bought her paper and pencils. The diner. June and her fake eyelashes and big smile. Adriel's terrified face in great detail. Kay's horse Niyol. The pressure of her memories was released, transferred to paper, no longer taking up too much space in her mind. And she would admit only to herself that she was a pretty dang good artist.

James was curious about what Molly remembered from the day she found Linda's body. They were going back there. James wanted Molly to draw it all.

They were on their way back from Vegas. Molly had never been, but she was underwhelmed. It was just another dirty city with more drunks and more lights. And the hotel walls were thin.

"Next time I'll take you to a show," James said.

"If we aren't investigating a murder," she answered.

He didn't say anything to that. Molly couldn't tell how he felt about the Linda situation. Sometimes he seemed eager to be investigating. Other times, slightly irritated.

But as soon as they pulled up at the gas station by the giant teepee, she could tell that he wasn't taking the case seriously. He was relaxed, smiling, strolling.

"Aren't you gonna, like, look for clues?" she asked. He smiled wider.

"I doubt there's going to be anything useful here. It's been weeks."

"So why are you doing this?"

"Because I told Kay I would. There's nothing else I can do right now. So why not come here? Check it off my list. Wait for the Codys to call."

"What did they say to you?" Molly asked, shifting her drawing pad from one arm to the other.

"Not much," he said. "I'm not sure they *will* say much. Even if one of them calls. But I'll try to get something. Then we—I—can gather some more information from the community. Sometimes the family hides things they're embarrassed about. Or sometimes they forget to tell you important things because they're grieving."

"So, you don't think it was the Codys?" Molly asked.

They stopped walking. They'd reached the site. The exact spot where Linda had lain.

"I don't think I know much about what happened at all. Kay's not giving me much. I might try to talk to George."

"You haven't asked her much," Molly pointed out. It was weird, Molly thought, the way James was handling this. Like he had agreed to help but wouldn't really. Like he wasn't that interested but still going through the motions.

James stood with his hands on his hips, looking around at the ground.

"Suppose you're right," he muttered. He shook his head.

"Useless." Molly wondered if he meant them being there or the cops. He looked at her.

"The most important thing is gonna be that drawing. If you think you can remember the scene accurately."

Heat rose to Molly's face. She was nervous now, but she nodded. She started listing things she remembered.

"Her right leg was over here." She pointed. "Sort of at a strange angle. Her hair was draped over the left half of her face. Her silk blouse was buttoned all the way up to the top button. She was wearing a turquoise necklace and turquoise earrings. She had lipstick on. She looked very . . . pretty."

She stopped. Linda had looked pretty. It made her sad. She shuddered. Why had this pretty woman—this mom— died here? James nodded enthusiastically, eyebrows furrowed, staring intently at the ground as if he could see Linda there.

Molly sat right on the dirt and began to sketch. She reached inside her mind as her hand moved across the paper. There was a stain, too, she remembered now, across the right side of Linda's chest. Just a streak. Spilled coffee maybe? She drew it and would let James decide. The pink eyeshadow. Teal fingernails. Brown platform clogs snug on her feet. The carving on her arm. The needle, inches from her hand.

Molly took longer than she wanted to on Linda's face. She wasn't so great at that part. When she handed the drawing to James, he said, "Her lips were parted a little more than that." She nodded.

She waited nervously while he studied the drawing, picking at her cuticles. He looked at her after a minute, eyebrows raised.

"This is good. And helpful. Want to know what I see when I look at it?"

She nodded again, eagerly.

"She's dressed nicely for something. Makeup, earrings, nice shirt. Not sure why there's a stain there. Could've happened that morning. Coffee, maybe." Molly smiled at that. "Buttons buttoned all the way up is strange. It doesn't seem like this shirt was meant to be worn that way. Most women don't wear shirts like that. The shoes are strange, too. Clogs come off easily. If Linda was high and collapsed here, I would have expected at least one of those shoes to come off."

He looked back up at Molly. "You sure they were both on her feet like that?"

"Positive."

"Huh," James said, staring at the drawing again.

"So, she was meeting someone, right?" Molly asked. "Or going somewhere special?"

"I suspect so." His forehead wrinkled in thought. "That stain bothers me. And the buttons. Even if she were meeting another woman. That's almost prudish."

"Maybe she got very conservative when she got clean. Maybe she found Jesus or Allah or something," Molly said.

James gave her a crooked smile. "How do you know about Allah?"

Molly shrugged. "Classmates."

James raised his eyebrows and said, "Huh," again. "I need to talk to Kay. Maybe George, too."

He put his hand awkwardly on her shoulder, and she looked at it before giving him a strained smile. Was he trying to be affectionate? It was a strange time for that.

"Good work today," he said.

"That's it?" Molly asked. "You're not gonna, like, dust for fingerprints or make shoe print castings?"

James chuckled. "Like I said, none of that would be usable."

"So, it was a waste to come here?"

He looked surprised. "No. I was hoping it would help you. Jog your memory. And it looks like it did. This—" He held up her sketch, "—is very useful."

Just as they were leaving, Molly spotted something underneath a rock about ten feet from where Linda had been lying. It shined a little. A coin?

"Wait! What's that?"

James squinted at it. He walked over and crouched down. "Give me a pencil, would ya?"

She handed him one. He carefully stuck it under the rock, tapping at whatever was lodged there. Finally, it slid out.

"Well, I'll be damned," James said. It was the syringe.

JAMES

JAMES HAD A GOOD MEMORY, too. It was why he had excelled almost immediately as an investigator. Maybe Molly had gotten that from him. He wanted to think so. The more time he spent with her, the more of her mom he could see in her. He hoped she had gotten something from him, too. Something good. Something useful.

But James hadn't been paying enough attention when they found Linda. Sure, some things he couldn't ignore. But mostly he had been thinking about getting out of there. About calling it in and distancing himself from the whole thing.

Now, he was in the thick of it. And kicking himself for not paying better attention in the first place. Molly's revelation was a gift. Her drawing priceless.

He thought about what he would do with the needle. Fingerprints, sure. Toxicologist, definitely. But he didn't have access to a lab anymore. He'd have to call up his buddy, Charles, with the FBI. Send it to him up in Denver. Charles had been CID with James until Charles's life came to be in great danger in Vietnam. Greater than most, on account of him being Black. The Vietcong weren't the only ones trying to kill him.

He and Molly were just about back at his house. She had picked the radio station, and Foreigner interrupted James's thoughts.

Molly hummed softly, tapping her foot on the floor of the truck. She tapped her fingertips on her thigh, too, as if playing those piano keys. She nodded to the beat. Every few words, she would sing a word. *"Never . . . someday you'll . . . I know . . ."*

"What other bands do you like?" James asked.

"Queen, Styx, Heart, Fleetwood Mac." Molly looked out the window, answering like she didn't care. Like she had just thought of those bands. Like music meant nothing to her, when James knew it did. He knew that much about fourteen-year-olds.

"A little bit of rock 'n' roll, huh?"

"I guess."

He turned into the driveway and shut off the truck. He watched Molly jump up out of her seat, throw her door open, climb out, slam it behind her, and run into the house. He wondered what that was about. Bathroom, he supposed.

He took his time stretching, walked around the truck, removed the air lines, squatted down to look at the underbelly for damaged beams and mudflaps.

When he finally went inside, he found Molly frowning at the answering machine.

"What is it?"

"No messages," she said. "The Codys didn't call."

He put their bags down in the hall and went to the kitchen.

"Want pancakes for dinner?" he asked.

Molly scrunched her nose. "I've had more pancakes these last few weeks than the whole rest of my life."

James opened the freezer.

"Hot dogs? Cheeseburgers?"

Just then, the phone rang. James and Molly looked at it. Looked at each other.

"I'll get it," he said.

He walked over and picked up the phone.

"Hello?"

"James Pinter?" a woman's voice asked.

"Speaking."

"I'm glad I caught you. My name's Gloria Fenwick. I'm a journalist with the *Santa Fe Reporter*. I was hoping we could set up a time to talk."

James thought about the documents he had just gotten signed for his last load. The date written on them. June 2. Past the anniversary of the occurrence. And not quite time for the trials. Sometimes James's name came up for those as an expert witness.

"Talk about what, Ms. Fenwick?"

"About Linda."

James kicked the bottom of the refrigerator, and Molly looked up sharply.

"Linda?" James asked, hoping he had heard wrong.

"Linda Morris," Gloria said. "I understand you think there was foul play involved in her death."

"Yeah?" James asked. "Who told you that?"

"George did," she said. "I cover the Navajo tribe. Try to get them the attention they need and deserve. Especially in matters such as this. George said you're ex-Army."

James bit his lip and let a stream of curses die in his throat.

"Ms. Fenwick, I don't have nearly enough information to speak on the incident."

"But you're looking into it, isn't that right?"

James didn't reply. He wondered why George would be so rash. So careless with this information.

"Look," Gloria said as if reading his thoughts. "Don't be angry with George. He loved Linda. He just wants to help in any way he can. The press I've helped them get over the years has been beneficial."

James remained quiet.

"Are you still there?"

"I'm still here."

"I won't publish anything yet," she said. "I understand this is a sensitive matter. The Navajo police can't do much with the death occurring off the reservation and with their limited resources. I believe you've met Officer Wayne Tully?"

James really could have smashed something. Wayne. The man who had taken them to Kay and George and Adriel. Why hadn't Wayne told him he was police? Why did this lady know so much more than he did? Molly was right. He hadn't asked nearly enough questions. If he was going to do this, he needed to really commit. This reporter was showing him just how much he'd been half-assing it.

"Yeah. We've met."

"I just think this is worth the *Reporter* being involved in. If you don't find much of anything, if you decide Linda really did just overdose, then fine. But I have some information that may be useful to you and your . . . investigation."

James did not want to talk to this woman. To any journalist. He knew how obtrusive they could be in an investigation. And this could barely qualify as one. But if she was familiar with the tribe, with their past troubles, it might be worth it.

"Fine," James said. "But I'm not due back in Albuquerque for two weeks."

"I'll come to you," Gloria said, her voice chipper. "Tell me when and where and I'll be there."

[16]

KAY

KAY HAD JUST GOTTEN home and taken her shoes off. She massaged her foot and rolled her head from side to side. She was a high school teacher on the reservation, and every part of her day was trying. The kids only got more defiant as they grew. Resisting authority, resisting learning, resisting their own history and culture. But Kay loved them all. The book-worms and the punks. She saw the kid inside each one of them. The curious innate being that, by fourteen, most had tried to bury. She loved the struggle of trying to pull it back out of them. To see just a glimmer of curiosity in their eyes. It made her whole day worth it.

She switched feet, rubbing through the ball of her foot, through her toes.

Her phone rang, and she let it go once, twice, three times before she stood to answer it.

"Yeah, it's Kay," she said.

"Kay, it's James."

Her heart beat faster as she leaned on her countertop.

"The Codys called?" she asked.

"No, but a reporter did. What is George doing, calling reporters?"

"Damn." She hung her head between her arms. "I didn't know he was going to call her. Gloria, right?"

"Yeah, that's her. What can you tell me about her?"

"Oh, I don't know." Kay sighed and stood up again. "She's like background noise around here. Always flashing a smile, handing out a card. Attractive. Fashionable. She covered the new high school that opened a few years ago. I did a lot of work on that. Obtained grants. Acted as a consultant at times. Gloria and I spent time together, then. She was around the house. Around my sister and George, too. She's nice."

"And her articles?" James asked.

Kay closed her eyes. Opened them back up and popped a walnut from the bag on the counter into her mouth.

"Never has a bad thing to say about us."

"Right," James said. "Well, look, she wants to meet and talk. Says she's got some information for me. Can you think of anything else I should know before going into this? Anything you might've forgotten to tell me? About Linda, about you, about anyone? Jobs, hobbies, friends? Sorry. Didn't mean to say her name."

Kay felt shaky. She had to sit down.

"Nothing," she said.

"Just take a minute and think."

Kay did think. There was plenty she could tell him that had nothing to do with *that*. Wasn't there?

"Ummmm," she said. "I work at the high school. My ex-husband works at the clinic. He's a doctor. George works at the post office."

"And what about her? Did she work? Did she have a job?"

Kay's mouth felt dry.

"Uh huh," she said. "Custodial job. At some offices." She grabbed her thighs with shaking hands. *Please don't ask anything else about her.*

"Offices?" James asked.

"Cleaned the bathrooms, took the trash out. For a company off the highway."

"Which company?"

"It's called the United Nuclear Corporation."

"And Adriel?" James asked.

"There's nothing none of you need to know about Adriel."

"All right, all right," James said. "Any other drug use in the family?"

"No," Kay said. "Our mom died when we were kids. Our dad raised us. He passed away seven years ago, now. Lung cancer."

"Mmhmm," James said. "You think you can talk a little more about . . . her? Molly and I went back to the site. Turns out Molly's got a damn good memory. Drew a sketch for me."

"Still learning about your own daughter, huh?" Kay asked. She hadn't meant to sound so spiteful, but her nerves were pulled tight like a wire.

"Sure am," James said, chuckling. He wasn't bothered.

"Yeah, go ahead and ask me," she said, sighing.

"She looked like she might've been meeting someone. Dressed nice. Jewelry on. Any idea who it could have been?"

"No," Kay said. And that was the truth. She didn't know. She *could've* guessed. But she wouldn't.

"Girlfriends?" James asked. Kay hated the accusatory tone she thought she heard in his voice. Linda would never have an affair. Even if she had done what Kay knew she had done.

"She had a few. You think she was going out with her girlfriends?"

"She just seemed awfully dressed up."

Kay was about to ask what he would know about why and when women dressed up, when he spoke again.

"Was she the kind of woman who would wear things with stains on them?"

"No," she said. "She liked all that homemaking and mothering stuff. She kept her things clean. She knew all the tricks when it came to removing stains. Ketchup, wine, anything."

"All right, then," James said.

"And, James, she *always* wore jewelry. That shouldn't tell you anything about where she was going or who she was seeing."

"How about a full face of makeup? Eyeshadow? Lipstick? The stuff you put on your eyelashes."

"Mascara," Kay said, quieter. "I don't think she normally wore mascara."

"Got it," he said. "Thanks, Kay."

"That's it?"

"That's it."

"Will you let me know what Gloria says?"

"I might."

Kay hated being treated like a suspect. That was what she felt like right then. She needed to get off the phone.

"One more thing," he said. She closed her eyes and waited.

"Do you remember much about that morning? Had you seen her? Spoken to her?"

Kay swallowed and tried to keep her tears from spilling out.

"I hadn't spoken to my sister in weeks," she said. "That morning, I did what I always do. I went to school to teach."

She barely waited long enough for him to take a breath before saying, "I've got to go. I'm late for something. Sorry." She hung up before he could say goodbye.

17

GLORIA

GLORIA SMOOTHED the front of her denim vest as she eased herself into a booth. James had wanted to meet for dinner. Nothing fancy, he'd made sure to add. She was fine with that. A burger restaurant like Bob's Big Boy or authentic Mexican or maybe Asian food. But he had picked Gloria's least favorite kind of restaurant. A cheap steak house where anyone with good taste wouldn't order the steak. But everything else on the menu was fried meat with some sort of gravy. And all the salads had eggs in them.

Gloria had tried to look casual. She would never normally wear something like a vest. But she didn't want James to see her as a threat. She wanted him to see her as an ally. Perhaps even a friend. Someone to work with, not against.

She'd dug up everything she could on him before flying out to Oklahoma City. James Pinter. Star quarterback at his high school in Sweetwater, Texas. Went to Baylor University until his parents were killed in an automobile accident.

Likely grieving his father, a World War II hero, he left college and enlisted in the Army. He kept in touch with his college girlfriend, Dorothy, and always went home to her in between tours. He started off as military police, eventually applying for the Criminal Investigation Division. Became estranged with Dorothy shortly after she had their baby, nearly nine years into their off-and-on relationship. He was stationed in the States for a while but went to Germany often. Then Vietnam. And the trial.

James breezed in four minutes before their scheduled meeting time. Gloria was surprised to see a teenage girl with him. His daughter? She hated that she hadn't expected that. She stood to shake his hand.

"You must be James," she said. He tried to smile, but it looked like a grimace.

"This is my daughter, Molly," he said.

Gloria smiled.

"It's a pleasure to meet you, Molly."

Molly gawked openly, and Gloria felt grounded again. It was the reaction she was used to getting. Gloria was nearly six feet tall and "prettier than the models," she was often told. She was getting older now, but even in her late thirties, she was mistaken for Hollywood actresses ten years younger. All through journalism school she had been encouraged to do broadcast. It was like she was made for it. But Gloria had never been very good at thinking on her feet or speaking on the spot. She liked to research. She was much more comfortable behind a typewriter, painstakingly weaving all of her hard work into a nice, neat package. To leave her readers shocked or breathless or ashamed or angry—or whatever emotion she wanted to evoke. Gloria did not do spur of the moment. She did methodical.

"Hi," Molly finally said as they all sat.

"I hope you don't mind, but I ordered us potato skins," Gloria said.

"I love potato skins!" Molly cried. She still looked starry-eyed.

"Me too," Gloria said.

"So, what is it you wanted to tell me about the case?" James asked, sliding into the booth beside Molly. "About Linda?"

Gloria glanced at Molly before sitting back down. She hadn't expected to talk about all this with anyone other than James. She might have to shift her strategy.

"I need to ask. Do you mind if I take some notes while we chat?"

James nodded once, and she assumed that meant he didn't mind. She took out her notepad.

"I'll tell you anything you'd like to know about the tribe and what I know about Linda and her family. But first, can you tell me a little about how you found her?"

"I found her," Molly blurted. She glanced at her dad for a moment, but he betrayed nothing. "Actually, I found the boy first."

"Her son?" Gloria asked. "Adriel? You found Adriel?"

Molly nodded.

"Sweet boy," Gloria said. "Doesn't talk though, does he? Did he say anything at all to you?"

James shook his head.

"He just took me by the arm and led me to her," Molly said.

"And what did she look like?" Gloria asked. "What made you think she hadn't overdosed?"

Molly was quiet this time, looking to her dad for answers. James sat back in the booth, arms crossed.

"What'd the family tell you?" he asked.

Gloria pressed her lips together. "George said he didn't know exactly what you saw. Kay wouldn't tell me. She said it was up to you to relay that information."

Gloria wasn't about to tell James what she'd come here to tell him until he told her what had made him get involved in the first place. She knew how cops were, and she knew how soldiers were. She had worked with both.

"Someone had done something to her body after she died."

"What?"

Just then the waitress appeared with their potato skins. "There you go!" she said. She was a young, bubbly thing.

"Thank you," Gloria said.

"Can I take y'alls orders?" she asked, smiling too big.

"Could you give us a few minutes?" Gloria asked.

"Sure thing! Y'all just call when you need me. Name's Sandra!"

Gloria gave her a strained smile, and the waitress bounced away. Gloria looked back at James, who had already put a potato skin on his plate.

"What had they done?" she pressed.

"Left a message," James said.

Maybe he didn't think she could handle hearing it. She almost laughed at that.

"What was the message?"

"The letters 'CC.'"

Gloria paced herself. Held her next question for a moment. "What does that mean?"

James took a bite and shrugged. He pulled the potato skin away from his mouth, and the cheese stretched until it broke. He stuffed the cheese into his mouth, too, and Gloria waited for him to finish chewing.

"Different things to different people," he finally answered.

Obviously. He was playing around with her, now.

"What do you think it meant to Linda?"

He drank his Dr. Pepper.

"That's the question, isn't it? What do *you* think it meant to Linda? You know more about her than I do."

Gloria chose her words carefully. Let them sit on her tongue for a moment. "Maybe it doesn't matter what it meant to Linda. Maybe the message wasn't for her."

"Well, yes," James said. "Linda is dead. A bit too late for her to get any messages."

Gloria blushed. She'd walked into that one. "What does it mean to you, James?"

"I seriously doubt it was meant for me, either." He chuckled. He took another bite of his potato skin. He was trying to frustrate her.

The waitress bounced over again.

"Y'all ready now?" she asked. James gave her a big smile back.

"Why don't you bring us a round of French onion soup and we'll look at the menu?" he said.

The waitress nodded vigorously. "You got it!"

"Did you know that George isn't Adriel's biological father?" Gloria asked, sick of talking in circles.

James's eyebrows went up. "No, I did not."

She tucked her hair behind her ear and cleared her throat. "George was Linda's husband but not Adriel's father. Adriel's real father lives in Albuquerque. White man. Soldier."

She saw the alarm go off in James's mind. Saw his eyes get wide for just a moment, and she smiled.

"Is that so?" he asked.

"Dale. Works at a restaurant downtown. Washes dishes there. Maybe you want to talk to him?"

Gloria knew that husbands and boyfriends and ex-husbands and ex-boyfriends were always the primary suspects in women's murders. She also knew this one looked a little unusual. Not how one would expect a crime of passion or jealousy to go. A murder made to look like an overdose was not typical in a domestic dispute. Still. Wives poisoned husbands. There was nothing to say that a husband couldn't do the same. James wouldn't be able to help himself. He'd have to investigate Dale.

"Got anything else on him?" he asked.

"Sure." Gloria pulled out a folder containing some papers and photos. "Served in the Army for six years. Did two tours in Vietnam. He and Linda were short-lived. She let him be a part of Adriel's life for a bit until he couldn't be trusted around the boy anymore. After his time in Vietnam, he became violent and unpredictable. He had a drug problem."

Gloria knew she didn't have to say the next thing. She didn't even know why she did other than the fact that she wanted James to know that she knew. He had been underestimating her this whole time. "This isn't the first time I've heard of the initials 'CC' being used to send a message. I've

heard of the ace of spades and CC being carved into someone's skin."

James looked up sharply, anger behind his eyes, sure. But
something else, too. Relief, perhaps? She went on before he
could say anything.

"And I know you have, too."

18

JAMES

JAMES SWORE the restaurant tilted after Gloria's little revelation. The theatrics he could have done without. If she had covered the My Lai trials, she could have just said so.

But now he had to address everything. He had to admit that Linda's death could be connected to someone who'd been in Vietnam. And it seemed like this Dale was the likely suspect.

If Gloria had wanted James to trust her, she had failed. Now he was on high alert. Now he knew who he was dealing with.

So, instead of giving Gloria any satisfaction, he said, "If you think that narrows down my suspects in any way, you're wrong. Most of the country paid attention to what happened in My Lai. Plenty of people might remember the details. A proud soldier or an ardent dissenter both could have left a message like that for different reasons."

"But it is strange that her ex-boyfriend, the father of her son, was a soldier, isn't it?"

She clearly wanted to solve this case for him. Of course

she did. Journalists thrived on being a step ahead of law enforcement. Not that James *was* law enforcement. Hell, Gloria was the closest thing he had to a partner right now. A thought that made him furious.

"Not that strange," James said. "Most young men were."

"You'll want to talk to him, though."

It was a statement this time.

"And why, I ask, would the boy's father just leave him there after killing Linda?"

Gloria shook her head, not bothered at all. "Who knows. Doesn't love the boy. Doesn't care about him. Doesn't want him. You know as well as I do that lunatics don't need a logical reason to do what they do."

"Other than knowing where he works, you got something else here that's going to help me?"

Her neck and cheeks reddened.

"I haven't spoken to him, if that's what you're asking. Not about this. Or about anything."

"Don't," James said. "Leave that to me."

Gloria nodded, looking down at the table.

"All right," she said, clearing her throat. "But if you need me for anything, please know that I want to help you."

Sure you do, James thought. The perky waitress brought them their soup, waited a beat with a closed-lip smile this time, and then turned and left when no one said anything.

"If I come across any other uncanny connections that are already public knowledge, you'll be the first to know," Gloria added.

James didn't consider himself a nasty person. The years he'd spent as military police and then CID had taught him that being spiteful got you nowhere with anyone. Plenty of other men who wore the badge had egos. James probably had at first, too. But he'd learned to shed anything and everything that wasn't useful to him. Which was why he'd needed to leave the Army when he did. He could never have shed the need to pursue the truth. It was all that was left.

He could see Gloria was embarrassed. Maybe even a little frustrated.

"Look," he said. "I appreciate the information about Dale. I'm going to speak to him because Kay wants to know what happened to her sister. But I'm not sure I'll ever get that answer. Anything short of a confession is still a question mark, isn't it? I'll likely never have hard evidence to bring to law enforcement. I'll only have hearsay."

Gloria studied him for a moment.

"That's where I come in. An article exposing the details of Linda's death—the unwillingness of the police to treat it as wrongful. It's the closest thing to justice that Linda might get."

James leaned forward to tell her that that *was* nothing. Her article would mean nothing. It wouldn't be justice, or anything close to it. The police wouldn't care, and neither would the rest of New Mexico. These were Indians. This was their affair. That was what everyone would think. That it wasn't their problem. James had seen it all before. No one had cared about those Vietnamese villagers, either. But Gloria put up her hands to stop him from speaking.

"I'll let you do your investigation first. Anything you can. You're clearly good at what you do if they put you on My Lai. Let's see what you can dig up with Dale."

James almost told her about the Codys then, just to see

what she might have had on them. But he kept it to himself. He still wasn't feeling generous toward this woman.

Instead, he took out a pen and tested it on a napkin. It worked. "What's the name of that place, now?" he asked. "The one where Dale works?"

It ended up being the loud Cody who they sent for James. His name was Byron, James would later learn, and he showed up at a rest stop bathroom just as James was leaving it.

He and Molly were on their way to Flagstaff with a load, and he was thinking of how he had left Molly with a locked truck and a baseball bat and how maybe he should teach her how to shoot instead.

Byron Cody followed James out of the bathroom, and it took him a full minute to notice the sound of the close footsteps. James knew then how out of practice he was by how little he was expecting such a surprise. Byron Cody grabbed him by the back of the collar and hustled him away from his truck, farther into the darkness, toward the trees. Fine. James didn't want this man around Molly, anyway.

"Listen, bilagáana," Byron Cody said in the loudest whisper James had ever heard. "We don't need you sniffin' around Indian affairs, trying to come to Miss Morris's rescue. We can handle it just fine, eh?"

Byron Cody still had James's collar clenched in his fist, so when James spun around to face him, it was tight and uncomfortable.

"You can handle it? I thought you people didn't like death," James said. "Skinwalkers and all that. Can't say I blame y'all, though. Sure have seen some strange things being around death."

For just a second, James saw a glimmer of fear pass over the man's face. So quickly it could've been the headlights of a passing car. But then Byron smiled.

"You've got the wrong Indian, bilagáana," he said. "Do I look like my pops? Like I still believe in ghost stories?"

"I just didn't know y'all were investigators, that's all."

Byron Cody laughed a raspy laugh. He wore a giant belt buckle and a tight ponytail.

"We are the law. On the reservation, we are the law. That's who we are."

"What about Wayne Tully? I thought he was the law."

Byron Cody got close to James's face.

"Wayne Tully is a fuckin' joke. You know who Diné respect? Codys. That's who."

"Fear, respect, same thing, right?"

Byron Cody smiled so wide James could see a gold tooth glinting in the dark.

"We learned from the best, bilagáana."

"You keep calling me that."

"Means 'friend,'" Byron said, still smiling wide. James knew it did not mean "friend."

"Why do you care about Linda Morris? I thought you didn't even know who she was."

"We care about you stickin' your nose in shit it don't belong in. We. Do. Not. Need. You. Got it?"

James shrugged dramatically, and probably without realizing he was doing it, Byron released his collar.

Byron looked indignant for a moment before smirking and continuing, "It's too bad. I kinda like what you got going on. Ghost of Jim Morrison vibes or somethin'. But I'll still kill you if I have to. Leave it to us. We'll find who did it."

"I appreciate the offer," James said.

Byron's laugh echoed in the empty woods beside them. "It's a promise, my friend. A promise."

They stared at each other before, finally, James tipped his hat.

"I'll be going, then," he said.

"Sure was nice to know you," Byron said, arms crossed. He didn't move.

James got in his truck, started it up, and turned it right around, back toward the reservation.

19

WAYNE

WAYNE SHUFFLED some papers around his desk and looked out the window. He had gotten off the phone with that reporter Gloria about ten minutes ago. She'd wanted him to know that James Pinter was going to look at Adriel's real father, Dale. It could have been him, Gloria explained, because Dale served in Vietnam, and what was carved on Linda's arm was a message from a soldier. Or could have been.

Wayne had asked for James's number, and now he flicked the small piece of paper he had written it on.

Just then, the bell to the station's door dinged, and two sets of footsteps entered. Wayne stood and listened to one of his younger officers—Ted, he guessed—greet whoever it was. It didn't sound like someone Ted knew.

Wayne needed to move, needed something to do, so he walked to the front to be nosy.

He saw Molly first. She was looking around the station with interest. She walked over to the corkboard with faces of the missing and wanted on it, as well as upcoming events and meetings.

But James looked serious, focused. He glanced up when Wayne approached.

"It's you again," Wayne said. "Good to see you both."

He stuck out a hand for James to shake.

"Wish I'd known you were the police lieutenant here when we first met," James said.

"It was my day off."

James smiled at that. They both knew there was no such thing, really. And apparently—by the look of James—even after you had left the job, the job didn't leave you. Still no days off.

"Can we get some coffee?" James asked.

"It's about to be time for my break," Wayne said. "How about an early lunch?"

"Sure."

"You both can ride in my truck again," Wayne said.

"Appreciate it."

Wayne held the door open for Molly, who smiled politely. Up close, he could see how tired she looked. How tired they both looked.

"Long night?" he asked, as they all loaded into his truck.

"We were on our way to Flagstaff. Had to double back after a little encounter at a rest stop."

"An encounter?"

"A Cody. In his late twenties. Has a voice like a trumpet."

Wayne chuckled. "Byron. What's Byron Cody want with you?"

"To threaten me. Told me to leave the whole Linda thing

alone." James glanced at him. "Sorry, does the name thing bother you, too?"

He shook his head. "Would be hard to do my job if it did."

"Byron Cody told me he doesn't need me poking around in Indian business. Said the Codys would take care of it."

Wayne sucked his teeth and shook his head again.

"Hey, what's that?" Molly asked from the back seat. James turned to see where she was pointing, and Wayne looked quickly, too.

"Line for the clinic," he said.

"Is it like that every day?" she asked.

"No," Wayne said. "It's dialysis treatment day. That's why they're all lined up like that."

"What's dialysis?" Molly asked.

"A treatment for when your kidneys don't work on their own anymore."

"Oh."

Wayne turned his attention back to James, still staring out the window. "So, you're saying you've got a Cody problem now?"

"And so do you," James said. "Carrying out whatever kind of justice they see fit. Or so they claim. But maybe it's as simple as an admission of guilt. What say you?"

Wayne didn't answer. He pulled into the parking lot of the buffet and sighed deeply, but he didn't move to open the door.

"Linda's death occurred off the reservation," he finally said. "It's not my jurisdiction, but it isn't yours, either." He cracked a small smile at that. "If I can help, I want to."

James nodded. "Appreciate that." He grasped the door

handle but stopped. "You don't feel the same way the Codys do? Like it's not my business?"

Wayne smiled wider. He thought about a time in his life when he would have been defensive toward James. But that time was long gone. Wayne knew to use whatever resources he could, whenever he could. The job, and the constraints that came with being a Navajo, with being on the reservation, humbled him.

"Nah," he said. "Now, maybe if you were BIA. They mess up everything they touch."

"I believe that," James said.

"I think we can work in a way that works for us both. Nobody breathing down our neck. Sound good?"

James nodded.

"I can handle the Codys on my end," Wayne said. "But if I were you, I'd watch my back off the reservation, too. They have people all over these parts. From Albuquerque to Flagstaff."

James glanced back at Molly. "Copy that," he said.

[20]
JAMES

WHEN KAY PULLED up to her house, James and Molly were already waiting for her. She looked exhausted, and James wondered if she wasn't sleeping well.

"News?" she asked.

He shook his head. "I was thinkin', though," he said, "you haven't gone to Linda's work, have you? I'm sure she left some of her things there. She had a locker or something. We ought to ask the people there about her, too. I was hoping you'd come with me. I don't think they'll hand her keys over to just anyone without a badge."

Kay tugged her hair free from its tie. It cascaded down her back. "You don't think the state police did that?"

"No, I don't think the state police—or the BIA—did squat."

She ran her fingers through her hair and took a deep breath. "I don't want to touch her things, okay?"

James didn't ask what that was about.

"Okay," he said. "I can get her things. But you'll need to get the key."

Kay nodded.

"Climb on into my rig. You and Molly will have more than enough room."

She smiled at Molly. "I'm sorry if I smell like teenagers."

Molly shrugged. "I am one. I won't even notice."

Kay laughed a tired laugh, and the three of them piled into the truck.

The offices for United Nuclear Corporation were not far off the reservation. The custodial crew were likely to stay later, but James hoped most of the office employees were still there, too.

The front desk was separated only slightly from the rest of the giant room of cubicles and desks. A woman just a few years older than James held a phone to her ear, and she put up a finger to ask them to wait.

"Yes, I can transfer you over to his line, and you can leave him a message directly. Yes. Okay, hold for just one moment, please." She brought the phone down just a little and dialed a few numbers on her switchboard.

The woman brought the phone back up to her ear. "Hi, Mr. Paulson. I have Gerald on the line. I'll put him through right now." More fiddling with the buttons. Then she hung up the phone and stared at James.

"May I help you?" she asked. Her smile was tight-lipped.

"Yes, I'm here with Kay Benally." He held his arm out to introduce her. "Her sister, Linda Morris, used to work here. She was a janitor."

"All right," the woman said.

"Linda Morris died a few weeks ago. We doubt anyone has been by to pick up her things, and we'd like to do so."

"Oh." The woman brought her hand to her chest. "I'm so

sorry to hear that." She turned to Kay and repeated, "I am so sorry to hear that."

Kay nodded but said nothing.

"Um. . . ." The woman stood up. "Let me find our building manager for you. He should be able to help."

"Thanks," James said.

He and Kay stood a few feet apart with their arms crossed. Molly looked up at the ceiling, then around the small lobby. James followed her gaze: a couple of chairs beside the door, a water cooler with small paper cups, a small table and lamp.

The woman returned, accompanied by a large man. His brown hair was thin and greasy, his face cleanly shaved, his neck wide and pimpled. He offered his hand to James.

"Sheryl told me about Linda," he said. "I'm sorry for your loss. She was a good worker. Always here on time. Never complained."

James shook his hand. "I'm James," he said. "And this is Linda's sister, Kay."

The man nodded once at her. "I'm Oscar Burnstead. I manage this facility."

"You say Linda was always on time? Did you call anyone when she didn't show for work?" James asked.

"Sure." Oscar nodded. "I called the home phone we have here on file. No one answered."

"And you left a message?"

"I did," Oscar said. "Two, actually. Once about a half hour after her shift started and then again later in the day."

"And what time was her shift supposed to start?" James asked.

"Seven in the morning."

"And what was that date?"

"I'm sorry," Oscar said. "Are you a cop?"

James was about to say he wasn't when Kay jumped in.

"Yes," she said. "A private investigator, actually. I hired him."

James bit the inside of his cheek to keep from laughing. Oscar stared at her for a moment, then shrugged.

"So, the date?" James pressed.

Oscar rubbed his chin. "I'll have to get back to you on that. Mid May, I know that much. It was a Monday, I think. But I'll have to check on that, too."

"I'd appreciate it," James said. "And no one ever called you back the day that she didn't show up?"

He shook his head. "No, sir."

"Did you think to call the police?" James asked.

Oscar gave them a half smile. "If I called the police every time an Indian didn't show up for work, that's all they'd have time to do. Respond to my calls."

"But you just said she was always on time. A good worker," James said. He could practically feel the heat radiating from Kay, and out of the corner of his eye, he saw her fist clench.

Oscar shrugged. "I've had plenty of good workers up and leave without warning. Especially women. I always figure their old man got sick of not having the house looked after or nothin'."

"So, can we collect her things?" Kay asked, abruptly.

Oscar looked startled for only a moment before saying, "Sure, sure, follow me."

He led them into the stairway and down into the basement. They walked down a long hallway before Oscar showed them into a room with lockers and a coffee machine and a big mirror along one wall. A man sat on a bench, lacing his boots. He didn't glance their way.

"Locker number 475," Oscar said, handing James the keys. Locker 475 was about five lockers down from the man lacing his boots.

Oscar waited by the door, arms crossed, while James opened Linda's locker and rummaged through its contents.

A jacket. A sweater. A pair of clean, rolled-up stockings. Her uniform with her nametag still attached. A pack of gum on the top shelf. James stuck his hand into her jacket pocket. Then the pocket of her uniform. He found a hair tie in one and a crumpled-up paper in the other. He opened it. *To Linda*, it said. The handwriting was messy. Legible, but barely. He slipped it into his own pocket.

Molly had the bag they had brought for Linda's things. He called her over and put everything else from the locker inside.

When James turned back around, Oscar was still studying him. Odd that he hadn't found something else to busy himself with, James thought. Odd that he was so invested.

"Well, thanks for your time." James extended his hand and Oscar shook it. He had big, sweaty paws.

"If I can help with anything else, give me a ring." Oscar handed James his card.

"Thanks," James said. "Could you point me in the direction of the nearest restroom?"

Oscar pointed a meaty finger farther down the hall. "On your right," he said.

James turned to Molly and Kay. "I'll meet you ladies back upstairs."

Just as James had hoped, Oscar led them down the hall and up the stairs. The man in the locker room was still there, combing his sandy hair in front of the mirror.

James walked up to him. "James Pinter," he said. The man eyed him carefully before nodding.

"Bo Coleman."

James could see his tattoos now. Prison tattoos all down both arms.

"Can I ask you a few questions, Bo? About a lady who used to work here?"

"Linda?" Bo asked.

"That's right."

"Sure," Bo said. "I'm not sure how much I can tell ya. The woman barely spoke. She came, did her job, went home."

"So, she didn't have many friends here?"

"Not that I ever saw," Bo said.

"Did she do her job well? Was that boss of yours ever on her ass about anything?"

Bo slowly shook his head.

"No, Linda wasn't ever gettin' yelled at."

James pulled the note from his pocket and unfolded it again.

"You happen to recognize this handwriting?" he asked.

Bo squinted at the note. "Can't say I do."

"And did you ever see Linda meetin' anyone here at work? Outside maybe? On her lunchbreak? Anything like that?"

"Like I said," Bo said, "she drove here in that beat-up Jeep Wagoneer, did her job, and left."

"Thanks for your time," James said, shaking Bo's hand. "What's the deal with your boss, anyway? He seemed suspicious of something. Maybe it was me. Maybe it was you."

"He's an ass," Bo said. "He always accuses us of stealin' shit. Like we want some staplers and pens. Give me a fuckin' break."

"Huh," James said. "Well, good luck with all that."

"Yeah, man."

21

KAY

KAY AND MOLLY had decided to wait by James's truck. That place made Kay uncomfortable. She could feel Linda's ghost. Restless in a way that Kay didn't know what to do with. She hoped that when she was dead herself, she would steer clear of the high school. She spent enough time there as it was.

She and Molly leaned against the front of the rig. Molly held the bag with Linda's things gingerly, like a bunch of articles of clothing might break. Better Molly than Kay, though. She would tell James to burn it all when he was done with it.

Kay had thought she'd feel annoyed, but actually, she felt at ease. Going to Linda's work, getting it over with, it was necessary. It was something closer to closure than Kay had yet felt.

James smiled a gentle smile when he saw them. "You ladies ready to hit the road?" he asked. Molly nodded.

"Let's get out of here," Kay agreed.

James unlocked the rig, and they all climbed in. He pulled something from his pocket.

"What is that?" Kay asked.

"I found it in her pocket," he said. "It's a note. It doesn't say much, but could you take a look? I'm hoping you'll recognize the handwriting."

Kay looked down at the crinkled paper. Even seeing her sister's name was painful.

"No," she said. "I don't recognize the handwriting."

"It's not George's?"

Kay stared at James. He was doing it again. Suggesting some sort of an affair. She took a deep breath. He was just doing his job, she reminded herself. She counted to three before answering.

"No, it's not from George. If he were to write her a love note, he would write it in Navajo. He would use her Navajo name."

"Can you tell me what her Navajo name is?" James asked, gently. Kay knew she should tell him, but she couldn't. Speaking that aloud would be worse than her English name. It was deeper, more personal. Kay shook her head.

"I'm sorry. Maybe George will tell you. Or Wayne. I can't."

"I understand," James said. He folded the note up and looked around his seat.

"Are you looking for something?" Kay asked.

"Paper bag. Swore I had a few lyin' around here somewhere."

Molly stood on the seat and reached behind Kay, sitting back down a moment later with a half-crumpled paper bag. James gave her a grateful smile and pulled a clean napkin and an empty beer can from it.

"This'll work," he said. "Thanks, Molly." He shook the bag then held it to his chest and tried to smooth it down.

Then, he slipped the note inside and folded the top down a few times.

"Keep that safe for me?" he asked Molly. She nodded.

James turned the key, checked his mirrors, and pulled out onto the highway. Fat pellets of rain splattered against the windshield. Kay watched one drip down, absorbing the one below it and the one below that with an insatiable appetite. James turned the wipers on, and the fat blob was carried away.

The gray sky surrounded them, and Kay had the urge to jump out of the truck and run through the storm. To feel the wetness on her face, her arms, her legs. Out here, rain felt like a promise. It felt like hope. Like maybe it could wash all of this away. The death. The pain. The secrets.

"I'm gonna pay Adriel's real father, Dale, a visit," James said. Kay's heart began to beat faster. "Today," he added. "Why didn't you tell me about him?"

"I'd rather try to forget he exists at all," she said.

"That's all well and good, but Dale is now my number one suspect. And I had to hear about him from the reporter."

"Dale's your number one suspect?" she asked.

"Yes," he said. "Dale served in the military. The message left on your sister . . . it could have military connections."

"But Dale would never have left Adriel there," Kay said.

"Why's that?" James asked.

"He's tried to get custody before. I know he wants to be a part of Adriel's life. But he can't be. He couldn't be."

"Was your sister in contact with him before she died?" James asked.

Kay tried to breathe normally. She didn't want to think about it. About how she had left things. What she had said.

"I don't know," she finally lied.

James nodded. "It's almost always someone close to the victim. And this guy looks too suspicious, so I've got to check him out. Will you hang out with Molly again? This could be a sticky situation."

"I want to come," Molly said. "I can handle it."

"Maybe, but maybe not. Sounds like this guy is violent. Drug problems. Unpredictable."

Kay shook her head. "Molly, you don't want anything to do with that man. Trust me. I'll make you some food at my place."

"Thanks," James said. Molly just stared out the window.

Lightning flashed in the distance, illuminating the mountains ahead of them. Kay hoped Dale lashed out. She wanted nothing more than that man dead. She hoped James would kill him. She knew it was unlikely, but it was what she wanted. Whether Dale had killed her sister or not, there was one thing that would always be his fault. The way Kay and Linda had left things. And for that alone, Dale should have to pay.

22

MOLLY

KAY TURNED up the radio as she scrambled eggs. It was too early for dinner, but Molly had eaten lunch so early that now she was starving.

Magazines were spread across Kay's coffee table, and Molly wondered if she liked to read them herself or had put them there for guests. *Mad. Cosmopolitan. Scientific American. Seventeen. Life.* Molly picked up *Seventeen* and flipped through it. Kay was listening to "Here You Come Again" by Dolly Parton, and every time the chorus came on, she would belt it out. Molly smiled. Kay had a nice, twangy singing voice. Deeper than Dolly's.

Kay's phone rang, and she turned the music down.

"Hello, this is Kay."

The radio got even quieter and then it was off.

"Listen, listen. You need to calm down. It's not . . ."

Silence for a moment and then Kay shouted, "Don't! Don't you dare, Al. Just wait. You don't understand. It's not what you think. I can explain. Where are you right now?"

Quiet again.

"Stay right there. I want to talk to you in person. To explain this."

Molly wanted to creep into the kitchen, but she didn't want to be a snoop.

"I promise you, that's not what happened. I'm coming now. Please. Just stay there."

Then, Molly heard the phone get set down and the pan get scraped. A minute later, Kay was rushing through the living room.

"I'm sorry," she said. "I really need to handle something right now." She grabbed her purse and hat. "You can't exactly come with me, but I'll drop you off at the station. Wayne will put you to work." She tried to smile, but it was strained and worried.

Molly nodded, dropping her magazine back on the coffee table and hopping up from the couch.

"Cool beans," Molly said. "Maybe Wayne can teach me a thing or two."

"That's the spirit," Kay said, hustling Molly out the door.

Molly had thought it would be weird and uncomfortable at the police station, but just as Kay had said, Wayne had plenty of work for her to do. Copying papers, sending faxes.

The other officers left around 4 p.m., and the station grew quiet. Wayne poured himself his third coffee since Molly had gotten there and then sat across from her. He sipped and then sucked his teeth.

"How do you like this, Molly?" he asked.

She didn't know exactly what he meant by "this," but she nodded anyway. "I like it just fine."

"Your dad seems to take you just about everywhere with him. Lets you in on things. Do you like helping him?"

Molly was eager to say yes again, because now that she knew what he was asking, she knew that she did like it. She liked it a lot. But a part of her didn't want to admit that she liked anything about her dad. Spending time with him. Making him proud, like she had with that sketch.

She sat on her hands and swung her legs under her chair. She looked down at her pink suede Vans as they moved. Out and under. Out and under.

"I guess," she finally said.

When she looked up, a piece of hair fell in her face. Wayne grinned.

"Your dad seems proud of that picture you drew." He tapped his temple with his finger. "You've got a knack. It's in your blood."

Molly couldn't help but smile. She shrugged. "Maybe."

Wayne set down his coffee and leaned forward, looking serious now. "What do you think he should do next?" he asked.

Molly felt the color rise to her cheeks. Adults never asked her opinion. Not like this. Not in a way where she could tell they really wanted to know it.

"Well . . ." she started. She wanted to say something.

"Take your time," Wayne said, sitting back again. "Didn't mean to put you on the spot there. But let's think. You're not working with much evidence, are you?"

Molly shook her head. "James said everything was ruined where we found her," she said. "But we did find the needle."

"You found the needle?" he asked.

She nodded. "He mailed it to someone. A lab, he said."

"Interesting." Wayne crossed his arms. "What else? We don't much like autopsies. Maybe if we had thought she was murdered from the get-go. But an overdose?" He shook his head. "No need."

"And he's talked to the Codys," Molly went on, the words tumbling out. She couldn't stop them if she tried. "I guess they were his first suspects?"

Wayne nodded. "But if it was the Codys, they aren't going to reveal themselves," he said. "They're professional criminals. They don't exactly get nervous. Or feel guilty."

"But they threatened him," Molly said, her voice getting louder and stronger. "Told him to stop investigating. That's pretty suspicious."

Wayne took another sip of his coffee. "I agree."

"He's talked to her family," she continued. "Well, I guess not all of them yet. But he's finishing that today. Right now."

"And what does he think of them?" Wayne's eyebrow rose. It was thick, like a fat caterpillar.

"He was frustrated that George told the reporter about all of this. But he seems to trust Kay."

"What did you think of Gloria?" Wayne asked.

"She's gorgeous," Molly gushed, and Wayne chuckled.

"Your dad doesn't like her, huh?"

"No." Molly shook her head. "That was obvious."

"I don't blame him," Wayne said. "But Gloria's all right. Actually—" He pushed his chair back a bit and propped his ankle up on his knee, "—I bet it'll be difficult for her to print this if it turns out a tribe member did it. Have your dad ask her about the Codys next time. I bet she'll get real squirrely."

Molly hopped up and walked to the window. Outside, a group of boys walked along the road, pushing each other and laughing. One rode a bike in wide circles around the rest.

"You think he's okay?" Molly asked. "Being alone with this Dale guy? Gloria made him sound kind of crazy."

"Your father has been in far more dangerous situations. I promise you that. He can handle himself."

Molly spun around and crossed her arms.

"We haven't talked to any of her friends yet," she said. "I think that's what I would do next. She must have had friends or coworkers or something. They might know something Kay doesn't."

Wayne stood up, too, slower than Molly had. He walked toward the open door of his office, then turned and smiled at Molly.

"That's exactly what I would do, too." He stuck out his arm, indicating the hallway. "I happen to know a few of them. Should we go?"

Molly beamed. "Really?"

Wayne nodded. Molly snatched a pen and the notepad Wayne had given her earlier and followed him out of the station.

23

JAMES

THE RESTAURANT where Dale worked was a pizza place with three booths and one lone, wobbly table. The pizza joint was sandwiched between a laundromat and a tattoo parlor. James's shoes stuck to the floor, as though it had been mopped without soap.

Fifteen minutes after the place opened at 5 p.m., James dinged the little bell on the counter. An aging man with a scowl and a full head of dark-gray hair came up with a small notepad. He grabbed the pen from behind his ear and said, "What can I get you?"

"I'm lookin' for one of your workers, actually," James said. "Dale."

The man's frown deepened. "I told him no side business at work."

James wished he still had a badge. Something to flash at this man.

"It's not that," James said. "Family matters."

The man shook his head and stalked away, clearly unconvinced.

James read the menu while he waited: mozzarella sticks, Caesar salad, antipasto salad, minestrone soup, chicken wings.

Dale appeared suddenly, quietly. He was a lean, wiry man wearing a tight gray T-shirt tucked into light denim jeans. His wavy blond hair poofed back almost into a mullet. They stood nearly eye to eye.

"Who're you?" Dale said.

"A friend of Kay Benally's."

Dale's eyes grew alert, sharp.

"What does that bitch want?"

"Nothing from you."

"Then why are you here?"

"No one's told you?" James asked, knowing good and well that no one would have.

Dale lifted his chin a little. "Told me what?"

"Linda," James said. "She's dead."

Dale wore the expression of a surprised man. His eyes wide, his skin going pale.

"Shit, man," he murmured. He looked at the floor and shook his head. Then, he took his hands from his pockets and crossed his arms. "What happened?"

"I'm trying to find that out," James said. "What time are you off?"

"Ten."

"There's a bar down the street. Moondance. I'll meet you there then."

Dale's eyebrows furrowed. He clearly thought all this was weird, but James was okay with that. He wanted the man to be curious. Maybe even a little nervous. He would have pegged him an innocent man right then and there. But James knew both addicts and soldiers to be good actors.

Finally, Dale nodded. "All right."

When James left RJ's Pizza, he wandered the city until he found a record store. He had let his record player sit for so long he could picture the dust in a thick layer on the top. He had bought it years ago. Single, with more money from tours and sign-on bonuses than he knew what to do with. He'd paid off the big rig in two years.

He had set some aside for Molly in an envelope tucked into his important papers file. He never had a plan for it. What was he gonna do, mail it to Dorothy one day? Maybe. He didn't know. Eventually, the envelope got so fat he couldn't justify keeping it in his house anymore. It was ridiculous for any officer of the law—current or not—to keep cash in his house. Especially when he was gone so often. But James was a contradiction in many ways he couldn't explain.

When he opened a USAA savings account for Molly's envelope, the bank clerk had fought to keep a neutral face. Why did James have all that money?

Still, he'd made the occasional extravagant purchase, and the record player was one of them. Extravagant not exactly for the price—which was high—but for how little time he would be spending with it. It wasn't like James was a music nut.

Now, he stood in the store, surrounded by employees with shiny necklaces and earrings hanging from their bodies, wearing tight bell-bottom jeans with bright patches—blue and white and yellow. He thumbed through the new releases and then the discount bin before moving on to the alphabetically stored section. He started at Z, and by the time he got to S, he finally found one of the names Molly had mentioned. Styx. *Pieces of Eight*, the album was called. The cover had an older woman on it. Her hair pulled up tight in some sort of twist or braid. You couldn't really see. You could only see half her face. The other half was covered by another picture of her face—this time, half of her profile. She was aging, James realized. The other half profile in the background was her at a younger age, and in the one in the foreground, she was older, with gray hair. Her earring was a profile, too. An ancient figure's face, though he couldn't tell from which civilization.

James grabbed it and made his way to the cash register to pay. A man across the street, smoking, caught his eye. He thought he was Mexican at first, but when James squinted, he looked more Navajo. Familiar, even. As James neared the window, the man disappeared behind a dumpster.

A Cody, James thought—though he wasn't certain. Still, he paid quickly and walked straight to the bar, where he found a seat at a table with his back to the corner and perfect view of the door.

James couldn't say if the Cody was there for him or for Dale. But he knew he needed to get this done, and quickly.

[24]

DALE

THE GUY, James, had told Dale he was a friend of Kay's, but Dale knew a cop when he saw one. Worse than a cop, an ex-cop. A cop who had no one to answer to. Not that most of them did anyway, even with a uniform on. They were still happy to bust up a junkie's face. But without a uniform? Much worse.

Dale wiped his palms on his jeans again before pulling open the door to the Moondance. Some cheesy bar owned by an Indian. Or not. But definitely making money off the theme. Wolves on the walls howling at the moon. Some sort of tribal pattern painted on the bar.

It was starting to fill up. Dale's gaze darted around the room, trying to find James before James found him. That tight-ass was probably drinking a Coke or a root beer.

Dale didn't know why he'd come. Curiosity, he guessed. All this about Linda. What he really wanted to know was what would happen to Adriel. Would George be able to keep him? Or would Dale finally get his chance? Now was the time to get him away from those people if he could. Adriel had Indian blood, sure. But he had white blood, too. Dale's blood. And Dale knew that was more important.

James was creeping at the back of the place, and Dale was not surprised. Eyes like a snake, ready to strike. Dale's heart beat faster, and he had to remind himself that punching a cop was never a good idea. Instead, when he sat at the table, he kept one leg hanging off the side of his chair so he could run if he needed to.

"Ordered you a Sprite," James said, nodding toward the sweating glass on the table.

"What do you want from me?" Dale asked, not touching the drink. "Is this about Adriel?"

"Why would it be about Adriel?"

They were both shouting over the jukebox, which played the Rolling Stones. "Miss You."

Dale's leg bobbed up and down but not to the rhythm of the music. To the ticking inside his own head. Telling him to get out of there.

"Because I'm his fucking father, that's why."

"And you want him?" James asked. "You want custody?"

Dale snorted. "They'd never let that happen. The state. Those people. Not for a man like me. It doesn't matter that I was their human shield for two years over in that shithole country. Still can't see my own son."

James drank. Dale had been wrong. James was drinking a beer. A real one. It didn't put Dale at ease.

"Vietnam, you mean," James said.

"Yeah, Vietnam. Where the fuck else would I mean?"

"Which platoon?" James asked.

"Scout dog recon 48th Infantry outta Benning," Dale

said. Wasn't shit this cop could say about that. Dale bet his ass hadn't been a recon soldier.

James nodded and pulled a pen from his back pocket. He slid a drink napkin across the table, along with the pen. "Can't say I know it. Can you write it down? Infantry number and all so I can get it right?"

Dale eyed him but did what he was asked. James wouldn't find any dirt on Dale. Dale had lain the same place everyone else did—in the rice paddies with the mud and the bugs and the cow shit. Shot at what everyone else shot at— every fuckin' gook that moved. He wasn't any crazier than his fellow soldier. This cop could knock himself out looking up Dale's record.

"When's the last time you saw the boy?" James asked, taking back the napkin and pen.

"I don't know," Dale said. "Recently. Hadn't seen him in years. Out of the blue, Linda starts reaching out again. Wants to set up a time for me to see Adriel." Dale chuckled. "That asshole husband of hers didn't know. I would bet on that."

"And where'd you meet up?" James asked.

"Between here and there. I sure as shit wasn't going to that reservation. Wasn't welcome there and that was fine by me."

"Where between here and there? McDonalds? Rest stops along the highway?"

James had leaned forward a little, and Dale didn't like all the prying.

"What's it matter?" he asked. "We met once, and Linda said she'd set up a time to meet again."

"When was that?"

"I don't know. A month ago? Two months ago? Three?"

"You haven't asked me anything about her death," James said.

"She overdosed, didn't she?" Dale asked.

James didn't say anything but looked at him real hard. Dale laughed. This guy wasn't much of a cop if he couldn't figure out that was how addicts died.

"Linda said she was clean, but once a junkie, always a junkie. Who knows that better than a junkie?" Dale asked.

James still didn't say anything, only pulled a cigarette from his shirt pocket. Dale watched him light it and thought about ripping it from his fingers and throwing it, setting this whole damn bar on fire.

Dale's mouth was so dry, and the Sprite looked so refreshing. He needed a sip, but he refused to take anything this man had paid for. And what he really needed was a hit. He needed to wrap this up. But what he needed the most—more than any of that, maybe—was to know where his son was. He was supposed to go back for him. And he would.

"So, where's Adriel now?" Dale asked. "With George?"

"Adriel's whereabouts are none of your concern."

Dale smacked the table hard.

"It *is* my concern! He's my fucking son! I'm not gonna let you dirtbags keep him from me!"

He stood and pointed a shaking finger at James.

"You tell Kay. You tell Kay he's mine. You tell her that!"

Dale turned and stormed out the bar, bumping men much larger than him on the way out. He didn't care. The fire was in him now. If he could kill a bunch of gooks in that godforsaken place and get out alive, he could get his son back. He would.

25

WAYNE

WILLA YAZZIE HAD ALWAYS BEEN AN ESPECIALLY small girl. Thin hair. Small eyes, small chin. Small footprints. She had been a nerd of all sorts, cycling through all the hobbies and interests that could make a kid an outcast until finally finding drugs. She was polite and apologetic. Folding into herself until you couldn't tell the difference between her and a gust of wind. She had been Linda's best friend for years, and now Wayne stood at the door to her trailer with Molly by his side, ready to tell this whisper of a woman that her friend was dead. He was sure she hadn't heard.

"Coming," said a quiet, scratchy voice after he knocked. He knew it was Willa. She lived alone, and though many drug addicts kept company, Willa didn't.

He looked down at the potted mammillaria beside the door. It was beautiful in a sad way. He was sure Willa had forgotten about it, but that didn't matter to a cactus. It bloomed out here, anyway.

Molly had pestered him the whole way there as to whether or not this was really a good idea. She was afraid, though Wayne could tell she was the kind who would never admit it. Not that most teenagers would. But Wayne wouldn't take her somewhere dangerous. This wasn't just any addict's house. It was Willa's. No guns inside, he knew. And Molly could push Willa over with one finger if she needed to.

Willa came to the door in Tweety Bird pajama pants and a long, hooded sweatshirt, despite the day reaching nearly one hundred degrees. Her hair was tied into a knot at the very top of her head, but loose strands slipped out even as she stood there greeting them.

"Hi, Wayne," she said, smiling. Then she looked at Molly and shuffled back a half step. "Who's this?"

"Molly. She's helping me out today. Can we come in?"

Molly and Willa looked at one another as if the other's stare was the only thing keeping them from clawing each other's eyes out. Finally, Willa nodded. "Okay."

The house wasn't too dirty, but Wayne suspected that was only because Willa didn't have much to clutter it up with. They sat on a mustard-yellow couch that sank down half a foot under the weight of their bodies. Willa stood in front of them, arms crossed. She bit her fingernail and then lowered her arm.

"Can I get you anything? Something to drink?"

"No thanks," Wayne said. "Why don't you sit down, Willa?"

Her gaze darted from Molly to Wayne, and finally, she sat on an ottoman in the corner, knees pulled up under her.

"Have you heard about Linda?" Wayne asked.

"What about her?"

He sighed. He brushed cat hair from his pants. "Linda

died. The state police said it was an overdose, but we're looking into it."

Willa clasped her hand over her mouth. Her wide eyes teared over.

"No," she whispered.

"I'm sorry," Wayne said. "I know how close you two were for a long time."

A little squeak escaped Willa, and Wayne realized she was sobbing. He let her for a minute. They sat in silence, and Molly stared hard at the carpet under their feet. It was a traditional Navajo rug. A black-and-white border that looked a bit like a zipper. A rich red background. Black diamonds inside of white diamonds inside of blue diamonds inside of gray diamonds.

"Where did they find her?" Willa finally asked.

"Off the highway," Wayne said. "Behind the teepee truck stop."

Willa shook her head and wiped her eyes with her sleeve.

"Had you two spoken recently?" Wayne asked.

"Yes, actually," Willa said, sniffling. "It was the strangest thing." She cleared her throat and stood up suddenly. She looked around the room before saying, "Excuse me." She left and came back clutching a wad of toilet paper. She blew her nose with it.

"After she got clean, she stopped coming over. She told me why. She said it was all we ever did together. It was . . ." Willa trailed off as she sat back down on the ottoman. ". . . Awful." She squinted at the setting sun coming through the window. It fell on the carpet, and Wayne could see dust particles dancing in the air.

"I can imagine," he said. "Kay said the two of you were best friends. And I remember you always being together."

"Kay doesn't like me," Willa said. "But I understand. I understand all of it, really, I do. Linda had to think about her son, and I'm a bad person. She couldn't be around me."

"You aren't a bad person," Wayne said. "You've had some bad things happen to you."

He remembered her father's reputation. The calls they would get back when Wayne first joined the force. The blood, the stitches, the bruising. Willa had spent her whole life looking for an escape.

Willa rolled her eyes and looked away.

"So, you saw her again? Recently?" This time, it was Molly who spoke, and Wayne and Willa stared at her.

"Ummmmm . . ." Willa sputtered. "Yes. Yes, I saw her not too long ago." She looked back at Wayne, unsure of who she ought to address. "Like I said, it was strange. I wasn't even high that morning. Not yet. I was having a coffee. Like a normal person. And I was just so happy to see her when she came to my door. She let me hug her. She seemed so concerned about me. She wanted to know if I needed anything. She offered to take me to that program at the church again, if I wanted to get clean with her. She told me she loved me. She wanted the best for me. And she wanted to be my friend again."

They sat quietly for a moment. Thinking. Molly scribbled something in her notebook.

"When was this exactly?" Wayne asked. "Do you remember?"

Willa bit her lip. She thought for a moment before shaking her head. "No."

"That's all right. And you didn't see her again after that?" Wayne asked.

Willa shook her head again. "She stayed for a couple hours, though. We talked a lot. It was nice."

"I'm glad," Wayne said. "I'm glad you had that time with her."

Willa smiled.

"Did she mention anything that you thought was out of the ordinary?" Molly asked. "I mean, I know you hadn't seen each other in years, probably . . ."

Molly looked to Wayne, apprehension in her eyes, and he nodded, encouraging her.

"You must have known her pretty well, anyway. All things considered," Molly finished.

Willa gripped the sides of the ottoman and let her legs hang. She looked at her feet. They waited.

"She said something about leaving her job. Which was too bad. It was a good job. I know it was only janitor stuff, but everyone knows the mill company pays good."

"The mill company?" Molly asked.

"Uranium mill," Wayne clarified.

"Did she say why she was leaving?" Molly asked.

Willa shook her head. "We were both so happy to be together, I didn't want to ruin the moment. I just changed the subject."

Molly scribbled on her notepad again. Wayne thought she was more diligent than some of his officers on payroll.

"Thank you for telling us about all of this," Wayne said. "If you think of anything else, you know where to find me."

Willa nodded. Wayne and Molly stood to leave.

"It was nice to meet you," Molly said.

Willa smiled. "It was nice to meet you, too."

Wayne held the door open for Molly and then turned back around to face Willa.

"And, Willa?" he said. "Linda really did care about you. Just because she isn't here anymore doesn't mean you can't take her up on that offer to go to that program. I'll even drive you, if you'd like."

Willa's gaze dropped to the floor.

"Thanks, Officer Tully," she said, quietly.

She had addressed him as officer. That meant "no."

26

JAMES

THE ROAD WASN'T empty yet when James left Albuquerque at half past ten. Not like it would be when he reached the reservation a few hours later.

Kay's house was completely dark. James assumed they were both asleep, so he knocked quietly at first. He waited. He thought about how awful he probably smelled from that bar. The beer and the cigarettes and the sweat from the bodies. No one answered.

He knocked harder, and when he still didn't hear any stirring, he started to shout through the door, "Kay! Molly!"

Nothing. He didn't want to break down Kay's door, but he would. He walked around to the side of the house and started peering in windows. He couldn't see anyone. He knocked on a few, but it was probably useless. The couches were empty. The bedrooms covered with curtains.

He went back around to the front and used an old credit card to work the door open.

"Kay?" he shouted again, as soon as he was inside. Still no response. All the bedrooms were empty.

"Shit," he hissed. Where the hell were they?

As he drove to the police station, he thought of George. He didn't know why Kay would have taken Molly there, but maybe she had. Still, he knew to go to Wayne first. Something could be terribly wrong. Then, he realized that Wayne was probably at home. It was very late. Too late for him to still be at work.

But he didn't know where Wayne lived, so he went to the station anyway. The lights were still on when James pulled in. In fact, he could see Wayne sitting at the front desk, head leaned back, mouth open. James banged on the door, and Wayne leaped up, reaching for his sidearm. He relaxed when he saw who it was. He opened the door.

"Kay isn't home," James said. "I was just at her house, and it's empty. I don't know where she and Molly went."

"Easy," Wayne said, putting a hand on James's chest. "Molly is here at the station. She's safe."

James threw his head back and took a deep breath. He let it out in a huge gust of air.

"Shit, Wayne," he said. "What happened?"

"Kay had something to attend to. An emergency, she said."

James narrowed his eyes.

"What kind of emergency?"

"She didn't say, but she seemed flustered. Glad to see you made it out of the city in one piece."

"Huh," James said. "So am I. Where's Molly now?"

Wayne jerked his thumb toward the back of the station.

"Got a cot back there."

James shook Wayne's hand. It was a solid shake.

"Thank you for your help with her."

Wayne grinned. "You've got a little detective on your hands. She did good today. I'll let her debrief you, but we learned some things."

"Oh yeah?" James asked.

"Yeah." Wayne handed him some keys. "There's an extra set of blankets back there, too. I'll see you in the morning." Then, Wayne headed for his pickup, locking the front door of the station behind him.

James switched off the lights, slumped into the same chair Wayne had been sitting in, and tried to close his eyes. He breathed. Four seconds in, hold for four seconds, four seconds out. Molly was safe. For now. How had he gotten them to this point so quickly? And where had Kay gone in such a hurry? He needed to keep a better eye on Molly. Not that being by his side was a safe place to be, either.

It had barely been a month since Molly had shown up in his life again. Since they encountered a dead body—something he'd hoped he'd left behind. And now, he had not one, but multiple dangerous men after him. Which meant they were after Molly, too. Because Molly was his now.

He had only known her for weeks, really, and the swell he felt in his chest when he thought about something bad happening to her physically hurt him. How had Dorothy done it for fourteen years? Alone? Was this crushing love what had made her turn to drugs? Did that make any sense at all?

Maybe he could have made sense of it if it were anyone other than Dorothy. But Dorothy's capacity to love others had seemed infinite. Overwhelming. It was what had made James feel so inadequate. Convinced him that he couldn't possibly handle being a father. And that that was okay, because Dorothy could give enough love for the both of them.

And now that he sat there thinking of Dale Fitzgerald getting anywhere near Molly, he thought maybe he had been right. A good father didn't drag his daughter into this sort of thing.

He sat back and crossed his arms. Closed his eyes. Let his thoughts become muddled and liquid and thick until he heard a banging.

He sat up, wide awake. It was only Wayne at the door. The rising sun lit up the room. He grunted as he got up to let Wayne in.

"I'll make the coffee," James muttered.

When he came back, Wayne was still standing there, staring at a piece of paper on the desk, hands in his pockets.

He looked up at James. "What'd Dale say?"

James handed him a mug.

"He wants Adriel. Wants to see him, at least. Don't know what else he wants to do with him."

Wayne blew on his coffee and took a sip. "That's not going to happen."

"According to him, it already did. He says Linda met with him recently. Brought Adriel with her. He said he was supposed to see them again."

Wayne crossed his arms, holding the mug handle with three fingers.

"Strange. Willa said something similar about Linda making contact with her. I'll let Molly tell you more. I don't want to take the wind from her sails."

"Willa?"

"Friend of Linda's."

"Hmmm," James said. "Think Dale's tellin' the truth, then?"

"Maybe."

"Wouldn't make much sense for Dale to be the killer, then, would it? Why leave the boy?"

Wayne shook his head. "Anything could have happened. Maybe Adriel ran."

James sipped. "Maybe."

"Besides, with the Vietnam thing? The carvings? Seems like something Dale might do."

James looked at him and chuckled. "What did Gloria tell you?"

"Sometimes I think that woman would wipe my ass if I asked her to," Wayne said.

James laughed heartily. "Man. What I wouldn't give for a cause of death," he said then.

"Welcome to my world," Wayne said. "The number of times I've pleaded with families."

"Why is that?" James asked. "If you don't mind me asking. What's all this about leaving them be, not speaking their name?"

"Oh, it goes way back." Wayne finally sat down. "Back to the Spanish. Like most things, I guess. They gave us all those horrible diseases. Wiped out whole families. Almost whole clans. All we knew was that if we got too close to the dead, too close to the dying, that we would be next. Thought it was the dead's spirit coming for us. Figured it was best to leave them alone. Give their spirit time to journey over to the next world. We still burn their things, you know."

"Damn." James shook his head. "Makes sense."

"So, what's your next move?" Wayne asked.

"Take this load to Flagstaff," he said. "It's got to get there today. I'll come up with a plan on the road. I should find somewhere safe for Molly to stay."

Wayne nodded, but said, "Molly will be disappointed if you cut her out now. She seems to really enjoy this. I think you'll find you two have plenty in common."

James looked out the window. Watched a hawk land on the fence post across the street.

"Yeah," he finally said. "Thanks, Lieutenant."

[27]
MOLLY

MOLLY SCOOPED her wet hair into a ponytail before climbing into James's truck. Wayne had let her use the station's shower, which, to Molly's surprise, had both shampoo and conditioner. James's bathroom had had only a two-in-one her first night there, but Wayne's hair was silky smooth and shiny. He clearly took care of it.

Molly carried both her sketchbook and the notebook Wayne had given her.

Wayne's wife, Barbara, had brought breakfast to the station. "I couldn't believe it when he told me he let you two sleep at the station!" she said. "I was horrified! You'll sleep in our extra bedroom next time."

Now, Molly bit into the round bread Barbara had given her for the road. It was covered in powdered sugar and jam, and Molly caught a drop with her napkin before it landed on her skirt.

"Mmmmm," she said with her mouth full. "This is amazing!"

James was quiet that morning, in his own world. Molly

waited for him to stop thinking about whatever he was thinking about, but he was still frowning when she wiped the last bits of sugar off her hands.

"Don't you want to hear about Wayne's and my day yesterday?"

"Hm?" he said, finally blinking and relaxing his face. "Oh yeah. Yes, yes, I do. Y'all talked to someone named Willa?"

Molly deflated. "Did Wayne tell you already?"

James sat back a little and glanced at her. "No. That's all I know. Wayne mentioned a Willa but said you'd tell me more."

"Oh!" Molly wiggled a little in her seat, pushing herself up straighter. "Well, we talked to a woman named Willa. She used to be Linda's friend, but she does drugs. So, when Linda stopped doing drugs, they stopped being friends. But then, one day recently—Willa doesn't remember when exactly—Linda came and saw her again. Wanted to be her friend again. Wanted to help her and stuff. Out of nowhere. Kinda strange, right?"

"Agreed," James said. "Kinda strange. Did she tell Willa anything? Anything we don't know?"

"She said she was gonna quit her job!"

"Hmmm, that's strange, too."

"I know! Well, hold on. Maybe she didn't say that exactly . . ." Molly opened her notebook and flipped back through the pages. "She said . . . she said she wasn't going to be working there anymore soon. Which sounds like quitting to me. Unless she knew they were gonna fire her."

"That's what Willa said?"

"Yeah, but . . ." Molly flipped through the notebook some more. "I don't know how good her memory is. Linda could have said something else. Kinda like that but not exactly."

James smiled. "Good," he said. "It's good to recognize when someone might be unreliable. And not just this Willa woman. Not just drug addicts. Most witnesses to crimes are unreliable. People in general. Our minds play tricks. We think we see things that we don't really see. Or we forget things and then reconstruct them in our minds the wrong way. And people hide things for all kinds of reasons, too. Sometimes people can tell us a lot. Sometimes what they *don't* tell us tells us a lot. But it's important to remain skeptical always."

Molly nodded. James probably knew a lot about this stuff. She was sure the Army had sent him to detective school.

"But, Molly . . ." James sighed. Molly knew that sigh. She hadn't heard it from James yet, but she knew it from her mom. It was the sound grown-ups made when they felt bad about something they were about to say, and so they would get defensive before they even spoke. She knew she would not like what was coming next.

"I think this case is starting to get too dangerous. First the Codys. And now this Dale knows who I am. These are not safe people."

"So, what are you gonna do? Stop investigating? You can't do that to Kay."

James rubbed the back of his neck. "No, I'm not gonna stop. But . . . I might need to find somewhere safe for you to be. Kinda like what we did with Adriel."

"I'm not a little kid like him, though."

"I know," he said. "But you're still in danger. With me and on the reservation."

Was she in danger? Why would anyone care about Molly? She hadn't witnessed a murder or anything.

"Where are you gonna dump me, then?" She knew she was starting to lose credibility as a mature adult, but she couldn't help it. She was angry and hurt. "I don't have a big family like Adriel does. I only have you."

"What about your grandmother?" James asked.

"Mom didn't want me with her. Clearly! Mom wanted me with you."

The truck got silent after that. Molly was trying not to cry.

"What do you mean?" James asked, slowly. "How do you know what your mother wanted?"

"Why else would Tricia have called you?"

"And how would Tricia know? You think your mom made plans with Tricia in case . . . in case she died?"

"Shit," Molly muttered. "Is this really the first time you've thought about that?"

James did look confused. His eyebrows were real low and wrinkled together.

"I guess I thought Tricia was making the decision the best she knew how. I didn't think it was planned. Didn't realize addicts had the time. But you seem to think so."

"That's because they don't, *James.*" There was so much bitterness in her voice. She could feel it dripping out of her. Why was Molly keeping the secret of a dead woman? She didn't want to anymore. She loved her mom so much, but her mom wasn't there now. Molly only had James, and it wasn't fair for Dorothy to keep asking her to lie. Not from the grave.

"Mom wasn't an addict," Molly said, quietly. James

leaned forward in the driver's seat, closer to the steering wheel. As if that would help him hear her better.

"She was dying. She had cancer. The doctors told her she might have a little time left. If she let them inject that poison into her body. That's what she called it, at least. Not much time, but a little. But Mom had other plans."

Molly listened to the hum of the road. The clatter of James's keys on the ignition whenever the truck hit a bump. She couldn't read his expression, and he wasn't speaking. Didn't even look to be moving.

"James?" Molly asked.

He cleared his throat a little. "You can call me Dad, you know."

[28]

JAMES

JAMES HAD NEVER FELT MORE inadequate than he did in
that moment. Inadequate as a father and as a man. To a
person he had loved for ten years of his life. He had failed
Dorothy so badly that she had wanted to die alone. To put
this burden on their teenage daughter. Maybe, underneath all
of it, James felt a burning rage.

But none of it was Molly's fault, and right then, he vowed
to stop making her feel like it was.

"Well, since we don't have anywhere for you to go, how'd
you like to learn how to shoot a gun instead?"

Molly grinned. "Really? Like a real gun?"

"If you're gonna be in my truck with me—if you're gonna
be conducting interviews with me and Wayne, knocking on
doors—you need to be able to protect yourself."

Molly's face got very serious. "All right, then."

"After we drop off this load, we'll get you a pistol and
head to Black Canyon."

"I can just . . . get a gun?"

"Well, *I* can just get a gun. And then I can give it to you, can't I? Who says I can't?"

Molly giggled nervously.

"Don't worry," he said. "I'll teach you."

The gun shop was right where James remembered it being. Two blocks off the highway exit, standing alone in the middle of a large parking lot: Lotsa Guns. Not the most creative name, but James knew the owner. Had met him enough times, at least, that James knew he'd be happy to see him.

Two other people—a couple—hung back at the front of the store, pointing and whispering. James walked right up to the counter with Molly by his side.

The man standing there was burly, and his bushy side-burns hadn't been maintained in some time. He grinned and stretched out his arm.

"Good to see you, Harry," James said, shaking the man's hand.

"How the hell you been, Jimmy?"

"Keepin' the bugs off my glass and trouble off my ass."

Harry's laugh was like an earthquake. So deep it seemed to shift the whole room.

"I don't believe that for one minute. Not if you're in here!"

James crossed his arms and leaned back on his heels. "I'm never in enough trouble to satisfy you, Harry."

"Hey, trouble's good for business. What can I do ya for today?"

"I'm lookin' for a snub nose, .38 cal. The smallest you got."

Harry's eyebrows went up a bit. It wasn't James's usual style.

"I know you're a Colt man, but I've got a Chief's Special over here. . . ." Harry started down the counter, and James and Molly followed.

"The Smith & Wesson Model 36 is the smallest I've got. Nice J-frame. More accurate than you'd think, too. Nice little revolver."

Harry unlocked the glass case and put it on the counter for James to inspect.

"You got a grip adapter?" he asked, flipping the revolver over in his palm.

"You better believe it."

Harry's gaze flicked to Molly for just a second. But James knew he would never say what he was thinking. Too good at his business for that.

"All right," James said. "Let's try it out. How much do I owe you?"

"I usually charge seventy-five dollars for that, but I'll give you a little deal." Harry winked. "You give me a note with Mr. Franklin on it, and I'll throw in a box of a hundred rounds and that grip adapter, and we'll call it even."

James reached for his wallet and handed Harry a hundred-dollar bill. They shook hands again.

"Pleasure as always," Harry said.

"Appreciate it, bud."

Harry boxed up their purchase and James gave him a little salute as he led Molly from the store.

"He knew you were buying that for me," Molly whispered as she hurried to keep up with James's long strides.

James chuckled. "Course he did. Now go on and get in the truck. You're gonna like this."

After they dropped the load, James headed south toward Black Canyon, about thirty miles north of Phoenix. Not quite two hours from where they were now.

"We'll get a hotel room tonight," James said. "A real bed. I'll promise you that."

"We better. Where else am I gonna sleep? That dinky bed of yours back there?" Molly jerked her head in the direction of his sleeper.

"The ground would be more comfortable. Why do you think I switched to regional?"

"Regional? What's that mean?" Molly asked.

"My trips aren't more than a thousand miles away. Used to do long hauls. Weeks across the country. I'm too old for that now."

The truck grew quiet. James didn't know what Molly was thinking, but he knew what he was thinking. What a waste that time had been. Time that could've been spent with her.

They still had a couple hours of sunlight left by the time they reached Black Canyon. They set up in front of a target about twenty yards away. James showed Molly how to load and fire the Smith & Wesson—pretty much idiotproof with those guns. Accuracy was another story.

"Your stance is important," he said. "You want to spread those legs a little wider than shoulder-width. Then, take that right foot and scoot it back just a hair. Toe in line with the left foot's heel."

Molly listened and adjusted her feet.

"Now stick your butt out."

Giggling, she moved her hips back just a little.

"More than that. You want your weight on your toes."

She moved her butt back further and put her hands on her knees.

"Right, now stand up all the way." James handed her the loaded gun. "Arms straight out in front of you."

Molly started to bring the gun up.

"Bring the front sight in line with the rear sight. Control your breathing. Keep your finger off the trigger until you're ready to shoot the target or kill someone."

Molly did as she was told, but her arms were tense. Reaching too far ahead. James touched her back, between her shoulder blades.

"Try to squeeze these muscles together but keep your arms straight. You feel how that takes the pressure off your shoulders and your arms?"

She nodded.

"All right. That looks pretty good. Fire away."

Molly cocked the hammer and fired. She hit the very edge of the target.

"Would you look at that!" James laughed a little. "First try, hit the target. Let's try again."

Molly slept good that night. She was in the hotel bed snoring before James had even started on his nightcap.

He sat outside on the room's balcony, looking at the stars,

watching the people pass below, their laughter rising and kissing the air like flames of a fire.

He was satisfied with the day. Molly hadn't seemed afraid at all, which surprised him. It was good, though. She didn't know what kind of men they were dealing with. What they were capable of. And she didn't need to quite yet.

He thought about how she would carry the gun. He'd like to buy her boots to tuck it into. Real, good boots. But she was a fashionable girl—he knew that much by shopping with her —and there was only so much anyone could do to convince a teenager of anything. The boots he had in mind weren't fashionable. They were reliable. Probably toxic to a teenager.

A bag would work, though. The kind that slung over her shoulder and sat on her hip. He was sure they could agree on one of those.

He breathed in night air that smelled of gasoline and old hamburgers. He had taken to wearing his holster again with his Colt Python visible for all to see. His other gun—a Commander—was normally wrapped in a T-shirt, sitting behind his seat in the rig. But that night, he had brought it into the hotel with the rest of their things.

Just having the guns on him again heightened his senses. It was like the extra weight had flipped a switch inside of him. This case was no longer something to be taken lightly. He had a duty to Molly. He needed to be prepared.

James stayed up late enough that the next day he drank two cups of coffee before they headed out, with a third in a to-go cup.

He gave Molly the Styx album he had bought in Albuquerque, and she spent most of the ride home gawking at it, studying the cover art and reading the names of everyone on the production team.

"How come you didn't tell me you had a record player?" she asked.

He shrugged. "My collection is a little embarrassing. This here's the start of a better one. Your collection."

Molly smiled at that. Probably bigger than she'd intended to, because right after, she turned away.

"A gun and a record," Molly said. "What would Mom think . . ."

She trailed off and didn't turn to look back at him. The comment dropped a stone in his stomach. Dorothy would be furious. Giving a fourteen-year-old a gun. But it was the only way James knew how to do this. He was sure Dorothy would have pointed out that maybe had he been a father before now, then he would have handled this the right way. Whatever way that was.

But Dorothy wasn't here. Molly could think about her all she wanted, but James was fighting to keep both of them alive. Dorothy had given up.

At home, James followed Molly inside, listening to the clomping of her clogs as she ran through the house, looking for the record player. When he came up behind her in the storage closet, she was talking to the thing.

"How dare he shove you away in here to collect dust! The disrespect!"

James chuckled. "All right, all right. Let me bring it out into the living room. We'll dust her off."

Molly stood back and crossed her arms.

"I think it ought to go on that chest table thing in the

corner of the living room. With those weird vases on it. Who even decorated this house? Some artsy girlfriend?"

James chuckled again. Most of it he'd bought from a catalog. Put the stuff wherever. Just didn't want an empty house.

"Well, go clear off those weird vases, then. Make some room."

Molly did, and when James came out with the record player, she was carrying two vases, one at least two feet long. Which meant both their hands were full when the phone rang. Molly hurried to find a place to put the vases but didn't catch the call before it went to the answering machine. Both Molly and James stood perfectly still as the shaky voice on the other end of the line filled the room.

"James, it's Kay. Please call me. Someone's killed Adriel's donkey."

BARBARA

TEDDY JACKSON WAS ALWAYS the last one to arrive to a council meeting. He would grin in apology—or maybe just acknowledgment—but he would offer no excuse or explanation. Rather, he would tear right into the day's work. He never wasted time. He had things to do. He was the head of the Navajo Nation, after all.

Cecil Cody, meanwhile, was always the first to arrive. He was there to watch others, Barbara knew. To pull them aside if he needed a word. But mostly to keep tabs. She supposed others could come before Cecil, but they never did. Like with so many other habits and practices, Cecil Cody arrived first because that was the way it had always been done. People respected this system.

And Barbara Tully, the only woman on the council these days, would arrive exactly on time. It was how she did everything. With precision. She believed in listening to others instead of thinking while they spoke. It was the key, for her, to being a good politician.

Barbara had run as the daughter of the great David Nakai

but also as a slow-spoken, stoic Indian. She'd relied on the stereotype during her election, but behind the scenes, Barbara was anything but slow. She spent her time reading up on laws, studying land ownership on and around the reservation, and visiting her people. She asked them what bothered them, what they needed, what would make their lives easier and more pleasurable. In council meetings, Barbara could afford to listen with her full attention. She didn't have to think about what she would say next. She already knew.

Barbara also already knew who the white man at today's council meeting was before he was introduced. He was from Armexx Coal, and he lurked at Jackson's shoulder like a vulture. They were to vote on the purchase of lands in Arizona today, but what that had to do with Aaron Hertz from Armexx, she wasn't sure.

"The Big Buck Boleman Ranch will come out to be about $33.4 million," said Jacob Dodge, a council member from the Jeddito Chapter. He was a tall man with a long face and permanent frown. He sat at the front of the auditorium-style conference room with Jackson and three other Diné councilmen and spoke into a microphone.

"But you all will only need to put down eight million at signing," Aaron Hertz said. The room went quiet. Beside Barbara, someone tapped their foot.

"This is Mr. Hertz," Jackson finally said, reaching out an awkward hand. "I believe I forgot to introduce him. He's the one who brought the sale to my attention. Now, nothing is moving on the Hopi front." Jackson looked back up at the room, pleading a bit. "This will give us much needed land."

"And when will the rest be due?" Lee Gordy asked from the row in front of Barbara.

"Let me worry about that," Jackson said. "We have the money."

"Chairman," Barbara said into her own microphone. Every eye in the room focused on her. Most with thinly disguised annoyance. "The Big Buck Boleman Ranch has been up for sale for some time now. Months, in fact. The original listing price was fifty dollars an acre. That falls well short of $33.4 million. Why the sudden price increase?"

Jackson's jaw clenched as he took a deep breath through his nose. Aaron Hertz peered at her with interest from atop his reading glasses.

"Sixty-eight dollars per acre is still quite the deal," Jackson said. "I'm not concerned about why the cost went up. But maybe it's why we ought to move quickly on this."

Barbara could feel Cecil Cody's eyes on her, too. He sat near the back of the room, across the aisle. She glanced his way and saw he was smiling. Close-lipped and sinister. A chill passed through her. Cecil's eyes were deep-set and dark. His skin tanned and weathered from a lifetime of sheep-herding and shearing. He wore both a cross and a pouch around his neck—the pouch filled with corn pollen and other protective items from his medicine man. But if Cecil Cody was ever worried, he didn't show it. The man looked at ease always, but especially in these meetings. Barbara knew he was untouchable for many reasons. Most council members who wanted to get on Jackson's good side had to show what they had to offer. But not Cecil Cody. His name alone was enough.

"Now, Barbara," Cecil said. "If you knew about this

incredible price for the land, why didn't you bring it to our attention sooner?"

"As you know, Cecil, over in Sanostee we are less worried about land acquisition than we are about schools and housing and hospitals and basic necessities."

"Land is our most basic necessity as Diné," Cecil said. "Your father would have known as much."

Someone behind Barbara chuckled.

"And yet, the land we do have is not being protected," she replied. "We are surrounded by companies who destroy it daily. Who have no concern for what they dig up and where they dump it. And what do you do about it? Nothing that would upset your brother."

Cecil Cody grinned wider, sat back in his seat, and laughed deep from his belly. Barbara could feel the heat rising in her cheeks and forced herself to ignore him.

"Actually, Mrs. Tully brings up a good point and one I meant to address," Lee Gordy said. "The mining in Red Rock was supposed to end last month, but they're still tearing into the earth."

Jackson nodded. "You are correct. I have the paperwork on that. I will meet with them. We will make them comply."

Next to Jackson, Aaron Hertz cleared his throat loudly.

"Anyway," Jackson said, glancing at him. "Let us vote now on whether the Navajo Nation will purchase the Big Buck Boleman Ranch for $33.4 million."

The room grew quiet.

"All in favor?" Jackson said.

Barbara's hand did not go up. But Cecil Cody's did.

KAY WANTED to know just how much the killer had known about that donkey. Did they know it was Adriel's? Or just Kay's? Did it matter?

Wayne thought it was the Codys. Was confident it was. Kay had called him second, and he had come right away. Why she had called James first, she didn't know. He wasn't anywhere nearby. It would take him hours to get there. But she supposed it was because she knew this was connected to Linda. The way the donkey had been slaughtered. A knife across the neck. It wasn't an accident. It wasn't a predator attack. It was a message. The donkey had been laid across her front step, its eyes looking up at her in everlasting confusion when she opened her door.

She was hosing the porch down when James and Molly showed up, the red water dripping from the steps. James looked disappointed.

"Wayne looked at the footprints and whatever," Kay said. "The donkey stunk awful, though. The flies were getting to be a problem."

"I'm sorry, Kay." James squinted into the sun. "Is Wayne still inside?"

Kay turned off the hose and brought a hand to her hip. "He left just a few minutes ago."

James nodded. Molly stepped carefully around the pooling water.

"How was Dale?" Kay asked.

"You probably know," James said. "Not the most pleasant man."

She snorted. "That's one way to put it. Did he have anything interesting to say?"

"Ah," James said. He looked at the ground and crossed his arms.

She draped the hose over the porch railing. "Let me shut the water off," she said. "And then I'll get you some drinks. Go on inside."

She walked around the side of the house and turned off the spigot. Weeds snaked up the siding and caught on her boots. When she got back inside, she took off her hat and hung it up. Whatever James had to say about Dale, Kay doubted it would surprise her. The man had been a nuisance to her family for more than ten years. Making threats. Causing scenes. He was like a recurring bad dream. That familiar feeling. The *oh no, not this again.*

James and Molly were sitting on the couch, James's arm draped over the top, Molly's back not quite touching the cushions behind her.

Kay washed her hands and brought them some lemonade.

"How are you doin'? You up and left Molly the other night. Wayne said you seemed frantic." James looked concerned. He stared at her intently, his green eyes piercing. She looked away and coughed.

"I'm sorry about that. But I knew she'd be safe with Wayne. He's good people." Kay sat across from them in the recliner.

"And your emergency?" he pressed.

She shook her head. "Taken care of. Thanks for asking."

"How's Adriel doin'?" he asked.

"He's fine," Kay said. "He loves to be with his cousins."

"Does Dale know about these cousins? Where to find them?"

Kay's jaw clenched, and she looked down at her hands. They were stained a little red, too.

"Do you think he'll go after him?" she asked.

James said nothing at first, so Kay looked back up at him. "Do you?"

"He seems to want to see him real bad."

She took a deep breath and nodded. "I don't know what Dale knows. He and Linda were always such a mystery to me. I don't know what their relationship was like. What kind of things she told him. They seemed so different. I didn't understand it."

"Dale will come looking for Adriel here first, though. Won't he?"

"Yes." She nodded again.

James threw his head back and gulped down the rest of the lemonade. "I'll stay, then. Me and Molly. We'll get a hotel or something. There a hotel around here?"

Kay laughed. "In Sanostee? I think you've seen all of it by now. It's not exactly a tourist destination."

He set his cup down on the side table and leaned his forearms on his thighs. He looked up at her. "I don't want to leave you alone here for Dale."

"Wayne's here."

"Wayne and his men have got too much to do already."

Kay knew it was true. She glanced at her extra bedroom and wished she could invite them to stay with her. She would sleep better. But if the Codys were killing her animals for working with James, what would they do if he stayed in her house?

She stood. "There are hotels in Gallup, but that's an hour's drive. Wayne and Barbara Tully will take you in. Their doors are always open."

"Can I use your phone to call him? I'd like to give him the heads-up," James said.

Kay nodded. "Sure."

When James got off the phone, the three of them walked back outside. Kay needed to run some errands. She had already wasted too much time on the donkey situation.

Her baby-blue Toyota Hilux pickup sat beside her house.

"Where'd you get this little thing?" James asked.

"My ex-husband was a car man. He would never have driven this himself, but he found it at an auction and got it for me. He wanted to see how the Japanese made trucks. He used to laugh when he looked at it. Like it was a joke." Kay shrugged. "I like it."

"I like it, too," James said, smiling.

"Where are you off to now?" she asked as she climbed into the driver's seat.

"Molly and I are gonna go visit George. I've got a couple of questions for him."

Kay didn't think George knew anything about what she knew.

She shrugged. "Good luck." She started the ignition and was about to drive off when James tapped on her window. She cranked it down.

"You want me around?" James asked. He jerked his head at her house. "If it *was* the Codys . . ."

Kay shook her head.

"They're just pets, James," she said. "I keep them because my father was a man of the old ways. He taught us our history, our language, our heritage. I want to pass that knowledge on. I want to show Adriel how important these animals are to the Navajo. But no one makes money herding sheep anymore. Or selling horses. I love those animals. I do. But I love my nephew more. And I need to find out what happened to my sister. I need your help. So yes. I do want you here."

"All right," he said. "That's all I needed to know." He rapped the roof of the truck with his knuckles. "I'll see you later."

Kay stared at him for a moment. She wished she could tell him everything, and yet, she didn't know if it even mattered anymore. She forced a smile and then put the truck in reverse and pulled away.

31

GEORGE

LINDA HAD FOUND it comforting to listen to George read Bible verses aloud while she struggled through detox. She would lie in bed, shaking, with a bucket next to her for the vomit, and George would read her favorite verses aloud in a strong and steady voice.

They'd met at the church, George having been saved as a teenager. He'd broken from the old ways, from his family, to become a Christian. Plenty of Navajo were taking bits and pieces of Christianity, slowly integrating it into their own teachings, but George went all in. He couldn't help it. He'd been called. George was one of ten children, and as a child, no one had paid much attention to him. How he would make little cuts on his arms and legs just to feel a little justice in his life. He knew nothing about him was special. He wasn't smart like his older brother John. Or funny like his younger sister Ruth. He wasn't particularly strong or likable, and he couldn't rope a sheep or a horse well, either. He made himself feel pain because he thought he deserved it. But God had shown him grace anyway

The day Linda walked into the meeting for addicts of all sorts, she never looked up. She stared at her hands and feet. But she kept coming. And one day, when she finally did look up, she saw George handing out cups of coffee. She smiled at him. George wanted to see that smile again, and so he started talking to her. Sitting next to her while the others spoke. He understood self-hatred. Could feel it in Linda. He understood wanting to make yourself better. He wanted Linda to know she wasn't alone.

But now George *was* alone, and he found solace in the same things he always had. The Lord and his teachings. And so George sat in his empty kitchen. No Linda. No Adriel. But still, he read aloud as if someone were there to listen. He missed Linda. He missed them both.

"'When you pass through the waters, I will be with you; and when you pass through the rivers, they will not sweep over you. When you walk through the fire, you will not be burned; the flames will not set you ablaze.'"

There was a knock on the door. George placed his sky-blue, tasseled bookmark into the center of the page before going to answer the door.

"How ya doin', George?" It was James and his daughter.

George shook his hand. "Come in," he said, moving aside so they could pass.

He poured them some tea while they waited in the middle of the room. James had his hands in the pockets of his jeans, and Molly chewed on her thumbnail.

George brought in the tea and led them both to the couch. It was still draped in Adriel's Star Wars blanket.

"Hey, I'm sorry I didn't give you a heads-up about Gloria. I was a little worried after you came by the first time. I didn't want Linda's death just swept away. She deserves better than that."

James's eyebrows went up at the sound of Linda's name. George wasn't afraid to say it. He knew there was no harm in it. Linda was with Jesus now.

"Don't worry about that," James said. "I understand."

He looked around the room, and George wondered what he saw. He hadn't moved much of anything since Linda died and Adriel left. It was all still the same.

"So, George, I'm trying to get a better idea of Linda's day the morning she died and her days leading up to that. When was the last time you saw her?"

"That morning," George said. "She wasn't awake yet. I leave for the post office at 3 a.m., and I left her in bed, like I always do."

"Did you know what her plans for the day were?"

"I knew she had taken the day off work. It was a Monday. She said she had errands to run that had to be done on a weekday. She was planning on taking Adriel to the museum, too, because the sitter was sick."

"What kind of errands?"

"I can't remember exactly. I think maybe she had to go to the DMV. She had some unpaid parking tickets, and her registration was about to expire."

Molly was studying George now. She had the look of a kid who wasn't ashamed to stare.

"Who is Adriel's sitter?" she asked.

"Umm . . . an older woman up the street," George answered. It was strange to be interrogated by a teenager.

"What's her name?" James asked.

"Thelma Long."

George watched Molly mouth the name to herself.

"He didn't go to school?" James asked.

"Schools around here don't have the resources to help a boy like Adriel. We're lucky. Thelma used to be a school-teacher. She taught him the best she could, and it seemed to work. They had a special bond. It was better than sticking him somewhere he would never receive any attention at all."

"So, Thelma knew Linda would be off work," James said. "You knew she would be off work. Did anyone else know?"

"Her boss," George answered.

"We spoke to her boss," James said. "He said he had called and left two messages."

"That was the next day," George said. "I got his messages on Tuesday, the day after she was killed."

"But you never called him back," James said.

George stared at him and didn't reply. He remembered thinking there was no point in calling back. Linda would never go to work again. He didn't care about her last paycheck. He didn't care about what her colleagues said about her. He didn't care about whatever she had left in her locker. He didn't care about anything but having her back. And he couldn't.

"Listen," James went on. "I talked to Dale. Adriel's father."

Prickles formed on the back of George's neck.

"*I'm* Adriel's father," George said. "That man's nothing but a sperm donor." He glanced at Molly, thinking he shouldn't say such things in the presence of a child, but he couldn't help it. He hated the man.

"Fine," James said. "I understand. But Dale's dead set on gettin' that boy back."

"Why'd you tell him?" George asked.

James gave him a strange look. "Dale's a suspect. If . . . uh . . . Linda really was murdered. Plus, he served in Vietnam. We believe the killer may be ex-military."

George swallowed the spit accumulating in his mouth and tried to be calm. His mind dutifully ran through the most useful verses in this situation. Matthew 5, Luke 6, Proverbs 25. *Love your enemies.*

"And does Dale know where Adriel is now?" he asked.

James shook his head. "We don't think so. Which means he might be comin' here. He could show up tomorrow loaded and ready for a fight, or he could get high, fall asleep, and forget all about it. Just be ready."

"And what's that mean? Being ready? How do you suggest I prepare for a man like Dale?"

"Well, there's safety in numbers. I'd like you to stay with Kay. I'm not sure how well she would do here. Around Linda's stuff."

George nodded. As much as he had tried to save Kay over these past few years, the woman held tight to the old ways. Kay and Linda's father had been an elder even as a young man. Passing along stories, the language, whatever he could. Drugs had brought Linda to Jesus, but Kay would never leave her father's teachings. George knew she was afraid of Linda's spirit. That was what she had been taught.

"Okay, I'll go to Kay's."

"And bring your gun?"

George chuckled. "If you think Kay doesn't have more guns than the Alamo, then you haven't spent enough time with Kay. But sure, I'll bring my gun, too."

"Okay, George," James said, standing up. Molly stood,

too, and awkwardly put her teacup down on the coffee table. They looked like they were about to leave, but then James stopped.

"What do you think?" he asked. "Do you think Linda was involved with drugs again?"

George sighed. He gazed into the kitchen at his open Bible.

"I sat through those meetings with her. I listened to people talk about relapsing over and over again. So, I suppose it's possible. But I didn't see any of it. If Linda was doing drugs again, she was very good at hiding it. And that would've been hard, since I've seen her relapse before and come back from it." He shook his head. "Someone did this to her."

"And if she wasn't using again," James went on, "would there be any reason for her to seek out people from her old life? Friends? Dealers? Did she owe someone money, maybe? Who did she get her stuff from?"

George wished he could help, but he couldn't. "We don't talk about that sort of thing. The sins of our past."

"Then one more question," James said, his hand on the doorknob. "And forgive my ignorance." He nodded in the direction of the kitchen. The sunlight was creeping into the room in such a way that it cast a beam onto the Bible. To George, it looked miraculous.

"Is the Native American Church where you met Linda?"

George let out a half laugh. "No, no, it's not. The Native American Church are blasphemers. It's not the old ways and it's not Christianity, but it thinks it's both. I'm not a part of that. I'm a true believer."

"And what's the name of your church?"

"The Church of the Open Door."

James nodded. "Thank you. You call the station if you need anything."

"Thank you," George said. Then James and Molly left, and he stared at the door for a long while, stuck on James's questions, thinking of Linda's secrets.

32

JAMES

MOLLY STARTED TALKING as soon as they were out the door.

"So, I know we have to talk to Thelma now, but I think we should try to go to the church, too. When Wayne and I were at Willa's, Wayne said something about her going to the program at the church. That must have been where Linda went, too. The program at George's church. For addicts or something."

James shoved his hands in his pockets and felt a swell of pride. Molly was quick. Picking up on everything. James looked down the road in each direction. The big rig was like a giant billboard announcing their presence. He'd have to put off the trucking for a bit. Maybe buy a used car out here on the reservation. Do this case right.

"I think those are some fine ideas," he said. "Let's go see Wayne at the station. We'll ask him about meeting times and where to find this Thelma."

James remembered the big parking lot behind the Navajo Nation Sanostee Chapter offices and the three big rigs he'd seen there the first time he and Molly came. He drove there now.

"This isn't the station," Molly said.

"We're walkin' there," James replied. "Think those floppy shoes of yours can handle it?"

Molly smirked. "I walk everywhere in these shoes."

"Famous last words." James chuckled. "You're too big for me to carry, now."

Things got quiet then, and James wondered if it would ever be normal for him to say something like that or if his fourteen years of absence would follow them around like a storm cloud forever.

"So, who do you think killed the donkey?" he asked, to break up the silence.

"The Codys, right? I mean, Kay said that's what Wayne thinks."

James nodded. "Sure does make more sense than it being Dale. It's not his style. It was a warning. The Codys would send a warning like that."

James and Molly walked past a basketball hoop. A couple of boys played, dust clouds rising every time one of them faked a shot.

"What was that note you showed Kay at the offices?" Molly asked. James wondered if she had been thinking about it this whole time.

"It said, 'To Linda.' That's all."

"Who do you think wrote it?"

"Well, you heard Kay. She didn't seem to think it was George. And it wasn't Dale, either. I had him write something down for me. Didn't match up."

They were at the station now. James held the door open

for Molly. An officer James hadn't met yet sat at the front desk. He was young. Strong. Serious face.

"We're lookin' for the lieutenant," James said.

"Back in his office," the man said. Begaye, per his nametag.

"Thanks, Officer," James said.

The door to Wayne's office was open just enough that James could see inside. Barbara was there, too. They both looked serious. Concerned. They spoke in hushed tones, and James couldn't make out what they were saying. He tapped on the door.

"Who is it?" Wayne called.

"James and Molly."

"Come in."

Barbara smiled at them both, but James could tell she was upset.

"Everything all right?" he asked. She waved her hand.

"Politics," she said. "Another council meeting."

"You're on the council?" Molly asked.

"Sure am."

"Wow, that's neat! What do you do?"

"Write laws. Vote on decisions."

"Is it fun?" Molly asked. Barbara laughed.

"Usually, no. But sometimes it is. Sometimes I get to watch those old men squirm." Barbara winked.

"How about you two?" Wayne asked. "Are you coming from Kay's?"

"Made a stop at George's, too."

"How'd that go?"

"Oh, it went all right," James said. "We asked him to stay

with Kay for a bit while we wait and see what Dale's gonna do."

Wayne nodded.

"How about that donkey? You plannin' on doin' anything with the Codys?" James asked.

"You know I don't have the evidence," Wayne said.

"Molly and I just ditched the rig," James changed the subject. "I was hoping maybe I could buy something here just to drive around for a bit."

Wayne shrugged. "I'm usually using the department's truck. And Barb uses mine. You're welcome to borrow our Oldsmobile."

"First your house and now your car? You're gonna get sick of me real quick." James grinned.

"That's the beauty. I can kick you out whenever I want."

Barbara shook her head. "Don't listen to him, Molly."

"We've got two more visits to make," James said. "One to the Church of the Open Door and one to a Miss Thelma Long."

Wayne nodded. "Are you looking to go to the addiction meeting?"

"Yes, we are."

Wayne turned to look at the clock on the wall behind him. "Starts in an hour," he said. "Every afternoon at four o'clock."

"Where is the church?" James asked.

"Take Route 34 until you've almost hit 491. It'll be on the left."

"I appreciate it, boss," James said. "And Miss Long?"

"I'll take you there tomorrow. It's about time I check in on her, anyway."

33

MOLLY

A GIANT CROSS STRETCHED into the sky, balancing on the top of the church like a ballerina on her toes. It was tall and proud and looming, and as Molly and James pulled up, its shadow enveloped them, blocking out the hot desert sun.

They had arrived about thirty minutes into the meeting, and James said it would be better to catch people on the way out. So, they sat on the stairs leading up to the front door, and Molly watched a lizard run from them, desperate for the sunlight.

"What's the plan?" she asked. "Are we just gonna grab random people on their way out and ask them if they knew Linda?"

"Pretty much." He pulled out a cigarette and stuck it in his mouth.

"Can I have one?" Molly asked.

James raised an eyebrow.

"Fine," he said, handing her one. "This is the last one, though."

"I thought you didn't care."

"I didn't say that. You *deserved* one after all that."

"But not now?" Molly asked.

"I think you're enjoying yourself now," James said.

Molly felt annoyed at that. He was right, of course. But she didn't want him to know that. She didn't know why she was holding on to this idea of being bitter. It was like her favorite childhood blanket that was dirty and tattered, but she still wouldn't let it go. It didn't serve her anymore. Still, she didn't think it should be that easy for him.

Molly took the cigarette. She would enjoy this smoke, that was for sure.

"What's enjoying it got to do with anything?" she asked after her first drag. She watched the end burn. "You're telling me you never enjoyed your job as a detective? I'm sure you had plenty of cigarettes."

He smiled. "I guess you're right. They ain't exclusive. You can enjoy a job that's pretty messed up. I did for years."

Well, at least she'd won that one, Molly thought. It made her feel better to hear James admit defeat. He didn't seem to mind doing it, though. Not to her.

Just then, the doors behind them opened with a loud creak, the bottoms dragging against the stone steps. She and James stood and took a few steps back. A short and chubby older man looked at them curiously.

"Are you here for the meeting? It's just wrapping up."

"No, sir," James said. "We were friends of Linda Morris. We knew she came here, and we were hoping we could ask some people some questions about her."

Molly was surprised he had said Linda's name so boldly. But then she remembered that George had, too. Maybe these people weren't afraid.

The man nodded slowly and walked down the steps toward them. "I remember Linda. She came years ago, though. I'm not sure anyone here tonight has been here that long." He stopped at the bottom step and looked out into the distance.

"You could try Pamela. She's been coming off and on for some time. She has a big perm. About your age. I'll point her out."

"Thank you," James said. "I don't think I caught your name."

"Fred," the man said, sticking out a hand for James to shake.

"Hi, Fred. I'm James. And this is my daughter, Molly."

Fred's smile almost took up his whole face. "Hi Molly."

She smiled back. "Nice to meet you." She was a little wary of church people. She remembered going with her grandmother and feeling like they always wanted something from her. *Come to youth group. Sing in the choir. Tell me about your school, about the city, about your mother.* She always felt like she was just a potential prayer to them. Not a real, living human being. But nothing about Fred felt threatening.

A moment later, a few people emerged from the church. A couple, followed closely by two older, skinny women. Then, Molly saw someone she recognized. Willa Yazzie stared at her, small eyes round and open real wide. Molly thought she would duck away, but she walked right up to them.

"Molly, right?" she asked. Molly nodded and thought about what Wayne might have said.

"Willa. It's nice to see you here."

Willa's gaze flicked to James.

"I'm glad to see you, too. There's actually something I'd like to talk to you about. Can we go somewhere to talk? Alone?"

Molly looked at James. His eyebrows were furrowed. He didn't like the sound of that, Molly could tell.

"How about just over here to my dad's car?" Molly asked, pointing at Wayne's Oldsmobile parked across the street.

"Okay," Willa agreed.

Molly turned to whisper in her dad's ear. "Can I have the keys? I just want to get my notebook."

James gave her the keys. "I'll be right here if you need me," he said, loudly.

Molly and Willa crossed the street, and Molly said, "Hold on one second." She unlocked the car and grabbed her notebook. She thought back to meeting Gloria. It would be professional to ask Willa if she could write this down, wouldn't it? Molly thought so.

"Can I write this down?" she asked.

Willa nodded quickly. "But I don't want to talk about it anymore after this."

"That's fine," Molly said, though she didn't know if it was fine. "What did you want to tell me?"

"I lied to Wayne," Willa said. "I was high that day. The day she came over."

Molly didn't know what to say to that, so she just nodded.

"And I don't remember most of what she said to me. And I wish I did, because I've been thinking my hardest about it. And I know she was afraid. And I know there was something she told me that she didn't want anyone else to know. She said I couldn't tell anyone. But now I want to tell someone and I can't because I can't remember." Willa started to tear up.

"It's okay," Molly said. "Anything is helpful. You said she was afraid?"

Willa bit her lip. "She was afraid and very serious. I couldn't understand why she was talking to me about it. We hadn't talked in so long. Maybe she didn't have any other friends to talk to."

"Maybe," Molly said.

"But last night I was dreaming and she was there and it was just like that day and then I woke up and I remembered something. I remembered that I was trying hard not to laugh at something she had said. She was so serious, but she said this name. Assman. Mr. Assman. I was trying so hard to listen to what she was saying, but I kept thinking about what a bummer it would be to be named Assman. Anyway, I thought it might help you."

"Assman?" Molly asked.

"Yeah, but like I said, please don't ask me anything else. I just can't remember. It was the last straw, it really was. I couldn't remember this super important thing. The one thing that might help you find her killer. So, I decided to do what Officer Tully suggested. I came here because it's what she wanted. And I'm going to keep coming, too."

"Good," Molly said. "That's great, actually! You should keep coming. And this is helpful. Thank you, Willa."

Willa frowned and looked at her feet. "She was a good friend. The best I ever had."

"I'm sorry," Molly said.

Willa looked up at her and said, "Please don't come by."

"I won't," Molly said.

Willa turned around and walked back across the street to the church parking lot, where a gangly man waited for her beside a car that might once have been white.

Molly scribbled on her notepad. *Assman. Linda was afraid. Told Willa not to tell anyone.*

When she looked back up, James was walking over.

"Anything good?" he asked. She smiled.

"You're right," she said. "I am enjoying this."

[34]

GLORIA

JAMES HAD NOT ANSWERED his phone in days. Gloria had left him three voicemails, but she could no longer wait.

He was probably on the road, driving that big rig from one city to the next, so she didn't intend to show up at his house—though she knew just where it was, nestled at the end of that long, lonely street. She'd go to the reservation instead. He would be stopping there at some point, she knew, before or after he talked to Dale.

She stepped harder on the gas pedal of her 1970 purple Plymouth Barracuda convertible and let the warm air kiss her neck. She dangled her left arm out the open window and thought of what she'd say to Wayne first and then to James when he showed up.

Dale was crazy enough for any of them to see just how likely it was that he had killed Linda. Gloria hadn't lied when she said she had never spoken to Dale. But she had followed him. Saw him go into his apartment. Come back out when it was almost dark. Swaying when he paused every few steps, fighting to stay on his feet. Sometimes, seemingly defying gravity to do so. Where was he going? Gloria had followed him for an hour like that—his eyes closed, his body independent of this world, unaware of what it was doing or where it was going until suddenly, at the sound of a siren, he jerked upward, looked around confused for only a moment, and then hurried to the corner store. He yelled racial slurs at the Mexican cashier and then pushed over a rack of potato chips before storming out. The man was volatile.

She shuddered. He reminded her of so many other men she had met in Vietnam. Men who were so vulnerable, so afraid, so broken that she would have hugged them had she not seen that same look in their eyes. The one that told her that underneath whatever show they were putting on in that moment, they were dangerous. They had learned to channel their fear, their anger, their confusion into killing. It had only taken her one bad experience to learn that, one close call. After that, she always carried a weapon. Always tried to create distance.

Dale was not special or unique.

Gloria pulled off the highway for gas and a drink. As she paid, she noticed a small stand of postcards and keyrings on the counter. Cacti. Mesas. A Navajo woman. Or maybe she was a Hopi. Even after years of reporting on both, she couldn't tell the difference. She wondered if anyone could. If the natives themselves could. If that was something she could admit or if she ought to be ashamed.

Gloria remembered covering the new high school opening on the reservation. The Morris family had been there. Kay had cut the ribbon. She had raised the most money and was going to teach there. Adriel had picked a blanket flower. Smiled down at it. Gloria remembered thinking that he shouldn't touch it. It might irritate his skin. But no one stopped him.

"Will that be all, ma'am?" the man behind the counter asked.

Gloria grabbed the postcard with the bright-red-and-yellow flower.

"This, too, please."

WAYNE

THELMA LONG USED to be married to Sanostee's most sought-after medicine man. But he had died almost twenty years ago, and Thelma still moved like a cat. She had flitty eyes and a smile that made you feel like you were part of a special secret shared only between the two of you. Wayne didn't think she was younger than ninety.

She was stooped in her garden when he pulled up with James and Molly.

"Wow," Molly said. "A garden."

"It's beautiful, isn't it?" Wayne said. "I don't know how she keeps up with it at her age. She's got a row of corn, some peppers."

"This was probably a wonderful place for Adriel to be," Molly said, quietly.

"I'm sure she misses him," he said.

They got out of the truck, and Wayne hollered, "Is that Mrs. Long? The most beautiful woman in the Navajo Nation?"

The old woman took her time standing up and turning around.

"Wayne Tully, I will tell that wife of yours that you said that."

Her smile faded just a little when she spotted Molly and James.

"How can I help you?" she asked them.

"This is James and Molly," Wayne said. "James here used to be a detective for the Army. He's helping me investigate a death right now."

Thelma's smile disappeared altogether.

"You know I wouldn't normally involve you in this," Wayne went on. "But it's about Adriel's mother."

Thelma shook her head slowly. "That poor boy. And that poor woman." She stared at James for a moment and then said, "Well, make it quick."

She unlatched the gate, and they walked through it, down her carefully marked vegetable rows and toward her house.

Wayne followed Thelma right to the kitchen.

"You sit down with James," he said, putting his hand on her arm. "I'll make the tea."

"This man," Thelma said. She gave him a knowing look.

"You can trust him," Wayne said.

"I don't trust anyone who chooses to be around death so much."

"So you don't trust me?"

"Of course not." She smirked.

"James wants to help. His daughter is the one who found Adriel all alone. They're concerned about him."

Thelma pursed her lips. "All right," she said, moving back

into the living room. At first, it was basic questions. How long had she known Linda? How long had she been watching Adriel?

When Wayne walked in, Thelma was explaining how their families were connected.

"And did you notice anything strange about Adriel before his mother died?" James asked.

Thelma looked down at her hands. "I did," she said. "And I told his parents, too."

"What did you notice?" Molly asked.

"He was upset. Anxious. It was difficult at times to communicate with him. He could read very well. Flew through books. Writing was much harder. I was teaching him, though. He knew his letters and some simple words. I asked him what was bothering him, but he just shook his head. So I asked if he wanted to draw it for me. He was still much better with pictures."

Thelma took a deep breath.

"It was an angry picture. Dark colors. Open mouths, glowing eyes. Then he wrote below it, 'Dad.' I asked him, 'Adriel, is your dad okay?' He shook his head—but as if to say I wasn't understanding him. Then he wrote, 'Mom.' I thought maybe his mom and dad had been fighting."

"And you told his parents about what he drew?" James asked.

"Not exactly," she said. "Adriel and I trust one another. I wasn't about to ruin that. But I did ask them, separately, if anything had been going on with Adriel at home. George seemed to have no idea what I was talking about. He said nothing was different."

"And what did his mom say?" Molly asked.

Wayne was impressed that Molly hadn't used Linda's name. The girl really did pay attention.

"She tried to brush it off, but I could tell she knew exactly what was bothering Adriel."

"But she never told you?" Molly asked again.

Thelma shook her head. "I pushed as much as I could. But she wasn't going to say anything."

"Did Adriel ever tell you anything else? Through his drawings?" James asked.

"No," Thelma said. "But he still wasn't himself the last time I saw him. Which was about three or four days before she died."

Thelma rubbed her neck and looked out the window. Her gaze was vacant.

It was time to wrap this up. "Thank you, Thelma," Wayne said. "We appreciate you talking to us."

"Yes, well, speaking about the dead drains me. I need a nap now." She gave a weak smile.

Wayne, Molly, and James stood.

"If you think of anything else, you know where to find me," Wayne said.

"Thank you," Molly said.

James smiled at Thelma. "I'm going to get to the bottom of this."

"As long as you don't involve me in it anymore."

"You got it," he said. "It was nice to meet you."

They drove in silence for a minute before Molly asked, "Do you think Adriel was talking about Dale when he wrote 'Dad'?"

"Maybe," James said. "He's certainly an angry man. Wayne, can you drop me at Kay's? I promised to help be the muscle for some horse stable project she's got goin' on."

"And George can't help?" Wayne asked.

James smiled and shrugged.

[36]

MOLLY

MOLLY HAD A CHART NOW. Suspects were in one column, motivations and evidence in two other columns. At the bottom she had random notes. *Key players* for one. She didn't know what to call them. People like Willa or Thelma or even Kay and George. She had told James about Mr. Assman, and he had spent the evening going through phone books, highlighting Assmans. There were more than Molly had imagined. Probably because James had looked through four different phone books.

She was drawing flowers around the corners of her chart when the door to the police station dinged.

James was still off helping Kay, and Molly sat in Wayne's office alone. Wayne was there, somewhere. Doing something. She wasn't sure what.

She heard a woman's soft voice and crept into the hallway to hear better.

"Yes, I'm here to speak with Lieutenant Tully."

Molly peered around the corner. It was the reporter, Gloria. Her hair fell in waves down her back, pushed out of her face with large, square-rimmed sunglasses that sat on top of her head.

The officer at the front desk wore a big, silly grin on his face. Molly would have rolled her eyes, but she sort of felt the same way. Awestruck.

"Sure, ma'am," he said, standing up. "Let me get him for you."

Molly took a deep breath and stepped out from behind the wall.

"Gloria! What's up?" she said, trying to sound glad to see her yet still cool. Gloria smiled.

"Hey, sunshine!" Gloria said. "I'm stoked to see you!"

Molly blushed. "Really?"

"Yes!" Gloria waltzed over. "I called your dad a bunch of times, but I haven't been able to get in touch."

"Oh," Molly said. "Yeah, he's here. Well, not here at the station. But he's coming back sometime."

"Oh?" Gloria gave Molly a closed-lip smile and raised her eyebrows, waiting for more.

"He's ummm . . . he's at Kay's."

"I see," she said. "I thought maybe he'd gone to see Dale."

"He already has," Molly said.

"Stellar." Gloria grinned. "I guess I'll wait for him here."

Wayne came up behind Molly and put a hand on her shoulder. She felt oddly relieved.

"Gloria," he said. "What can I help you with?"

"Officer Tully! Yes, I came to see if you had heard from James, actually. But here's Molly! She told me he's around the reservation. At Kay's?"

Wayne took a moment to respond, and Molly could see

something behind his eyes. Hesitation, definitely. Distrust, maybe.

"He might be," Wayne finally said. "He had a few things to do."

That was a lie. James had said he would be back as soon as he finished at Kay's.

"You're welcome to take a seat and wait for him. Molly and I have some work to do."

"A little detective, huh?" Gloria asked, winking at Molly. Though she felt stupid, Molly smiled anyway.

"Uh huh," Wayne said in a way that suggested he was done with the conversation.

"Wait." Gloria held up a finger and then rummaged through her purse. She dug out a postcard with a flower on it.

"I know Adriel is at some undisclosed location. But I was thinking of him earlier, the poor thing, and bought this for him. You don't have to tell me where he is. But could you send it to him for me?"

Wayne took the postcard and flipped it over, reading whatever she had written.

"Sure," he said.

"Did James see Dale?" Gloria asked hastily, which Molly found strange since she had just confirmed that he had.

Wayne glanced at Molly.

"Yes, but you'll have to talk with him about that."

"Of course," Gloria said. "I'll let you get back to your work."

With his hand still on her shoulder, Wayne guided Molly to his office, and once he had shut the door, he shook his head.

"Reporters," he said. "You always give them the least amount of information possible."

"I'm sorry," Molly said.

"Oh, it's all right. You're new to all this." He smiled warmly, and Molly felt her shoulders relax a little. "Next time, just let me or your dad handle her. We're used to it."

Molly nodded. "But she seems like she wants to help."

"She probably does," Wayne said. "But that doesn't mean that she won't use information you give her to twist up a story. She may have some strange . . . fascination with us Indians, but at the end of the day, you have to assume that Gloria is looking out for herself and her career."

"That's pretty negative," Molly said.

Wayne chuckled. "You have to be a skeptic when you're a cop. And an Indian."

JAMES

THE BARRACUDA LOOKED out of place on a reservation full of pickup trucks and station wagons and Frankenstein cars. James peered into the window. A woman's blazer hung in the back seat. He sighed and tried to get his mind right before stepping into the station. The reporter had been real eager to point James in Dale's direction. He had a sneaking suspicion that she would not welcome the Codys as suspects. Or anyone else he was considering.

He found Gloria sitting in one of the metal chairs by the front door. She flashed him a smile.

"Just the person I was looking for. You haven't returned any of my calls."

"Didn't know about them," he said. "I've been a little busy."

Kay entered behind him.

"Kay Benally!" Gloria chirped. Kay gave her a quick hug.

"Good to see you," Kay said, her smile strained. "Can't keep Wayne waiting."

Gloria watched her stride down the hall, then picked up her purse and swung it over her shoulder. "Can we have a chat?"

James glanced outside. The sun was setting, turning the horizon a deep purple. Molly was probably starving.

"They got a bar around here?"

"You've got to go to Farmington or Gallup for that."

James whistled. "A whole damn hour to get to a bar. That ain't right."

Gloria laughed, and James tried to ignore just how beautiful she looked in the early evening light with that easy smile on her face.

"How about a couple of beers from the gas station, then?"

Gloria smirked. "Romantic."

James made a show of rolling his eyes. "I'm tryin' to do the opposite here, lady. Scare you away."

"Well, it isn't working."

"Let me tell Wayne. I'm stayin' over at his place, so we can take the beers back there."

"All right, then," Gloria said. She didn't sit back down.

Kay, Wayne, and Molly were deep in conversation when James entered.

"What's this little powwow about?" he asked.

Kay groaned and Wayne shook his head. "This is not a powwow, bilagáana," Kay said.

"Byron Cody called me that, too," James said.

Kay laughed loudly. James noticed how her nostrils flared when she laughed—really laughed, like she did then.

"We don't mean it in the same way, I promise," she said.

"What's it mean?" Molly asked.

"'White man,'" Wayne said.

"We were just talking about your little *girlfriend*," Kay said, rolling her eyes.

"I thought you two were buddies," James said. She shrugged.

"Well, *not* my girlfriend, but she is comin' over tonight, Wayne," James said.

Wayne raised his eyebrows, and Molly looked away.

"Well, that's my cue to go," Kay said. She waggled her fingers at them as she left, calling over her shoulder, "See you tomorrow for lunch, Wayne!"

"I know what I'm doin'," James said after Kay left.

"You better," Wayne said.

"Molly, you must be starving," James said.

She grinned. "Barbara's making us a real, traditional Navajo dinner! My mouth has been watering for hours thinking about it."

James laughed. "You've never even had real, traditional Navajo food. How do you know you'll like it?"

"I trust Barbara," Molly said. "After that bread she gave me for breakfast? Off the hook!"

"'Off the hook?' And that's a good thing?" James chuckled. "I'll tell you what. It sure ain't a good thing if my truck's air lines are off the hook."

Molly rolled her eyes. "I don't even want to know what air lines are. You're such a dork."

James winked. "Don't worry. I'll give you a lesson someday about all the parts of a semitruck. But not now. Gloria and I will be there soon. Don't eat it all."

"Do we have to feed her, too?" Wayne asked.

"Ah, sorry," James said. "I should have asked. Well, I only invited her for beer." He shrugged.

"Barb won't allow that," Wayne said. "But you're the one that'll get an earful! I'm telling her it was your idea."

"Maybe I'll buy Gloria a gas station pizza. She can eat it on the steps." James grinned.

"Don't!" Molly shrieked, laughing. "You can't! I'll be horrified!"

James grabbed a balled-up piece of paper from the trash bin and tossed it at her. She shrieked again.

"Maybe *you* should take her on a date since you like her so much," James teased.

Molly's mouth fell open before she bent down, picked up the balled-up paper, and threw it back at him. James was out the door before it could hit him. He chuckled to himself as he walked to the front and decided he might actually enjoy being a dad to a teenage girl. In some ways.

Barbara's dinner was fantastic. She had even tried to serve Gloria a second helping, but Gloria declined. Barbara had only glared at James once, and that was because he'd suggested that Gloria could have his portion if there wasn't enough to go around.

"Do you think I didn't make enough food for half this reservation? Don't you know anything?" she scolded. "You sit down and eat."

"Yes, ma'am," James said.

Now, he and Gloria sat in lawn chairs behind Wayne's trailer, looking at the black night sky, the rock formations reaching toward the bright stars, and the nothingness that stretched below them. It was one of the most calming sights James had ever seen.

"I think you hurt Barbara's feelings in there, refusing more food," James said.

Gloria smiled. "Tell her I'm a diabetic. I have to watch what I eat."

"That true?" he asked.

"Yes, it's true."

For a moment, they listened to the distant calls of the owls. The coyotes. The firing of car engines.

"I was there, too, you know," Gloria said. She sipped a drink Barbara had made for her, and James supposed he was on his own with the gas station beer.

A light shone from the trailer behind them, only partially illuminating Gloria's face.

"Where?" he asked.

"Vietnam."

"You were there? Reporting?"

"Yep."

"Damn. Was hard enough being a man there. Were you with the troops?"

"Sometimes."

"Why? Why'd you go there?"

She sighed. "I had to do something. My little brother came home. Had these . . . just . . . *awful* stories about what he had seen. Messed him up really bad, you know?"

James took a sip. Didn't surprise him. It went with her personality to think she'd be the one to make a difference while hundreds of thousands of others floundered around, trying to figure out what to do with that heap of mess.

"Do you think you did somethin'?" he asked.

"Yeah, I do." Gloria's voice was hard. She had probably heard his touch of sarcasm.

"What?" he asked. "What'd you do?"

"Told people!" she cried. "Told them how terrible we were being to the Vietnamese. I wanted people back home to see how backwards it all was. We weren't helping a single person. I had to watch women and children and old people get murdered by Americans. I had to risk my own life to tell people back home exactly what was happening."

"Hmmm," he grunted.

"I can tell you think it didn't make a difference. But I think you're wrong. Lots of people believed what I wrote. Believed all of us who spoke out against it. It stopped because of us. We showed them all how meaningless it was."

James didn't argue with that. It had been a useless war.

"How about you?" Gloria asked. "Why did you go?"

"It was my job."

"And why did you make being an investigator your job?"

James smiled to himself; he doubted Gloria could see much of his face, either.

"I guess I was kinda like you. Wanted to make a difference. Thought I knew who the bad guys were. Thought I could weed out the Army's bad apples."

"And?" Gloria asked.

"Don't believe that anymore."

"What do you mean?"

"After My Lai? All those boys massacring four hundred some civilians? I think we're all just apples on the verge of decay. Some further along than others."

Gloria didn't say anything.

"Those men stabbed babies. Babies. And you could've plucked 'em out of any town in America. Just the boy next door. Stabbin' babies."

"So, is that why you left?" Her voiced cracked a bit, and James wondered if he had gone too far. But if Gloria had been there, in the shit, she ought to have a strong stomach. "Did Vietnam destroy your sense of self? Did it crumble that hero persona you had created?"

"I wasn't there to be a hero. I was there to see justice done. And it wasn't. So yeah. I left."

"You gonna stay around here until you see justice done?" she asked.

James shifted in his chair. "I'm gonna sure as hell try."

"So. Dale. You think it was him?"

James almost said "no" outright. "No" would've been the truth. But he didn't want Gloria to ask the next question. Who, then?

"Maybe," he said. "A couple of things add up, and a couple things don't."

"What doesn't add up?" she asked.

"Adriel. Why'd he leave him there? That's what Dale wants. Adriel."

"Why does he want Adriel?"

James thought it was a pretty stupid question, so he just waited for her to gather her thoughts.

Then Gloria asked, "What's he got to offer the kid?"

"It's not about that. It's about pride. Adriel's his son."

Gloria sipped. "It was Dale who did it. It has to be. It makes too much sense."

"Don't you go writing anything yet," James warned.

"You got it, boss."

James could hear the attitude behind her words and wanted to smack the drink right out of her hand. But he didn't.

Instead, he said, "So, tell me. What do you know about Charlie Company?"

38

DALE

DALE THOUGHT he had been awake for two whole days now, but he didn't know for sure. He had taken just about every upper he could get his hands on, and now he was driving to the reservation. Or he thought he was, at least. All this shit looked the same to him. He didn't know if he'd remember where to find Kay's house. That was where Linda had been living when he met her.

Sometimes he saw balloons falling from the sky. Red balloons. Hundreds of them. Then, they'd burst right before they hit the ground, shrapnel flying at his windshield. He ducked every time, and he was surprised he hadn't been hit yet. Just like those fuckin' Indians to use balloons to attack him. They acted like they weren't violent, but Dale knew they were.

When he first got back from Vietnam and got so high he saw gooks in his own kitchen, he knew on some level they weren't really there. It was the drugs. The memories. Still, he smashed every plate he owned trying to make them go away.

He no longer knew—on any level—what was real and

what wasn't. Was that cop who'd come to tell him about Linda real? He thought so. He had been pretty sober that day. But what about the Indians who had been following him ever since? Real sketchy motherfuckers. They were probably the ones behind these balloons.

Dale blinked real fast and this time only saw the road stretched in front of him like a long roll of duct tape. The tape started to roll up, and Dale braced for his car to flip, but it didn't. He just kept driving up and around. He looked to the seat next to him. The Indians might have exploding fucking balloons, but they didn't have an AK-47 pried right from the cold, dead fingers of a commie.

He was taking Adriel today. He had to. Adriel would make it all better. Adriel would give Dale a reason to wake up in the morning. To go to a shitty job at a pizza place. To get his life together, even. He could be a good dad. Would raise Adriel right.

His cheeks were a little wet, and he swiped at his eyes with his sleeve. He had to focus.

Up ahead, he saw something he thought he had seen before. A picture in his brain. Sort of like a memory he didn't know he had. The old woman selling jewelry out of her pickup. Linda giggling. Linda picking up a bracelet, putting it on her wrist, turning it over and back. Showing it off for Dale like she was a model or some shit. Damn, Linda had been a looker.

Dale jerked the wheel to the left and pulled down the road just past the jewelry stand. This was the way to Kay's.

39

JAMES

GLORIA HAD DRIVEN BACK to Santa Fe the night before, and now it was Sunday morning. Apparently, the Native American Church didn't meet weekly like the Christians did. They only gathered for big, important things. But Wayne and Barbara were Catholics, and so James watched them pull out of the driveway on their way to Mass.

He and Molly did crossword puzzles and listened to the radio over their morning coffee. Barbara had invited them, but James hadn't gone to church since his parents died and Molly made a face when Barbara's back was turned, so he politely said maybe next week.

James thought about George going to his own church. The only *real* Christian church around, supposedly. He had a strange urge to go see Kay. He didn't have any specific questions to ask her. At least none other than the big one: What was she not telling him? But he wanted to see her anyway. She seemed like the answer to all of this.

He looked at Molly, guzzling down her orange juice and

breakfast. He had forgotten what it was like to be a teenager. Hungry—always. Tired—always. And, well, one other thing that he hoped Molly wasn't feeling all the time. There weren't any teenage boys in her life, anyway. Not now. James jerked his head toward the window, like maybe he would see one just then.

"'Star of *Blazing Saddles* and certainly not big.' Six letters, ends with an E," Molly said, her mouth still partially full. She swallowed. "Brooks and Wilder are six letters, but they don't end with an E. What's the sheriff's name?"

"Little," James said. "His name is Cleavon Little."

"Ha!" Molly cried. "I get it! 'Certainly not big.' I thought they meant the actor was small."

James would hold on to the memory of this morning for a while afterward. The quiet time before hell broke loose a few miles away. Molly's unbrushed hair, a little frizzy around her face. She wore her pajamas still, and James, a T-shirt. The ease with which they sat in one another's company. James marveled at Molly's resiliency. Her lack of complaint. She had been through too much these past few months.

The phone rang, and Molly looked at James. He stood up.

"This is the Tully residence," he said when he picked up.

There was only heavy breathing at first, and then, in a whisper, "James. He's here."

"Kay?" James asked. "Who's here? Dale?"

"Yes." Her voice was steady but quiet. "He's outside and high as shit. He was shouting at me before, but now he's stopped and I don't know where he is."

"Your doors and windows are locked?" James asked.

"They are now."

"And where is George?"

"At church."

"I'm coming," James said.

"I heard him shooting into the air. He said he doesn't want to hurt Adriel, but he's got a gun out there."

Just then, James heard from a distance, "Open up this fuckin' door, bitch!" And a bang.

"Kay, are you still there?"

"Damn it. . . ." she hissed. "I'm here. But he's banging on the back door now."

"Stay there and stay down." James looked out the window at the driveway. Wayne and Barbara had left their Oldsmobile, the keys on the counter. James grabbed them and handed the phone to Molly.

"Stay on the phone with her. And don't leave this house. If Wayne gets back, tell him Dale is here. At Kay's."

Molly's eyes went wide, and she nodded, gingerly taking the phone.

James laced his boots as quickly as he could and grabbed his guns and ammo from the bedroom. He took off, the screen door banging behind him.

He tore out of the driveway, dust covering the car and, for a moment, his vision. He drove entirely too fast, swerving around a tire in the middle of the road and a bike laid on its side at the corner of an intersection.

When he pulled up to Kay's, he could see Dale circling the trailer, an AK-47 pointed at the ground while he raised up on his toes to peek into windows.

James parked with the passenger side to the house, got

out, and crouched behind the car. He peered around the bumper, but Dale hadn't even noticed him.

"Dale!" he shouted. Dale didn't answer. He was kicking things now, muttering to himself. James aimed his revolver near Dale's feet and fired.

"What the fuck!" Dale cried, jumping into the air.

"Dale! It's me, James. Remember? I just wanna talk."

Dale had taken cover behind the other side of the house. "Yeah, I remember you, pig!"

"Soldier, actually," James said. "Just like you."

Dale laughed. "Still a pig!" This time, James could see Dale's profile, gaze darting all around.

"Adriel's not here, so you can go ahead and leave Kay alone," James said.

"No way, man. You think I fuckin' believe you? I'm not leaving without Adriel."

"He's not here."

"Then one of you is gonna tell me where to find him. Where's his house?"

"He's not there, either," James answered.

"Fuck you and your bullshit," Dale cried and disappeared from view. "He's here somewhere, goddamnit." His voice grew more muffled. Then, the crash of a window breaking. James ran to the house. He pressed his back up against the siding and started to creep around.

But then, another car came screeching to a halt across the street, and out stepped a Cody boy, shooting a damn M16 at them both. Bullets everywhere.

"Jesus!" James breathed, running to the back of the house. He got there just in time to see Dale ducking and zigzagging.

"Fuck!" Dale yelled.

James crouched low with his back to the house, trying to make himself as small as possible. He could hear the Cody boy—James thought this one's name was Ronnie—getting closer, still shooting. Dale vanished behind the neighbor's trailer.

"Hey!" James yelled. "We want him alive!"

Ronnie stopped next to James and squinted at the neighbor's house, dropping the gun to his side.

"Maybe *you* want him alive."

James stood and put his hands in the air, letting his Colt dangle from one finger. "I need to ask him some questions." He shook his head and then brushed off his jeans. "Come on, man."

"Ask me if I care what you want," Ronnie said.

"Look, he's not going anywhere," James said. "His car's right here. Let him give himself up."

"No one comes onto *my* reservation, shooting at *my* people. I'm not letting him do anything."

Just then, the neighbor's truck roared to life. Dale in the driver's seat. James tried to shoot out the tires, but the truck was long gone before he could even get a round off.

Ronnie muttered to himself, then turned and stared at James.

"You brought this shit here. We told you to fuck off and you didn't. And now you're next, you hear me?" He got real close to James's face. "You and that pretty little daughter of yours are next."

James clenched his jaw and willed himself not to pummel the man.

"Leave," Ronnie said. "Get. The fuck. Out of here. Bilagáana."

James remained motionless. Ronnie spat on the ground, turned, and strode off. James took a deep breath and as soon as Ronnie's car was out of sight, ran into the house. Kay was on the ground, bleeding.

"What happened?" he asked, rushing to her.

"I don't know," she said. "It hit me."

"Just now?"

She nodded.

"Come on." He helped her up onto the couch. It was her forearm. He grabbed a clean towel from the hall closet and wrapped her arm tight. She winced.

"Is Dale gone?" she asked.

"Yeah," James said. "Stole the neighbor's car. Ronnie Cody showed up shootin', too. Looks like he might've gotten you instead."

Kay bit her trembling lip.

"Let's get you to the hospital," James said. He helped her to her feet.

"I'm fine," Kay said.

"We need to get you closed up."

He led her out the door, down the steps, and into the Oldsmobile.

"You keep that towel on, okay?"

She nodded.

"The Codys are going to come for you," she said.

The towel was already soaked in blood.

"I know," James said, kneeling beside the open passenger door. He took off his belt to make a tourniquet. It was worse than he'd thought.

Kay closed her eyes.

"You keep those eyes open, now," James said.

She moaned a little when the tourniquet tightened and opened her eyes.

"Shit. That hurts."

"I know," James said again. He closed her door and got in the driver's seat. Kay grunted and shifted, trying to get comfortable.

"You better not have broken my arm, James . . ." She frowned. "What's your last name?"

"Pinter," he said, backing out onto the road, lurching Kay forward a little.

"James Pinter," she said. "Hospital's in Shiprock."

"Roger." He glanced at her every few minutes, watching her eyes open and close, her breath deepening and then quickening again. James sped along the dirt road of the reservation until he got to the main road. Then, he pulled off to get Molly.

He threw the car into park and ran inside Wayne's house, hollering, "Molly!" She was right where he'd left her. Shaky and watching out the window.

"Come with me," he said. "We've gotta get Kay to the hospital." Molly just nodded. She climbed into the back seat, and he pulled away before she could even buckle her seat belt.

"You with me, Kay?" James asked, loudly.

"Mmmhmm." Kay opened her eyes again. Furrowed her eyebrows.

"I've got to tell you something," she said.

"All right," James said. "You can tell me when we get you fixed up."

As much as he wanted to know, he wanted Kay to stay calm. Calm but alert.

"Why don't you tell me about something else right now?"

"My father," Kay said.

"Yeah, your father."

"Hated Dale," Kay went on. "Used to fight with her all the time about him."

"What was your father like?" James asked. He wanted to get her mind away from Dale.

"My father was . . . even when he was younger, it was like he knew the history of the whole world. It was in his bones. A forever old man. He was tall and strong. Knew who he was."

James wondered if Kay even realized Molly was there. She was speaking so openly. She closed her eyes but then opened them again.

"I miss him. I always thought he knew the answer. I felt like he would keep me safe from everything."

She let her head tilt toward James. "Am I making any sense?"

"Lots of sense," James said. "Sounds like a guy I would've liked to meet."

Kay looked up at him as if studying him.

"What?" he asked.

"I'm trying to decide if he would've liked you."

James chuckled. "I don't think you know me well enough to make that sort of judgment."

"He'd have liked that you served the country," she said. "Us Navajo are volunteers."

"Sure. The Code Talkers of World War II. Legends."

"Wayne Tully's father was a code talker," Kay said.

"No shit."

James breathed a sigh of relief as they pulled into the hospital's parking lot. "Let's get you fixed up so you can tell me that secret of yours."

Kay laughed. "You'll make me now, won't you?"

He turned off the ignition. "Yup."

40

WAYNE

As soon as Wayne came home to an empty house with the door wide open and Molly's orange juice glass on the floor, he ran out the door and pushed the truck into gear. He found no one at Kay's, but he did find a pool of blood and droplets leading to the couch. He went back outside and circled the house, studying the casings littering the ground, the footprints in the dirt—four sets besides his own. He followed the fourth set away from the house, where they ended at the Bahe's driveway. Wayne knocked on the door. Mrs. Bahe answered, her face relaxing at sight of him.

"Wayne." She sighed with relief. "I've been calling the station, but no one answered. My truck's been stolen."

He glanced at the empty spot where the truck normally stood.

"I see that," Wayne said. "What happened?"

Elva Bahe's eyes grew wide.

"Oh, Wayne, it was awful. So many gunshots! I made my boys lie on the ground, on their stomachs. So, I don't know who took it. I was lying flat, holding Sterling's hand, when I heard the truck screech out of here. Then the shooting stopped. We all waited a long time before getting up. I was so relieved. And then a little upset with Darren for leaving the keys in the ignition. I've told him so many times to stop doing that."

Wayne nodded. "When you got up, did you see anything or anyone outside?"

Elva glanced sharply at him, like she wasn't sure she should say.

"Ronnie Cody was here to see what the fuss was about. But I'm sure he wasn't involved in this mess."

The Codys, Wayne thought. *What the hell were they doing here?*

"And before all this started? Did you happen to notice anything strange?"

"I was clearing the dishes when I heard yelling. I saw some white man poking around Kay's place. I was about to call the station when I heard a gunshot. That's when I made us all get down. That man sounded crazy."

"He's not a good guy," Wayne agreed.

"You know him? You think he's the one who stole my truck?"

"It's likely," Wayne said. "I'm gonna call some of the other stations to look out for him. We'll try to get your truck back."

Elva pursed her lips. "Don't know what we'll do without it."

"I'm sorry, Elva."

She nodded once. Wayne tipped his hat as he left. "We'll tell you if we find it," he called as he got into his own truck.

Elva held up a hand and closed the door.

Wayne went straight to the station. He made coffee and listened to the voicemails Elva had left.

The coffee pot dripped, and he could hear Elva's voice in a panic, then growing to irritation, and in the last few messages, frustration. He poured his coffee and watched a tarantula crawl across the window outside. He took a sip and then picked up the phone. Dale wasn't going home, Wayne guessed. He dialed and listened to it ring.

"Window Rock PD," the voice said. Wayne breathed a sigh of relief.

"Kelsey," Wayne said. "It's Wayne Tully. We've got a situation."

"What's up, Wayne?"

"Armed known drug addict left Sanostee. I don't have an exact time. An hour maybe? In a stolen vehicle."

"What are we looking for?"

"Red Chevy LUV, license plate 5769RTF."

"We'll keep an eye out. You said he's armed?"

"Yes," Wayne said. "Heavily. I've got steel casings that look like a 7.62 and a bunch of 5.56."

Kelsey whistled. "Casings? So he shot someone?"

"I'm trying to find that out. Tried to, at the least."

"Who is this guy?"

"White guy. Dale Fitzpatrick. He's got a son on the reservation. Not here right now. Down by you. I don't think he knows that, though, since he came here first. The man is incredibly dangerous. Ex-Army. Vietnam."

"That explains the AK, then."

"Suppose it does. Call me if you arrest him."

"You got it, Wayne."

Wayne hung up and called Chinle PD, Kayenta PD, and

Crownpoint PD. He had similar conversations with all of them and made himself another coffee while he waited to hear from James. He was getting antsy. Maybe he ought to call Albuquerque PD, too, in case Dale did go home. Or the state police to watch for him on the highway. But he just couldn't see Dale going home after all that without Adriel. And he knew Dale didn't have Adriel.

Wayne paced. He was about to radio his officer on duty when the station door opened and he walked in.

"Where have you been all morning?" Wayne demanded.

The officer shook his head. "Mrs. Ellison was missing again. Got a call from her daughter, Mary."

"Did you find her?"

"Down by the creek."

The phone rang, and Wayne snatched it up.

"Shiprock PD, Sanostee," he said.

"Wayne. It's James."

"What the hell happened? Is Kay all right?"

"Kay's all right. She's gettin' cleaned up and stitched up. She's on some pain killers right now. Kinda loopy. And her arm's gonna be hurtin' for a while. But she'll be all right."

"Did he shoot her?"

"She got shot all right. Lucky ricochet."

"Damn."

"Don't believe it was Dale's doing, though," James said.

"What do you mean?"

"I mean, I didn't see Dale fire his weapon at all. Which was an AK, by the way."

"He fired it," Wayne said. "Found the casings."

"Huh," James said. "Well, I'll tell you who I did see rain hellfire down on all of us. Ronnie Cody. The man had an

M16. Shootin' to kill Dale but didn't seem to mind if anyone else got in the way. Dale ended up stealin' a truck and high-tailin' it."

"Yeah, I talked to the owner. How did Ronnie Cody know that Dale was here?"

"Only thing I can think of is that he was following him. Or me," James said.

Wayne sucked his teeth. "This is getting serious, James."

"You're tellin' me," he said. "We got feelers out for Dale?"

"Called my buddies at the other reservation chapters."

"You need to get the State Troopers on this, too," James said.

Wayne heard the goings-on of the hospital in the background. Faint beeps. The soft voices of the nurses.

"The troopers will pick up a vehicle theft," Wayne finally said. "But they won't let us question him."

"You decide," James said. After a beat, he went on, "I need to deal with the Codys."

Wayne nodded even though James couldn't see him.

"You got any ideas how?" James asked.

"Naw. But we'll come up with something. I'll send George. You come back to the station. We need to talk."

"Roger that."

41

JAMES

KAY HAD SAID few words since they gave her the pain medicine.

"I'm not taking those with me," was one thing she had said. James waited until she fell asleep to slip the pills into his pocket. He didn't think she knew just how much pain she would still be in later.

James watched Molly adjust the pajamas she was still wearing. She kept fiddling with her hair, too. Trying to rake her fingers through it. They sat on opposite sides of the hospital room, Kay between them.

He thought about Dale, on his way to who knew where. James didn't care whether Wayne called the state police or not. Dale might be one hell of a loose cannon, but he wasn't Linda's killer. If the man wanted his son badly enough to brandish an AK on an innocent woman, there was no reason he wouldn't have just shot Linda and taken Adriel. He was sick enough to leave a message like that, sure. But he wasn't sophisticated enough to cover his tracks. Didn't care enough to, either, it seemed.

Did Cecil Cody know about My Lai? About the carvings on the bodies there? Is that why he left that card in her pocket? Or did the ace of spades mean something completely different to the Navajo? The symbol could be significant for any number of reasons. The Vietnamese had been fearful of it. Might as well have been the mark of the beast to them.

And what about this Assman? The Codys' thug, maybe? James would have to find out if there had been an Assman in Charlie Company. Maybe Gloria could help with that. There certainly wasn't an Assman in the group of thirty-one James had investigated. But Charlie Company was much bigger than that, and James didn't know the rest of their names from memory. Not even an Assman. Or maybe the CC didn't have one thing to do with My Lai after all. Maybe it was as simple as Cecil Cody leaving a message. For whom, though, James wasn't sure.

Kay snored a little and then turned her head toward James. He had wondered about her at first, sure. But someone who killed their own sister would have to be pretty arrogant to hire an investigator. Seemed unlikely. Though, it wouldn't be the weirdest thing James had seen. Once, in Vietnam, a soldier had confessed to a crime in the third person. "Duck sends the drugs," Duck had said to him, on the verge of tears. "Duck sends the drugs with the bodies back to America." Duck trembled. "That's how the drugs get there."

Duck was truly surprised when James arrested him. He had separated himself, the good Duck from the bad. It was the only way for him to move forward. For him to do the heinous deed and keep a bit of his old self.

Kay was not a sociopath. But she knew something. Something she wasn't telling him.

George finally arrived. James heard his loud footsteps before the man stormed into the room.

"What happened?" George asked.

"Dale showed up," James said, rising from his chair.

"Wayne said that. So he shot her?"

James looked at him, trying to figure out how much he ought to tell him. "Maybe," James said. "Ronnie Cody showed up, too. Started shootin' at Dale. A few stray bullets tore into Kay's house."

George's eyes narrowed. "What's Ronnie Cody got to do with this?"

"I don't know," James said. "Other than the fact that the Codys don't want me workin' on this."

George looked surprised. "How do you know that?"

"They told me."

"That's . . ." George searched for the word, ". . . strange. Wouldn't you say?"

James shrugged. "Told me it wasn't my place. Great point, actually."

"Gloria know about this?" George asked.

"About Kay? No, not from me."

"About Ronnie Cody being there," George said, flatly.

"Why? What's it to her?"

George crossed his arms and looked at Kay.

"Maybe you ought to hand all this over to Wayne."

"Wayne could handle it, I'm sure, if Wayne weren't stretched so thin as it is. He's asked for my help."

"Has he?" George stared so hard it made James question whether Wayne really had asked for his help at all. Maybe it was James who had asked for Wayne's.

"If Wayne wants me off the case—if Kay wants me off the case—then I'll leave. Not sooner."

George nodded but looked away again. "Let's hope no one else has to get hurt before then."

"Yeah, let's hope," James said. "Say, George, I'd like your help with something. You still got your phone bill from the month of May?"

"I'm sure I do."

"How about April?"

"I can check."

"Thanks," James said. "I'd like to have a look, if you can find them."

George stared at his feet. "I'll see if I can dig them up."

James knew George had a stack of bills sitting by his front door. He'd seen them there.

"Appreciate it," he said.

42

KAY

A WAVE of nausea hit Kay even before she opened her eyes and realized she was home again. From fear or pain, she didn't know. It was all jumbled inside her like that snow globe Adriel used to have. Like someone had shaken her and now all the pieces of her life were slowly falling and she didn't know where any of them would end up.

She reached for the glass of water George had placed beside her bed. She didn't know how she knew it was there. She didn't remember much of the car ride to the hospital or much of anything after either.

She squinted and saw the pill bottle next to the water. She cursed James for sending the pills home with her. She knew there were some Navajos desperate for those pills. She could sell them for a good price. Not that she ever would. But having them felt like another thing she didn't need.

Still, the pain throbbed and tore at her arm. She couldn't even think it hurt so much. She reached for the pills and swallowed one, and within minutes, her arm and mind began to calm. She took some deep breaths.

The drugs made her mind a little heavy, a little slow, but clear.

Her first clear thought was, *I need to tell James.* It didn't matter now how relevant Kay might think it was or wasn't. It didn't matter that damn near everyone had accepted that Linda hadn't overdosed. Kay had information. Information that might help James. Kay didn't even care what happened to her anymore. She just wanted to find her sister's killer.

She was tired again, and when she closed her eyes, she saw Linda. Tears streamed down Kay's face, and she didn't know if she was still awake or if she was dreaming.

"I'm sorry," Kay said to Linda. "I'm so sorry for everything."

Linda didn't speak, but she held Kay, and Kay felt more at peace than she had in a long time.

[43]

JAMES

WAYNE STILL LOOKED STRESSED EVEN after James assured him that being at church wasn't his fault. James had left Molly with Barbara. It had been a long day for the girl.

Wayne was opening and closing his mouth now, rubbing his jaw.

"The troopers won't let him get very far," James said. Wayne nodded.

"I have to deal with the Codys now, too," Wayne said. "You sure it was Ronnie that shot her? I found casings from Dale's gun, too."

"I don't know for sure, but Kay said it had just happened. And like I said, Dale did not fire that AK while I was there."

Wayne sighed. "There were thirty damn casings from the M16."

"You could put it on Dale for now if you need to. Let me handle the Codys."

Wayne looked at him and sighed again.

"What are you gonna do?" he asked.

"What can you tell me about Byron and Ronnie?"

"Ronnie's what you just saw. The muscle. Byron's real outgoing. Helps out a lot in the community. He's a part of ONEO. Which is a pretty wonderful organization here on the reservation. If someone wants something done, they go to Byron. He's the brains, too. He'll take over Cecil's day-to-day eventually."

"What's ONEO?"

"Office of Navajo Economic Opportunity. We were given a grant in the sixties as part of that war on poverty. ONEO does legal services, the cultural centers, the neighborhood youth corps, community development, alcohol dependency programs, Head Start. If it's a service for the people on the reservation, ONEO is probably involved."

"Shit, and he still goes around threatening people?" James asked.

"Well, for one, you aren't Diné. You've got to understand the politics on the reservation before we go any further into the Codys." Wayne glanced at the clock: 8:35 p.m. "Let me call Barb and tell her we'll be late. I'm gonna need another coffee."

"Pour me one, too, if you don't mind," James said.

While Wayne was gone, James studied his desk, the shelves behind it. A college degree. Certificates. Awards. A photo of Wayne and Barbara smiling big in full Navajo attire, the sun bright on their faces.

Wayne returned with two steaming cups of coffee. "Molly's doing all right," he said, handing a mug to James. "She and Barbara have eaten, and Molly's going to bed soon."

"Glad to hear it," James said. "So, tell me about the politics."

Wayne took a deep breath. "Teddy Jackson is the

chairman for the Navajo Nation. He's like our president. He ran on a platform that promised to take care of Navajos first, always. He railed against outsiders of all sorts, whether it was the BIA or the coal companies. None of them had Diné interest at heart, he said. Which is true."

Wayne scratched his cheek. "It's become very popular to blame all of our problems on everyone else." He paused again.

"Speak freely, Wayne," James said. "You won't hurt my feelings."

Wayne chuckled. "I hate the BIA. I have to watch them—along with the state of New Mexico—disregard my people, think they know what's best for us, and implement rules and laws that misunderstand us on the most basic levels. Every day I try to help my people, and they try to do the opposite. I wish I could just do my job the right way, but at every turn, I run into their wagging fingers, their walls of paperwork."

He leaned back in his chair and interlaced his hands behind his head.

"I voted for Jackson. I wanted to see the Navajo Nation stand tall and proud. I didn't even want to believe the things Barbara told me at first. But she sees things so clearly. She's a woman, you know? They're just better at not being tricked."

"See what?" James asked. "What did Barbara tell you?"

"She's suspicious," Wayne said. "There's this land deal coming up. A ranch that's been for sale for months now. All of a sudden, Jackson is hell-bent on purchasing it for the Nation. But only once the price went up. Barbara believes that Jackson is about to make a whole bunch of money."

"How's that?"

"She thinks there's a middleman. You see, this new higher price? She can't find it listed anywhere. Jackson claims it's the price the landowners gave him, but Barb doesn't think so. She thinks Jackson is working on getting some of that extra money from the sale for himself."

"Why does she think that?"

"If you saw the way the man dresses, the way his office building looks, the cars he has, you'd understand. The chairman of the Nation doesn't make that kind of money. Plus, he hasn't been the tough bulldog he promised to be when it comes to these outside companies. He's been downright lenient to any company with Navajo ties. Cecil Cody's brother, Ken, is middle management for the uranium company, for example. Jackson doesn't ever question what *they're* doing for Diné. Which is absolutely nothing."

"So, Cecil Cody and Teddy Jackson are scratchin' each other's backs, is that right?"

"Not bothering Cecil's brother's company is just a favor to get Ken promoted, I'm sure. What I worry about is Cecil's connection with drugs. I'm sure Kay mentioned it."

"She did," James said. "But not much. Tell me more."

"The Codys are best known for their support of the Native American Church. And of peyote," Wayne said.

"The hallucinogen," James said.

"Correct. Used for ceremonial purposes only. Not recreation. *But* it's also an excellent front for what the Codys really specialize in."

"Cocaine?" James guessed.

"Cocaine, marijuana, heroin now. Anything in demand on the reservation. Not that Cecil is directly involved in any way. His sons handle it. But they are *very* good at covering their tracks. Never been able to nail down anything solid. But it seems to be a well-known fact around these parts, anyhow."

"And Jackson knows about this?" James asked.

"Jackson would never question it, even if he did hear rumors. It's understood that Cecil is untouchable. He does too many good things for Diné. People would rather see the Codys' good side. Their generosity. Their compassion for their people. Even if people knew Byron threatened you, no one would be bothered by it. You *are* just another white man who thinks he knows how to fix a Diné problem."

They were quiet for a minute. A car drove by outside.

"You want me off this case, Wayne?" James asked.

"Now I thought you said you weren't going to get offended?"

James smiled. "You'll have to get nastier than that. I'm just thinkin' that maybe I *am* making things more difficult for us both."

Wayne rocked himself back and forth in his office chair.

"If this *is* somehow tied to the Codys and their secrets, I'm going to need outside help whether I want it or not."

James nodded. "I can see that. Well, we've got a name from that Willa lady you and Molly spoke to. Assman. She remembered because it was funny. That name ring any bells?"

Wayne shook his head. "Can't say I've heard of an Assman." He cracked a smile.

"Oh, I've met plenty of Assmen in my day," James said.

Wayne laughed. "All right, so you think this Assman is important?"

"Could be," James said. "We both know the state of mind this Willa girl was probably in, but she told Molly that Linda seemed scared."

"I can have one of my officers look through our records. See if an Assman ever comes up."

"Thanks, Wayne. I've got something for you to look at real quick." He pulled a list from his pocket.

"This here is the list of names from Charlie Company. Charlie Company is the group of soldiers who massacred those villagers at My Lai."

"Charlie Company. C.C.," Wayne mused.

"Exactly. These are only the thirty-one I investigated. But it's a place to start. I'd like you to take a look and tell me if you recognize any of these names. Maybe while your officer is looking for an Assman, they can see if any of these names come up, too."

Wayne took the list and scowled at it for a moment. "Nothing here means anything to me. But I'll put the new kid on it."

Just then, the phone rang. Wayne picked it up.

"Officer Tully."

He leaned forward on his desk.

"Kay," he said. "How are you feeling?"

He looked down intently.

"Sure, James is here. Hold on."

Wayne handed the phone over.

"Hey, Kay."

"Hey, I need to talk to you."

"Yeah, you said that in the car. You feelin' up to it?"

"Not really, but it can't wait. Please. Come by tonight.

These damn pills keep making me fall asleep, so just have George wake me up if you need to."

"All right," James said. "I'll come by now."

KAY

KAY THOUGHT she'd be fighting to stay awake, but after hanging up with James, she couldn't stop her heart from pounding in her chest. She was about to tell him. The reason she and Linda had fallen out. The reason Kay had been less than helpful with this investigation.

She heard the knock on the front door, the soft, low murmurs of George talking to James. She tried to prop herself up a bit. Smooth her hair down. She took a long gulp of water before she heard a knock on her bedroom door.

"Come in," she said.

James shut the door behind him quietly.

"How you feelin'?" he asked.

"Like a cow trampled my arm."

"Are the meds helping?"

"Yes," Kay sighed. "Thank you for bringing them back."

James gave her a sideways smile, and Kay ignored the melting feeling at the back of her head. She gave her head a little shake.

"Please sit," she said.

He was about to sit in the chair in the corner until she said, "Scoot that closer."

When he did, he was right beside her bed. Close enough to touch. She had a fleeting thought that she ought to be embarrassed. This was all too intimate. But truly, she didn't care. She trusted him and had since she first laid eyes on him. She didn't quite know why.

"My sister and I had a big fight," Kay started. It felt like the safest place to begin. The easiest place. "A few weeks before she died. I found out she was seeing Dale again and bringing Adriel around him. I blew up on her."

James reached for his back pocket but stopped. He folded his hands instead and leaned in even closer. Kay's heart sped up even more.

"Did she tell you why she was seeing him?" he asked.

"No," she said. "All she could get out was that it wasn't what I thought."

"And what did you think?" James asked. "That she was having an affair?"

"I thought she was using again," Kay said. "Actually, I'm pretty sure she *was* using again."

The backs of her eyes stung. The ache in her arm intensified. She looked at the clock on the wall above the door. It wasn't time for more medication yet. She coughed a little.

"And why is that?" James asked.

"Because I got her the pills," Kay said. "I got her the pills just like I did in the beginning when she first started using."

Kay felt like she could almost hear James's heart beating, too. Beating in time with hers. She looked down at her shaking hands and kept going, because that wasn't all.

"I met my ex-husband my senior year of high school. He

was older. In medical school. Basically the catch of the town. When he graduated medical school, I was still partying a lot. He would get us pills."

She paused and searched James's face. He was good at staying focused. At not judging.

"Please don't tell Wayne," she whispered. "I don't want Al to get in trouble. I don't care what happens to me, really. But Al could lose his medical license."

James nodded. "I'm not concerned with Al. Go on."

"He was young and cocky and trying to impress me. I shared some with Linda, and after that, she was hooked. Al and I got married. I stopped partying so much. He stopped getting her drugs. That's when she turned to Ronnie Cody. Just like everyone else on the reservation. I tried to help her, and eventually she let me. But not for years. Not until she had met Dale and had Adriel and crashed her car. I thought it was all behind her."

James ran his fingers through his hair and sat back again.

"I can understand that. You were both young. It happens all the time."

"I know," Kay said. "Still. If it wasn't for me, she might never have gotten hooked in the first place. It was my fault. Anyway, I don't like George's church. But they have the best addiction program around, so I took her there. And to be honest, I didn't like George much at first, either."

"And now?" James asked.

Kay shrugged. "He loved her."

"That's what you've been hiding?" he asked.

"There's more." For a moment, Kay couldn't speak. James leaned forward again and put his hand next to hers on the bed. Close enough to grab and hold if she wanted to. And she did. She swallowed and sniffed. She had to tell him all of it.

"She came to me. It was probably sometime in late April. She told me she had hurt her back at work. That she really needed some pain medication. That it was hard to get through her day. But she was on the clinic's blacklist, so to speak. A known addict that's only allowed ibuprofen. She said it wasn't helping. She asked me to call Al. And I did."

James rubbed the back of her hand with his thumb.

"He obviously wasn't thrilled. But I wore him down, and he wrote the prescription. Enough pills to last her some time. I don't think he wanted me to ask again. But then I found out that she had gone to see Dale. I still don't know why. I was so angry at her. She lied to me to get pills! She was seeing that piece of shit again—and worse, bringing her son. I told her Dale ought to be dead to her. That if she was going to be a junkie again, couldn't she just hang around with useless Willa?"

Her muscles tensed, and a sharp pain jolted through her arm. "Ah," she hissed, her face scrunching up.

"You all right?" James asked. "That can be enough for now."

Kay shook her head. "I think she was trying to tell me something, but I wouldn't listen. She told me that the pills were for Dale. He was trying to get sober or something, but he needed some pills to wean himself. That it was impossible to do that with pure heroin. She said she was sorry she lied. But that made even less sense. I couldn't understand why my sober sister would want to see Dale at all. Even if she did want to have an affair. There were much better options much closer. But I don't think that was it. My sister was so loyal to everyone in her life. I just kept thinking she was using again, and she just kept saying, 'It's not what you think.' But I wouldn't have any of it. We stopped speaking after that. It was the last time I saw her."

James clucked his tongue and shook his head. "Gosh, that must be hard. I'm sorry, Kay."

"She's haunting me, you know. It probably sounds ridiculous to you, but it's true. She wouldn't leave after she died. She pestered me. She wouldn't let me sleep very long. She was telling me that I was wrong about all of it. Because I thought she *did* overdose. I was convinced she did and that it was my fault. She was telling me that I needed to trust you. To work with you. I'm sorry I've been keeping this from you."

"I don't think it's ridiculous," James said. "Losing someone you love is hard. It's hard for all of us. Whether it's their ghost or their spirit or just their memory talkin' to us, I think it's important to keep them with us as long as we can. And in this case, it sounds like she's on my side."

James let go of her hand and brushed her hair out of her face. "Your sister didn't overdose, you understand? Whatever it is that happened before this, it doesn't change the fact that she was killed."

A small sob escaped Kay, and she nodded.

"Whatever you need me to do, I'll do it," she said in a small voice. "I promise. Please find whoever did this."

"I will," James said. His voice was strong. Assured. Kay breathed deeply. She felt so much relief, it was almost overwhelming. She wanted to cry and sleep and laugh. Then she thought of one more thing.

"Oh, and that's where I was the night I left Molly at the station with Wayne. Al called. He found out that Linda had overdosed, and he was furious and terrified. He was threatening to tell the school if I let it slip where she got the meds. I had to go explain it to him. I'm sorry."

"I forgive you," James said. "Turns out Wayne's a pretty good guy."

"I agree," Kay said. "I don't want him to think any less of me. That thought is worse than him arresting me."

"He's not gonna arrest you," James said. "And he's not gonna think any less of you."

"You're gonna tell him?" Kay asked.

"I think I should."

She nodded. She'd known it was coming.

"Let's solve this case," James said. "You know any Assmans?"

Kay laughed. A real belly laugh. It felt good. "Assmen? Plenty."

JAMES

JAMES STOOD in Wayne's kitchen, staring into the sink of dirty dishes. He had just gotten off the phone with his friend Charles at the FBI's Denver office. Charles had the lab results from the syringe. No match on the fingerprints. And even more interestingly, no trace of heroin or any other narcotic. He had also asked Charles to check the records for any Assmans in New Mexico or Arizona or Colorado. Charles had been able to find only one Assman with a record. Wayne had found none. Turned out, Assmans were pretty square dudes in general.

Jerry Assman from Albuquerque had been arrested ten years ago for breaking and entering and then for possession two years ago. It was marijuana and not much of it. Small potatoes compared to what Cecil Cody was probably involved in. James didn't see this being *his* Assman. Still, after his conversation with Kay, he knew he needed to talk to Cecil. Linda had been using again. Or had been involved with folks who were. It didn't matter much which it was. All signs pointed to the Codys.

James had also asked Gloria to track down the names of the remaining sixty-seven members of Charlie Company. She had agreed to try. James hoped one of them would be an Assman, though he knew it was unlikely.

Molly was getting dressed now. James had heard the shower turn off and the blow dryer run for a while. Sometimes Molly hummed as she got ready. Sometimes he'd hear her laughing to herself. But she usually tried to act cool around him. He wished he had been there to see that carefree Molly more. To see the raw, unedited version of her. But this was what he had now, and he grabbed onto every moment he could.

When Molly emerged from the bedroom, she breezed past him to pour herself some coffee.

"What's it gonna be today, boss?" she asked. Not "dad" yet. But getting closer.

"Today's the day I go see Cecil Cody," he said. Molly's eyes grew wide as she sipped.

"How do you know you're gonna see him? Didn't his sons block you last time?"

"I'm going to his office," he said. "I've got a little bird on the inside, told me when he likes to hang around."

Molly picked up a piece of toast from the plate James had left for her. She smeared jelly on it.

"Am I coming, too?" she asked. "I want to see this guy."

"I have a different mission for you. A very important one. Are you up for it?"

Molly squinted at him. "I feel like if it were *that* important, you'd be doing it yourself. But, sure. Lay it on me."

"Oh, it's important, all right," James said. "But it'll take fortitude."

Molly groaned. "Why are you giving me the bad stuff?"

"Every private's got to earn her stripes."

"Whatever that means," she said.

"The library in Gallup," James said. "They've got archives there. Newspaper archives, local high school yearbooks. I'm gonna drop you off there on my way to Window Rock. I need you to look for Assmans."

Molly swallowed. "What? How? I'm supposed to read every newspaper ever and just hope I find a guy named Assman?"

James poured his own cup of coffee and leaned back against the counter with her. She had her feet crossed. He crossed his, too.

"No. We know which high school Linda graduated from. You can start there. Look for Assmans her year, the three years behind her and the three years ahead. Then, you can move on to the newspapers. There will be an archivist there. Start with this year—1979—and go backwards. Ask her for anything about the United Nuclear Corporation, where Linda worked. This Assman doesn't seem to have a criminal record. So, he won't be in any kind of news like that."

Molly took another bite of her toast and raised her eyebrows.

"If we can't find any Assmans doing that, we'll have to get creative."

"How many years should I go back?" Molly asked.

James grinned. "Until I pick you up."

She sighed. "I better get a raise for this."

James rubbed his chin and thought. "Maybe a bonus. A celebratory cigarette if you find an Assman."

Molly smiled. "Something better than that."

"A Twinkie?"

Molly giggled. "Lame. Come up with something better." She popped the rest of the toast in her mouth. "I'll get my shoes on!" she called over her shoulder as she left the kitchen.

James smiled and shook his head. Then, he tipped back his coffee and went to get his boots.

The offices at Window Rock were impressive, and James wondered how he would feel about that if he were Navajo. Especially seeing the state of some of the trailers and buildings in Sanostee. But it wasn't really any of his business, and when he arrived at Cecil Cody's door, he knocked loudly three times. He knew the man would be inside.

He heard nothing at first, and then, suddenly, the door opened. Cecil Cody stood in the frame, his mouth downturned, his frown lines deep. His braids were the longest James had ever seen. Past his belt buckle and completely gray. Cecil said nothing, only stepped aside enough to let James in, and then shut the door behind him.

Cecil went back around his desk and sat in his large leather chair. "Sit," he said, gesturing to the chair opposite.

James sat. "Mr. Cody. Pleasure to meet you."

"James Pinter. The man who left me his number on an ace of spades playing card. You a gambler?"

"Not much of one, sir, no."

Cecil nodded. "I guessed as much."

"Why's that?"

"You don't have much of a read on this situation."

James couldn't help himself. He smiled. "Wouldn't be the first time I was in over my head."

Cecil raised an eyebrow. "To what do I owe the honor?"

"We haven't had a chance to chat yet. I'd like to ask you some questions about Linda Morris."

"Don't know Linda Morris."

"But you knew her daddy," James said. "Didn't you?"

Cecil stared, more curious than anything.

"Sure, I knew Ned."

"Do you think Ned would have liked to see his daughter become addicted to drugs?"

"No Indian would," Cecil said.

"And yet plenty do."

"Some things can't be changed. Only controlled. Man cannot stop a storm or a drought. They can only respond to the damage and perhaps plan accordingly for the next one. Which is why I funded the new addiction program at the Native American Church."

"Is it better than the one at the Church of the Open Door? I hear that's the best one around."

"It's a white man's church and a white man's program. No wonder it's failing our community."

"Linda went to that one before she died," James said.

"Like I said."

"You know of a Jerry Assman?" James asked.

Cecil frowned and shook his head. "I do not."

"He doesn't do any work for you down in Albuquerque?"

"What sort of work?"

James paced himself. It wouldn't do any good to outright accuse Cecil of anything in the man's own office.

"Any sort of work," James said.

Cecil leaned over his desk and smiled. "Albuquerque is full of common criminals. I don't work with criminals. And I don't work with outsiders. Assman isn't an Indian name."

James let the silence hang. And then Cecil went on like James had hoped he would.

"You see, Mr. Pinter, my work is done here on the reservation. I help Diné. I represent them here at Window Rock. Make sure their needs are met. I'm not concerned with you. I'm not concerned with this Assman, either. That is, until you interfere in the lives of Diné. So, my suggestion to you is that you learn real quick when to fold that losing hand of yours."

James nodded. "That's some good advice. Problem is, I'm hardheaded. And I'm persistent. If there are cards left in that deck, I'm not gonna stop." He stood. "Thank you for your time today. I'll be seein' you around."

Cecil shook his head. "I hope not."

46

MOLLY

THE LIBRARY WAS the same color as the land and seemed to fit in as seamlessly as the mesas, rising up from the dust as a fixture of the earth. It was stout and wide and shaped like a maze. Molly had expected the archivist to be old and solid, too, but she was young. Probably just graduated from whatever program a person had to go through to be an archivist. She had long, straight bangs and stylish tortoiseshell glasses that covered half her face. Her name tag read Ruiz.

"How can I help you?" she asked Molly.

"I'd like to see your yearbooks, please," Molly said. "For um . . ." She reached into her purse's pocket and pulled out a piece of paper. "West Newcomb High School."

Miss Ruiz stared, waiting for more.

"For the years . . . 1955 through 1964."

Miss Ruiz stood from her desk. "School project?" she asked.

"Not exactly," Molly said. "Just curious about some local history."

"Uh huh." But she didn't sound convinced. She

rummaged in her top drawer for a moment and then said, "Well, follow me."

She led Molly through a door behind her, down a hallway, and into a room that could've been an office space or a conference room but was lined with filing cabinets and barrister bookshelves. She unlocked one in the far corner and started pulling out yearbooks.

"I'll put them right on this table here, all right?" she asked.

"Thanks," Molly said.

For the next half hour, Molly flipped through the senior photos of each yearbook, looking for an Assman. There were plenty of Ahkeahs, Allens, Austins, Arvisos, and Ashleys but no Assmans. She rubbed her eyes. The newspapers would be worse, but she guessed James would still be another hour or so. She went back to Miss Ruiz.

"Find what you're looking for?" she asked. Molly shook her head.

"How about newspapers? Do y'all have newspapers?"

"Yes," Miss Ruiz said, dragging out the word inquisitively.

"Do you happen to know if you have any articles about the United Nuclear Corporation?" Molly asked.

Now Miss Ruiz was truly intrigued. She sat back in her chair and tapped her pencil against her lips.

"United . . ." she muttered. She stood again and walked back to a different room this time. Her heels clicked on the floor, her yellow skirt suit perfectly tailored and spotless. She pulled out a giant drawer.

"I believe that's the company off the highway near Church Rock, correct?"

Molly thought back to her visit with James and Kay. Was that what the exit sign had said? Molly was sure it was.

"That's the one," she said.

"United just started milling uranium here in 1977. So, we'll only have to look at the past two years."

That still sounded like a lot to Molly.

"I don't know what you're looking for," Miss Ruiz said, glancing at her. "But the biggest story will probably be its opening. After that, maybe significant hires."

She pulled out a large bound volume of newspapers and placed it on the table behind her. "These are all the articles from 1977. I believe it opened in the summer."

Molly opened the book and carefully turned the pages until she got to May. "Thank you," she said.

Miss Ruiz smiled for the first time. "I hope you find what you're looking for," she said.

Molly looked through all of May and found no mention of the United Nuclear Corporation. But on June 20, 1977, there it was. Front page of the *Gallup Independent*. *Uranium Mill Begins Operations*. Below the headline, a photo of three men shaking hands with the governor of New Mexico. Molly read the caption: *Henry Fields, Senior Manager of Operations; Robert Feeney, Engineering Director; and Carl Assman, Director of Finances for the United Nuclear Corporation, meet with Governor Apodaca to discuss the future of uranium in New Mexico.*

Assman! Molly could've cried with happiness. She let out a shaky laugh and then raced back to Miss Ruiz.

She was so excited she was nearly out of breath. "Could you copy something for me?"

47

JAMES

THE SECRETARY at United Nuclear Corporation had given James the new phone number for Carl Assman. At first, Carl didn't answer his phone or return James's calls. But James waited him out and made his messages more and more intriguing until, finally, Carl called one evening when the Pinters and the Tullys were all watching television.

"Hi Carl," James said. "I see you got my messages."

"Yes," Carl said. "I want nothing to do with that company anymore and had no idea who Linda Morris was at first. But then I remembered."

There was silence on the line after that. "I'm sorry to hear about her death," he finally said. "But this is the last time I want to speak with anyone about this."

James didn't know what "this" was, but he only asked, "Can I meet you somewhere?"

"Farmington," Carl said. "I'll meet you there this Sunday."

"I'll buy you some lunch," James said.

"There's a diner on Main Street," Carl said. "Near the park."

"I'll see you there at noon," James said. Carl hung up the phone.

Molly wanted to come, of course, and James saw no harm in it. They set off that Sunday morning and drove toward the mountains. The roads were almost empty, and it played tricks on their eyes.

"That mountain never seems to get any closer," Molly said, pointing ahead. "I keep thinking we're gonna drive right into it."

She carried her purse with her revolver, her notepad, and her drawing tools. James didn't know what else. Some lipstick, he noticed, when she pulled some out and painted it on her lips, smacking them together.

They were fifteen minutes early and got a table in the far corner, where two large windows met. Molly sat with her back to one so James could see out them both and watch the parking lot. An older couple. A very young couple. A family. And then a man in his sixties, alone. He had a trimmed gray beard and glasses and wore a striped polo shirt and well-tailored tan pants. When he entered the diner, he looked around. James stood and walked toward him. He hadn't mentioned bringing Molly.

They shook hands.

"James Pinter," James said.

"Carl Assman," Carl said.

"I brought my daughter with me."

Carl glanced over at her.

"She's good at keeping secrets," he added. Carl shrugged.

The diner was getting busier now, and a little kid

shrieked in frustration. A table of teenagers laughed loudly. Carl sipped on the lemonade James had ordered for him.

"We won't take up much of your time," James said. Molly munched on some onion rings but kept looking at Carl. James wondered what she was noticing. He would ask her later.

"How did you know Linda Morris?" he asked.

"I didn't," Carl said. "She cleaned my office, and one day I asked another janitor what her name was."

James pulled out the note he had found in Linda's pocket. "Did you write this?"

"I did," Carl said. "It was taped to a large folder containing documents that I wanted Linda to have."

"Documents?" James asked. "What kind of documents?"

"Damning ones," Carl said. He scowled. He cleared his throat and looked over his shoulder before continuing. "About things the company was doing. Illegal things."

"And why did you want Linda to have documents like that? You just said you didn't even know her. That all she did was clean your office."

Carl sat back a little and took a deep breath. "I don't want it to get out that I told you this, you understand me? I'm telling you because you're ex-Army. So am I. But this stays between us." He looked at Molly. "And her, I guess."

"Understood," James said. "I appreciate it."

"United was being reckless. See, I was just a numbers man. The highest numbers man at the company, but still. I had nothing to do with the operations side." He paused and squinted at James. "You know how a uranium mill works?"

"I'm guessing it's got something to do with turning uranium into a usable nuclear product, but no, I don't know the ins and outs."

Carl nodded. "After the uranium ore is dug up from the ground, it's brought to a mill and ground up. Then, some chemicals are added to dissolve the uranium. That's how they separate it from the rest of the stuff they pull up out of the earth. Once they have the uranium separated, they solidify it, dry it, package it, and send it off. Got that much?"

"Sure."

"So, the rest of the stuff left behind is all toxic. There's radioactive decay products in there, heavy metals, all kinds of waste. They've got to put that sludge somewhere, don't they?"

"I suppose they do."

"That stuff is called 'tailings,' and United—and every other uranium processing company—has holding ponds to store it. Except, United cut a lot of corners. They didn't line the holding ponds properly, and once cracks showed up, they didn't move quickly enough to fix them. Basically, the whole thing is a ticking time bomb. Soon, the dam that holds the tailings in is going to give out. All that harmful waste is going to seep into the ground, flow into rivers and creeks."

"Holy shit." James sat back and stared at Carl. Then he ran his fingers through his hair. What the hell had this man done?

Carl took off his glasses and carefully wiped them with a handkerchief from his pocket.

"Listen, Linda isn't the first person I went to," he said. "What could a janitor do? I'd been fighting this for a while now. First, I argued with people inside the company to no avail. I tried to help them see that they could afford to fix those ponds. And that they had better, because what they were doing was against the law. They told me it was a waste of money. It was no big deal. No one would care. And you know what? I had to find out that they were right."

Carl put his glasses back on and frowned. Molly had stopped moving, her pencil hovering above her notepad. Right then, the waitress brought their lunches over. James had ordered club sandwiches all around before Carl arrived. Carl barely even glanced at his sandwich before taking a bite. James waited for him to swallow.

"What did you do then?"

"I went to the police. New Mexico State Police. They took down my information. Wrote down what I said. And didn't do anything at all about it. I called them twice to see what was going on. They said they were looking into it." He took another bite. James wasn't feeling so hungry anymore.

"But they never came by. Never even made a phone call as far as I know."

"And so you gave the documents that proved all of this to Linda?"

"Copies of them, yes," Carl said. "I knew if I couldn't do anything, she couldn't do anything. But I wanted them to know. The Indians. It's their land. They're the ones that are about to be poisoned."

James looked out the window. He watched the cars passing on the highway. The semis. He thought about how none of those drivers knew what he knew and how he'd once been one of them. A simple life. James felt grief, then. Suddenly and from nowhere. He cared now. He cared about Wayne and Barbara and Kay.

"Has this happened before?" he asked.

"Hell if I know," Carl said. "Not because of United, but there are plenty of oil and coal and uranium companies on and around those New Mexico reservations that don't give a damn about those people."

James thought of Jackson railing against such companies. He thought about Wayne, and probably plenty of others, believing him. And then he thought about Cecil Cody's brother, getting a promotion because Jackson had made it a habit to look the other way.

"The dams haven't burst yet, though?" he asked.

Carl furrowed his eyebrows. "I quit a couple of months ago. On May 12. The same day I left Linda those papers. If it's happened between then and now, I wouldn't know. I'm not sure if anyone would know other than United."

James didn't know what to say. How many showers had Molly taken on the reservation? How much water had she drank? His stomach turned over.

"I'm telling you all this because I'm worried that it did have something to do with her death," Carl said. "If you think she was killed, this might have been why. I haven't been able to sleep since you told me that. I guess I've got to live with the fact that I killed a woman with this information."

James watched him take another bite of his sandwich.

"You did what you could," he said.

Neither James nor Molly had touched their food. When the waitress walked by, James asked, "Can we get these boxed up?"

James's first thought was to tell Gloria. She could put this out there quickly. Could probably do the most to stop it. But what did he really have for her? Missing copies of documents. A source who refused to speak to the press.

James's next thought was to call his buddy Charles. But still, the same problem existed. And on top of that, it wasn't technically on Navajo land and so it wasn't the feds' jurisdiction.

James thought again about Duck. About how many American soldiers and officers had been involved in that operation. Sending their fellow Americans home to be buried in a national cemetery with a flag draped over their coffins and heroin stuffed under their armpits and between their legs. For major crimes like that, James had found there were usually more people involved than you would first think. Logistics guys, paperwork guys, transportation guys, so many people down the line who had to, at the very least, look the other way.

He wondered how far this crime reached. How many people had to know about blatant neglect beyond those Carl Assman had told? Had Cecil Cody's brother known?

And who had Linda told? Not Kay. It didn't seem as if she had told George, but James couldn't be sure. Was Willa the only one? Carl had sworn that no one else knew he had left those documents with Linda. And James supposed if someone from the company had found them first, those papers would never even have made it to Linda. Linda must have told someone else.

James was pretty sure now that the Codys' threats had nothing to do with him being an outsider, a white man. Whether they had been involved in Linda's death or only informed afterward, James guessed that they knew she was killed. But if they were hiding Linda's murder for the uranium company, why? This was their land. Their water.

By the time James and Molly got back to Wayne's, the house was dark. But James knew he wouldn't be able to sleep. He told Molly not to drink any tap water unless she boiled it first. To keep her mouth shut during her shower. To brush her teeth with a bottle of Pepsi. He sat on the hood of Wayne's Oldsmobile after Molly went into bed, back against the windshield, listening to Kenny Rogers sing about a gambler. Almost the exact words Cecil had used. What had Cecil said? *You better learn real quick when to fold that losing hand of yours.*

James closed his eyes and tried to imagine what it would have felt like to be Linda. To be asked to carry this enormous secret. The day James had helped Kay fix her stables, she had told him that Linda was a big fan of Teddy Jackson. She told him what Linda had been like. How she was finally looking toward the future. Trying to find out how to be more involved in her community beyond the church. That when Linda listened to Jackson speak, her life made a little more sense. The hand-me-down clothes, the spurts of time where they had no electricity, no running water. The meal after meal of scrambled eggs and spam. The addiction. Jackson had made it make sense for Linda. She trusted him.

Could Linda have gone to Jackson? It would have made sense. Of course she would think he would want to help. Could he have done this? Or could he have told the company what she knew and left them to handle it? Jackson would've had to do *something* with the information. Make a stink about it or keep Linda quiet. And it clearly hadn't been the former.

James wished he had a better timeline. According to Carl,

at least a week had passed between Linda receiving those documents and her death. What had she done in the interim? Other than go to Willa? James wondered what George knew. Could Linda keep that sort of secret from him? Would she? George seemed oblivious, but maybe James just hadn't asked the right questions.

The sound of the screen door closing jolted James's eyes open. Wayne was coming over.

"You all right?" he asked.

"It's even bigger than we thought," James almost whispered. He cleared his throat and looked at Wayne. His hair was down. Not in a ponytail or braids. Just loose. He had basketball shorts on. His eyes were wide awake, though. His mouth pinched tight.

"Should I get us a few drinks?" he asked.

"I could use a beer, sure," James said.

Wayne came back with two beers, opened James's before handing it to him. He hoisted himself up onto the hood, too, and James waited until Wayne had had a couple of sips. Until he could see Wayne's shoulders loosen a bit.

"The uranium company that Linda worked for," James finally said. "Their dam won't hold. A whole bunch of toxic waste is about to leak onto this land. Into the rivers, the creeks. Maybe it already has. He didn't know."

Wayne said nothing at first. He even took another sip, his eyes set ahead on the house. Then, his fist came down on the hood hard, and James jumped.

"It's all we have left!" Wayne shouted. He brought his fist down again. "It's all we have left," he said again, quieter now, his voice quavering. He turned to James with fury in his eyes.

"When is enough, enough? When we're all dead and gone? Only then?"

James shook his head. "Linda knew. Carl Assman left documents for her."

"Damn it!" Wayne yelled. He held his beer tight in his lap and looked down at it. "Who did she tell?"

"I don't know," James said. "Kay doesn't know. Could you imagine if she did?" He paused and smiled at the thought. Kay would burn the place down. That was what she'd do. He would have to keep an eye on her once he told her. He sat up a little straighter. "I'm wonderin' if Linda went to Jackson. Kay said Linda was a supporter. You think she might've?"

"Certainly possible," Wayne mused. "But I don't like where that leaves us with Linda's killer." James watched him try to slow his breathing. Shake his head a few times. Mutter under his breath. Then he looked up at James again. "What are we going to do?" he asked.

"The papers that Linda had, the proof. They're gone. Whoever killed Linda has them. Right now, I've got nothing to back up Carl's statement, which he wants to remain anonymous. I think he got spooked after the state police did nothing."

Wayne scrubbed his face with his hand. "He told the state police?"

"So he says."

"We need some help, James. The two of us can't handle this. You aren't a sworn officer of the law anymore, and my badge is next to meaningless off the reservation."

James sighed. "Who do you know on the state level?"

"I could write to our representative, I guess," Wayne chuckled. "But I doubt he cares. Beyond that, a couple of officers at the state level that I trust, but it sounds like they already know."

"You got any Navajo in those positions?"

Wayne shook his head.

"All right," James said. "Call those guys up tomorrow. See what you can get out of them. Maybe they don't know. Maybe they've got someone else we can go to. A superior. Hell, I don't know. We've got to try."

Wayne sipped his beer. "You want to know what else I'm going to do tomorrow?" he asked.

"What's that?"

"Open up an official investigation into Linda's death. To hell with jurisdiction. If nobody else is going to do their damn job, I'm going to have to do it for them."

"Looks like you will," James said. Wayne muttered a few more curses.

"Sorry, Wayne," James said. "Now you're gonna be up all night like me."

"At least it's company."

James raised his beer up a bit, and Wayne clinked it with his own.

48

CECIL

CECIL SAT on the rocking chair on his porch, watching his sheep graze. He thought about Ned Benally. About how that white cop had brought him up as if he knew Cecil's business. As if he understood the relationship between two Diné men.

Cecil and Ned hadn't been the closest of friends, but he respected the man. Both cared about their people. About the reservation. They had both tried to keep the language alive. The storytelling.

At one point, Ned had even been on the Tribal Council. And when he gave that up, it wasn't because of arguments or bad blood. Ned just wasn't a politician. He took things personally. Was too honest. He admitted that it was affecting his health and left, but he and Cecil understood one another on some level. What in the hell would James Pinter know about that?

Cecil assumed Ned's other daughter—not the one who'd died—had accused Cecil of something. Or maybe it was the dead woman's husband. Cecil knew very little about him. Didn't see the man many places. But why? Why would either of them point their finger at him? What did they think they knew?

And now Wayne Tully was involved. Cecil despised Barbara Tully. It was only because of her father that she'd gotten a seat on the council. But she didn't understand what it took to govern the reservation. The sorts of compromises and sacrifices that had to be made in the name of progress and greatness.

She was stupid for an Indian. She didn't seem to know that everything given had to be taken from somewhere else. The lizard gave its life so the coyote could keep living. The sheep its wool so that people could stay warm. Barbara Tully acted like she could make something out of nothing. Like they should all be able to do that. She was already too close for Cecil's comfort. He didn't need her well-meaning but simple-minded husband messing things up.

Cecil didn't underestimate Wayne Tully so much that he would kill this James Pinter on the reservation, though. Then it would be Wayne's problem, and that would be Cecil's problem.

No, he needed to get James off the reservation first. Then, Byron and Ronnie could take care of him. Cecil stood and adjusted his belt. Watched his smallest sheep wander away from the herd, ears twitching quickly.

Cecil walked inside, picked up the phone, and dialed a number. When he heard someone on the other end, he said, "I need a favor."

49

KAY

THEY HAD CAUGHT DALE. He'd swerved off the road when they tried to pull him over, grazed a tree, and stumbled out unarmed. He was being held at the jail in Shonto without bail. This was the first piece of news James delivered to Kay. They were sitting in her truck, and she didn't know why she hadn't invited him inside yet. When she'd driven up to her house, he was already there waiting for her, petting Niyol. She rolled down her window to greet him and he asked, with a somber expression, if they could talk. So she unlocked the passenger's side door, and he climbed in.

Now, Kay knew he wasn't done. There was something else. Something bad.

"And?" she pressed.

"Remember how I asked you about an Assman?"

She looked down at her arm. It was no longer bandaged and the stitches had come out, but the scar was fresh and deep.

"Did you find him?" she asked.

James nodded. "Molly did, actually. I thought he'd be

connected to the Codys, the drug trade. But he wasn't. He worked for the same company as your sister. He was in charge of their finances."

Kay furrowed her eyebrows. "And she emptied his trash-can? What's the connection?"

"Correct," James said. "And when Carl Assman left the company, he also left your sister a little gift. A secret."

"What do you mean?"

"The company has been doin' some bad things," he said. Now, Kay knew for sure that whatever he had to tell her was going to make her upset. He always started talking all folksy and simple when he was nervous.

"Tell me," she said.

"They have a holding pond where they keep all the toxic waste that comes about during the process of extracting uranium."

He paused and glanced away before looking into her eyes.

"It's gonna leak into the land and into the water. Or maybe it already has. We don't know. But it hadn't as of May, when Mr. Assman was still with the company. He tried to tell people. He argued with his colleagues. He reported it to the state police. But nothing has been done. He wanted the reservation to know."

Kay was trying to put the pieces in place, but her frustration was getting the better of her. It didn't make any sense.

"Why would he tell my sister and not . . . not . . . Jackson or someone?"

"Who knows? He wants to stay anonymous. I know that much. Maybe he thought this was the best way to do that. Or maybe Mr. Jackson was too friendly of a face."

The reality of what he was saying slowly started to crash down onto Kay. She took quicker breaths now. "Are you saying this is why she's dead? Because she knew? And someone killed her for it?"

"Maybe," James said. "I'd say there's a good chance."

"What the hell?" Kay yelled. "This man! This . . . this . . . Assman! This piece of shit!" She'd almost called Mr. Assman an ass. She could have laughed at the absurdity of it all. If it weren't her sister's life—and all of their lives at stake now—this might be funny. It might be one big joke.

"Who does that? And now we're all being poisoned? That's criminal! That company! This man! They're murderers!"

She needed to hit something. She couldn't see straight anymore. She pushed herself out of the truck, tipped her head back, and shouted as loud as she could. Tears poured down her face. She started walking and didn't look back. She would walk until she couldn't feel her feet anymore. Until her legs screamed for rest. She would walk until she couldn't see her car or her house or that stupid, incredibly handsome man anymore. Until it was just her and the earth and the sky. She hated those people. She hated what they had done to her and to her land and to everyone she loved. She hated what they had done to her home. *Her* home. The only one she had ever had.

50

WAYNE

OFFICER SANCHEZ with the New Mexico State Police had told Wayne to come meet him. Sanchez felt they couldn't talk about it on the phone. Wayne had a strained feeling in his throat as he and James drove over.

In the passenger seat of Wayne's pickup, James fiddled with the radio.

"He didn't sound surprised," Wayne said.

James rubbed his palms on his thighs. "Wayne, if this is a true cover-up and not just incompetence, if the state police know and aren't doing anything, this is a big fuckup."

Wayne was quiet as they passed the sign announcing they were leaving the reservation. He smirked.

"That should be on the Navajo Nation welcome billboard: This Is a Big Fuckup."

James chuckled. "You're a sick man, Tully."

"Very healthy, actually. Especially my eyes. They see very clearly."

It surprised Wayne that James wasn't more incredulous about it all. Wayne was seasoned in fighting for his very existence each day. But he'd thought James would be more surprised. Though, he supposed James had seen enough in his life to make him open to the idea of people being shitty to each other.

"You worked My Lai," Wayne said. "That must have been awful."

James didn't say anything but reached into his pocket for his cigarettes.

"You see anything else like that during your time in the service?"

James selected a cigarette and lit it. "That's all Vietnam was," he said out of the corner of his mouth. "Scared, angry American boys. Scared, angry Vietnamese people. On opposite sides. The American boys had bigger guns, though. And body counts to hit. Those body counts went up, so with it Vietcong recruits. It was a bloody hamster wheel that everyone wanted off of."

He cranked his window open and tapped his cigarette ash out. "Except maybe the brass. Talk about cover-ups," James chuckled. "Every time you took a step, it was into a pile of shit. But the generals and the full bird colonels acted like they were in a field of fuckin' roses. You should have seen the ridiculous pamphlets they handed out about being culturally sensitive and not using racial slurs. War crimes and torture, on the other hand? They weren't so worried about those. Every person was a combatant to them. A possible Vietcong. That's how they hit those body count numbers. And that's how they got those promotions. So, their troops could do no wrong. *They* could do no wrong. All that blood on their hands, and those commanders slept like babies at night. The soldiers, on the other hand? The ones actually doing the killing? They'll never stop having nightmares."

Wayne pulled into the state police parking lot. "And what's this case look like to you?"

"Haven't quite decided yet, but I'm leading toward a much shoddier cover-up," James said. "The kind where the person doing the killing isn't worried one bit about being caught. Or maybe they just ain't worried about the consequences. If they were, they'd have done something with Linda's body."

"You might be wrong there," Wayne said. "I think most Navajos would want to leave that body be. Off the reservation. Undisturbed. Let her spirit roam elsewhere."

"So the killer's Navajo, then," James said.

Wayne grunted and opened the truck door. James followed him out.

"I don't want to believe Jackson's involved," Wayne said. "He might be a cheat. But not a killer. I don't want to believe that he could be bought off about something like this. And I don't want to believe that the Codys are involved, either. That they're just fine with radioactive waste spilling into our water."

James put his hand on Wayne's shoulder. "One thing at a time. Let's hope the spill hasn't happened yet. Let's see if we can stop it."

"Don't hold your breath," Wayne said.

The New Mexico police station in Gallup was big and airy. The door was heavy and slammed shut behind Wayne as soon as he let it go. The woman at the desk looked up and smiled sweetly.

"Hey there, Chief Tully," she said. She had a big perm, curly hair framing her round face.

"Hey, Sue. I've got a meeting with Officer Sanchez."

She nodded. "He just popped in. Let me get him for you."

She pushed back in her chair, and Wayne listened to her heels click away on the tile floor. He sat down in one of the padded waiting area chairs, crossed his arms, and leaned his head back. Two sets of shoes echoed down the hall a few minutes later, and Wayne looked up. Officer Sanchez was short with a thin frame. Wayne stood and shook his hand.

"I'm buying lunch," Officer Sanchez said. Wayne nodded.

"All right, then. This here's James Pinter. Former special agent for the Army. CID."

Sanchez's eyebrows went up. "Impressive," he said, shaking James's hand. "And what do you do now?"

"Trucks," James said. "I drive one."

"Well, that's quite the change."

"Yup. That was kinda the point."

"But you're not here with Wayne today because you drive trucks."

"No, sir," James said.

"Let's grab a burger."

James finished his burger first, and Wayne was still only halfway through his when Sanchez started talking.

"I'm just gonna put this out there. New Mexico State Police aren't gonna do anything about this uranium thing."

"Why not?" James asked. Wayne swallowed.

"We were actually already tipped off about it. A guy who worked for the company, believe it or not."

Wayne sipped his iced tea.

"You don't say," James said. "Aren't y'all supposed to report something like this to the Environmental Protection Agency?"

Sanchez shrugged. "It's a mess dealing with them. They're brand new, you know. Not that all federal agencies aren't a mess. You've got to fill out twenty hours of paperwork, and then good luck finding an address or a phone number."

"Does the governor know?" James asked.

"Probably. He's buddies with the chief."

Wayne shook his head. "This affects my people, my reservation, and you *know* there's nothing I can do about it."

"I'd help if I could," Sanchez said. "It's messed up. It really is."

Wayne popped a French fry into his mouth.

"How'd you two find out?" Sanchez asked. "That guy from the company come to you, too?"

"Yeah," James said.

"He give you his name when he called?" Wayne asked.

"Nope." Sanchez leaned back in his chair and crossed his arms. "He just said he worked for the company and had documentation to prove his claims."

James slurped down the rest of his soda and stood. "Well, it's been enlightening," he said.

Sanchez huffed. "I want you two to know it's a dead end."

"Appreciate it," Wayne said. He stood and shook Sanchez's hand. "Got to get back. Thanks for your time."

"I hope it doesn't leak, Wayne," Sanchez said, standing up. "I hope it's all a hoax."

Wayne put his hands in pockets and looked down at the checkered tile floor. "Thanks, but I very much doubt that it is."

51

JAMES

JAMES FELL asleep on Wayne's couch while watching a new sitcom called *Detective School*. It had actually made James laugh once or twice before his heavy eyelids dropped closed.

The loud ring of Wayne's phone startled him awake about an hour later, and he knocked over his glass of water trying to get to it.

"Damn it," he murmured, grabbing the hand towel hanging from the oven door. The phone rang again as he sopped up the water, and he answered on the last ring.

"Tully residence."

"It's Gloria!" she practically shouted into the phone.

"Hey there. I'm sure you've heard by now about the melee?"

"Yes. No thanks to you or Wayne, though. George called."

"Of course he did. We've been kinda busy around here."

"I know. I'm not upset," Gloria said. James almost laughed. Like he cared if she was upset.

"Did he tell you Ronnie Cody showed up?" he asked.

"Ronnie Cody does not like outside interference. Rightfully so. Besides, he's right. Dale is a menace."

James let the silence hang in the air for a moment. He wasn't sure what to say to that, anyway.

"That isn't why I'm calling, though I would like your comment on it at some point. I'm calling because I just got off the phone with a man claiming to be Dale's roommate."

"Dale's in jail."

"I know. I've already spoken to Shonto PD. I'm trying to get in to talk to him, because—listen to this—Dale told this roommate that he killed Linda. He said he killed her and now he's going to get his son back."

James stared at the wet towel in his hand.

"What's this roommate's name?" he asked.

"He wouldn't tell me."

"He's lying."

"Why would he lie? Why would you think that?"

"We have a new lead. One that makes much more sense."

"Really? One with connections to My Lai?"

The comment quieted James. Both because that was the part that didn't seem to fit, and also because Gloria somehow knew that.

"You're looking too hard at that," he said. "My Lai could be a ruse. You've got to see the big picture instead."

"Listen, I could go to Albuquerque to get the records and find out who lives with Dale. It might be multiple people because of the kind of apartment it is. But I bet I can just go to Shonto and get Dale to confess."

"Great. I hope you do. Good luck," James said.

"I don't understand your problem," Gloria said. "A

confession is the closest we're going to get to proof, and you know it."

James started to say something, but Gloria cut him off. "I'm going, James," she said, the irritation thick in her voice.

"Meet up with me first, then," he said. "You said you could go to Albuquerque and try to track down the roommate. Let's meet there."

"Tracking down the roommate is a waste of my time."

"Won't you want to know if Dale doesn't confess?"

Gloria sighed. "Fine. Albuquerque. Tomorrow."

"I've got a favorite bar there now. Meet me at the Moondance."

Gloria snorted. "That place is a dump, but I'll be there."

"Drinks on you this time," James said before hanging up.

What the hell was this woman doing? James threw the wet towel into the washing machine in the hallway along with a pair of Molly's dirty socks sitting outside her bedroom. A part of him wanted to tell Gloria everything. Any other journalist would never run a story with such little information—with only hearsay from a man who wouldn't go on record. But Gloria seemed to really care about the Navajo people.

But that would mean convincing her that Jackson might have been involved in Linda's death. Maybe the Codys, too. He had just seen how she reacted to Ronnie shooting Kay. Brushed it off like it was nothing. Why was she so intent on only positive stories about all Navajos? She didn't think them real people, capable of horrible things?

Maybe he could tell her about the spill but let her think what she wanted about Linda's death. As much as he wanted to solve this homicide and bring justice to the killer, he wanted to prevent the spill more. If Gloria could help him do that, he'd have to tell her.

The door to Molly's bedroom creaked open, and she stepped into the hall just as James was starting the washing machine.

"Did the phone wake you up?" he asked.

"It's ten o'clock, Dad. I wasn't asleep."

Dad. James grinned without meaning to. Molly must have realized why, because her face reddened.

"Who was it?" she asked, quickly. She tucked her hair behind her ear and peered over his shoulder like the caller might be standing right there in the kitchen.

"Gloria," James said.

"She knows about all this?"

He gestured for her to follow him into the other room, and they sat on the couch in front of the TV.

"She knows Dale came here. She knows Ronnie shot Kay, though she didn't seem surprised or concerned. She doesn't know about any of the uranium business, though."

Molly bit at the cuff of her sweatshirt. She curled her knees up under her chin.

"Are you gonna tell her?"

"Barbara wants me to. She's been givin' Wayne an earful. And I agree. Anything that can stop this."

Molly looked at the TV. At some summer variety special. Two women dancing. The rest of the room was dark, and the screen lit her face.

"I want her to stop this, too. Do you think she will?"

"I don't know. I hope she'll try. She doesn't have much to go on, though. You heard Mr. Assman."

Molly nodded.

"I'm going to see her tomorrow. To tell her all this. And to try to convince her that it wasn't Dale who killed Linda. She says he confessed to an anonymous roommate."

Molly gaped at him. "Confessed to killing Linda?"

"That's what she said."

"So you don't believe it?"

"The only thing that points to Dale is that carving. And honestly, it doesn't fit his MO. My guess is that it was meant to throw someone off. Makes me think it wasn't the Codys. They wouldn't leave their own initials on a dead body, even if it was supposed to be a distraction."

"Who do you think did it, then?"

James sighed. He wondered if he should be telling Molly all this. He was putting her in more danger.

"You promise not to tell anyone?"

Molly nodded slowly, hesitantly.

"I think it was Jackson," he said. "Or one of his cronies, at least. I spoke with Kay again after she cooled off a bit, and she's convinced Linda would've gone straight to Jackson."

"Isn't he the most powerful man in the Navajo Nation?"

"In theory, yes."

"So how are you going to get him? Will it have to be Wayne?"

James sat back and crossed his arms. "It'll have to be Wayne who convinces the state police to investigate, since it was done off the reservation. And we've got to find some pretty damning evidence for that to work."

They fell quiet, watching the women on TV singing into the same mic.

"Can I come?" Molly said, quietly. "To meet with Gloria?"

"Why not?" James said. "It's just Gloria."

She grinned. "Thanks, Dad."

James was close enough to reach out and put his arm around her. He didn't know how she'd take it, but he tried it. She leaned into him. Rested her head on his shoulder.

52

BYRON

His FATHER HAD PROMISED that the confession would get James off the reservation, and it worked.

Byron watched Wayne start up the truck with James and the girl inside. Watched them drive to the Nation's Sanostee offices.

Byron parked down the street as James and the girl climbed into the big rig. He hadn't expected James to bring her.

Ronnie sat next to him, M16 in his lap, set to full auto. Byron knew without even asking. Cecil wanted the man dead, no question. That much had been clear. The trickiest part would be getting out of the truck's way once they hit James. A bleeding or dead man didn't have control over his actions. And a big rig could easily crush Byron and Ronnie.

The girl's face flashed in his mind and made his stomach flip. She shouldn't be there. But he cleared his throat and pulled out onto the road after them all the same.

Ronnie spat out the window.

"We should try to separate the girl," Byron said.

"How would we do that?"

"Wait till they stop."

Ronnie shook his head. "I'm not doing this in a place where we can't get the hell out of there and quick. People can see us at a gas station. Identify us."

"So put on a fucking mask or something."

"Does it look like I have a mask?"

"She wasn't part of the deal," Byron said.

"Man the fuck up. Everything is part of the deal. Always. Because you're a Cody. So handle it."

Byron clenched his teeth and kept driving. Ronnie laid his head back. "Tell me when we're off the reservation," he said. Then, he closed his eyes.

Byron was supposed to have gone to college. He was smart and everyone knew it, even early on. He had been talking in full sentences before his second birthday, and from that moment on, Cecil brought him along to council meetings. He couldn't remember ever getting lower than a B in school, but still, that hadn't been enough for Cecil. After his homework, Cecil would give him books about the history of the Diné written in Diné. He'd make him recite things from memory. Byron thrived, despite the pressure and the high standards, mainly because of their mom. She was the fun one. She taught Byron how to laugh. How to joke, even in the face of despair. For the boys, Helen Cody was their relief. Their love. Their shining sun. She was everything.

The year Byron was supposed to leave for college was the year Helen Cody died. Ronnie was at the worst age. Fourteen and volatile. Helen would have straightened him out. She would have showed him how to love things. But Cecil didn't know how to do that. Cecil only knew responsibility and honor and pride. The only thing Cecil knew to do with Ronnie's anger was to harness it.

Cecil held on to his power with a closed fist. If even one finger tired and started to slip, it might all unravel. So, he made sure his sons carried that burden, too. That they walked around with tight shoulders. The Cody brothers were constantly rolling their heads around, trying to stretch out the knots in their necks. They couldn't slip up. Cecil made that clear. Helen's death had made Cecil an even bigger pain in the ass for everyone. Especially his sons.

But Byron had inherited something from both his father and his mother that couldn't be taught. Byron loved his people. He lived to serve them. He knew one day he would go back to school. Maybe become a lawyer. Cecil wanted him on the council, and it was possible that one day he would be. Everyone liked Byron. People would vote for him. But he didn't have any interest in the *other* work his father did. That would all be up to Ronnie. Still, Byron was a Cody and fully devoted to his father. Whatever his father asked him to do, Byron would do it. Even if he didn't like it.

Ronnie started to snore. His gun's muzzle slipped from his hands and banged against his leg every so often. Byron turned the radio up loud, but Ronnie just kept on snoring.

The white girl wasn't his people, but she was still just a child. Byron wanted to leave her out of it. It was what his mother would have done. Hell, Byron didn't even think Cecil would be okay with hurting an innocent kid. Ronnie needed to learn that sort of shit was unacceptable. Sometimes his brother scared him. But mostly he just made him angry. He wanted to shake him and tell him to use his fuckin' brain. And his heart, sometimes, too.

The truck pulled off at a gas station, and Byron decided to do exactly what Ronnie had said they weren't doing. He pulled over on the shoulder and waited until the girl had climbed down from the passenger side and went into the gas station. Then, Byron pulled back onto the highway, smacked Ronnie in the chest as hard as he could, and shouted, "Wake the fuck up!"

Ronnie looked around, wide-eyed and panicked.

"They're stopped up here," Byron still shouted for some reason. "Point that thing out the window and shoot!"

Ronnie blinked furiously and did what he was told. The bullets sprayed the truck. The window glass shattered, and the truck tilted violently as the air left the front tires.

Then, Byron sped off down the highway, listening to Ronnie curse and spit and shove him with the butt of the gun. Byron smiled. Ronnie needed to learn some fuckin' manners.

53

MOLLY

THE GUNSHOTS and the breaking glass sounded like screaming inside Molly's head. She had dropped to the floor instinctively and put her hands over her head. The floor smelled like soda and dirt and bleach. Her heart pounded so loudly she thought it would burst.

When the ringing in her ears stopped, she could only hear whimpering, and she realized it was coming from her own throat. She pushed herself up onto her hands and knees and then stood, shaking. The clerk hurried over to her.

"Are you okay?" he asked her.

She swallowed and tears started to pour from her eyes, but she nodded anyway. When she looked out the window and saw the truck with its windows shattered, she screamed.

"Call 911!" she begged the man. "Call 911!"

He took a couple of steps backwards, looked where she was looking, and then ran into a back room.

Molly felt dizzy. Sick. She forced herself toward the truck.

Everything outside was still. So quiet. She opened the

passenger door and held her breath, trying to make sense of what was going on.

James was hunched over, his forehead on the steering wheel. Blood poured down the side of his face from the very top of his head. He groaned and shifted, and Molly let out a relieved cry. She clambered up next to him.

"Dad! Dad, are you with me? Can you hear me?"

James breathed heavily. "Yeah," he finally said.

She was sobbing now. "Hang on, Dad. He's calling 911. The ambulance is gonna come."

"Okay," James breathed.

The iron-like smell of blood made Molly even dizzier. "What should I do?" she asked. She looked down at her own hands. They were bloody, too. She must have cut herself on the broken glass, but she couldn't feel anything.

"Go. Back inside," James said.

Molly looked down at the foot of the passenger's seat. At her bag with her revolver inside. Then she glanced behind James's seat, where he kept his own guns. She could protect them, she told herself. She could fight back.

"No." She shook her head vigorously. "I'm staying with you."

"They could. Come back," he gasped.

"I don't care!" she shouted. She had to stop the bleeding, didn't she? She got on her knees, carefully pushing the glass out of her way, and rummaged around in James's tiny bed area. She grabbed the sheet from the mattress and balled it up.

"Should I put this sheet on your head?" she asked.

"Okay," James said. "Push down real hard."

Molly did what he said. The hole in his head didn't seem

all that big now that she could feel it. It was more like a dent. Why was it bleeding so much?

"Head wounds. Are messy," he said, as if reading her thoughts.

"You'll be okay, right, Dad?" She couldn't stop sobbing.

"Right," James said. "Molly. Are there any. Cars around?"

She looked up and down the highway. Swiveled around to take in the gas station parking lot.

"I don't see any," she said.

"It isn't. Safe for you."

"I'm not leaving you!" she screamed.

"All right," he said. "All right."

Molly shifted her weight and pushed down even harder on his head.

"Tell me. About. School," James said.

"School?" Molly couldn't remember anything about school in that moment. Not the name of it. Nothing.

"It's better. If I keep. Talking."

"Oh. Okay. Okay. I was a majorette," she said. She dug in her brain for something. Anything. "My favorite subject is chemistry. I have a chemistry teacher whose last name is Spock. And everyone gives him that salute. I don't know what it's called."

James chuckled. "Vulcan. Live long. And prosper. You watched it. As a tiny thing."

"Well, I don't remember, of course."

"It's one of the few. Memories I have," he said.

Molly bit her lip. Normally this would make her mad at him. Bitter that he hadn't been there. That he didn't have more of these memories. But right now, her heart felt like it was leaking right out of her. That some part of her wanted to give all of the love she had left to James. She felt angry and sad still, but in that moment, her love for him overwhelmed her. She'd just lost one parent. She didn't want to lose another.

"Tell me," she said, softly.

"Me and your mom. On the floor. *Star Trek* on the TV. I was home. For a few months. You were talking. Really talking now. Small. So small. But so smart."

James breathed heavily, and Molly thought he was done. But then he kept going. "We had. Spaghetti that night. Your face. Was still covered. In sauce."

He chuckled again. Molly smiled, though the tears still ran down her cheeks.

"You had. Your hands. On your hips," he went on. "You called me. Captain Daddy."

Molly laughed too, now. Then, they heard the sirens in the distance. She shifted her weight but didn't release the pressure. Her foot was falling asleep. She felt relief. So much relief.

"They're coming," she said. "Captain Daddy."

Molly dialed the payphone with shaking hands. It rang only once.

"Hello?"

"Hi Barbara. It's Molly."

"What's going on, Molly?"

"I'm at the hospital in Gallup. Dad was shot."

Barbara gasped into the phone. "Is he . . . okay?"

Tears tickled the backs of Molly's eyes again.

"Yeah," she said. "The doctors say he's gonna be okay." She sniffled and wiped her eyes. "It was his head," she blurted. "The bullet grazed his head. They said he was lucky. So lucky."

"Oh, honey," Barbara said. "Are you okay? You're not hurt, too, are you?"

"No." She shook her head and looked down at her bandaged hand. "No, I'm okay. But Dad is sedated. The nurses keep asking me if someone is coming to pick me up. I don't want to leave him."

"I'm coming right now," Barbara said. "You stay right there. I'll talk to the nurses. You tell them . . . tell them your aunt is coming."

"Okay," Molly said. "Thank you."

"Hang in there, sweetie."

"I'll see you soon," Molly said. She hung up and looked around. The parking lot was full of cars, but she was the only one outside. She took a deep breath, tipped her head back, and looked at the sky. The clouds were so sharp today. And so close. She felt like she could reach up and grab one. Pop it in her mouth like a marshmallow. Instead, she reached into her pocket for more change, inserted it into the phone, and waited for the dial tone. She had one more call to make. A call that James had asked her to make before they wheeled him out of the ambulance and into the hospital.

He hadn't been thinking straight, but she would make the call anyway, just in case. She listened to the phone ring as she toed a cement rock at the base of the pay phone.

"Hello. You've reached Gloria Fenwick. I'm not available

to take your call. Please leave a message after the beep and I'll get back to you as soon as possible. Thanks!"

Molly heard the beep and hesitated for a moment. Gloria was long gone at this point, but Molly started to speak anyway.

"Hi Gloria. It's Molly, James's daughter. You've probably already left, but I wanted to tell you that Dad's been shot. We're at the hospital in Gallup. So, we won't be at the bar later. Obviously. Dad wants . . . for you to come here. If you can. If you get this message. Okay. Bye."

She hung up and stared at the phone. That was done. She felt her fascination for Gloria fading. The woman's act was tiring. And Molly was beginning to trust her dad. His instincts were to be wary of Gloria, and so now Molly was, too.

[54]

JAMES

THE LIGHTS WERE BLINDING when James opened his eyes. It took him only a second to remember where he was. To recognize the searing pain in his head. The machines beeped steadily, and when he tried to sit up, he got tangled in wires.

"Easy there, cowboy," Wayne's voice came from the corner of the room.

"Help me up," James said. "I can't even see you with these damn things in my way."

Wayne chuckled and came to his side. He propped some pillows up behind James and helped him sit.

"Where's Molly?" James asked.

"With Barbara. They went to get food."

"She okay?"

"She's fine. Had a gash in her hand from the glass, but that's all."

James shook his head. "The girl's as hardheaded as I am. Wasn't expecting that. I told her to go back inside, but she just wouldn't."

Wayne adjusted his belt and took a seat at James's bedside.

"Believe it or not, I think she loves you."

Though James smiled, fear clutched at his chest. This was why he'd never been able to reconcile these two parts of his life. Being a dad and being a detective. They were incompatible. He'd chosen to let the dad part go a long time ago. But now. Now it was here again.

"Poor girl," James said. "If only she had a dad who isn't an idiot."

"Oh, stop it already," Wayne said. "You're new to the whole parenting thing."

James looked down at the IV sticking out of his hand.

"Anyway," Wayne went on, "what the hell happened?"

"Ronnie Cody."

"You sure of that?"

"The man thinks he's special forces with that damn thing."

Wayne raised his eyebrows. "The M16 again?"

"You should see my truck," James said. Then he groaned. "If they haven't towed it already. Could you call a buddy of mine? He owes me a favor. He'll tow it free back to Oklahoma."

"I'll handle it."

"Thanks, Wayne."

"So the Codys tried to kill you off the reservation. That's not good."

"They look guiltier and guiltier every day. Still, I don't think Cecil Cody would leave his own initials on the body. That would just be plain stupid."

Wayne shook his head. "I don't believe it, either."

"I need to tell Gloria about the uranium. I was on my way to meet her."

"Where?"

"Albuquerque."

"I'll call the station. Have them send her here. I'm sure that's where she'll look for you."

James nodded. "You think that's the right thing to do? To tell her?"

Wayne glanced past James into the hallway.

"It's the only option now, isn't it? No other journalist will run this. Not without some sort of proof."

"I was thinking about that. . . ."

"Oh yeah?"

"What if we had proof?"

"That would help. But we don't," Wayne said.

"What if I got inside the uranium offices? Poked around a bit. After-hours, maybe."

Wayne crossed his arms. "You're asking a cop if you should break the law?"

James smiled. "No one likes breaking the law more than cops do."

Wayne guffawed. "I don't know anything about that. But I will repeat that it sure would be helpful if we had proof."

"Say no more," James said.

The sharp pain made him dizzy. He closed his eyes.

"Some water, Wayne?" he asked.

He heard Wayne cross to the sink. Turn on the water. Walk back.

James opened his eyes, and Wayne held up a small plastic cup. James swallowed the whole thing in three gulps.

"Give me that tow truck driver's number, and I'll make some phone calls. You rest up for Gloria."

"I hope she comes."

"She'll come."

55

MOLLY

THE NEXT MORNING, Molly and Barbara were eating breakfast at a picnic table outside the hospital. Molly was just dipping her breakfast sandwich in the ketchup and yoke covering the foil when Barbara murmured, "Here she comes."

The clacking of Gloria's heels grew louder, and Molly could see genuine concern on her face. Barbara waved her over.

"I came as soon as I heard," she said, sitting down. "What happened?"

"Someone," Barbara said, pointedly, "shot at James's truck while he sat on the side of the highway waiting for Molly to pee."

Gloria's hand flew to her mouth.

"But he's okay?" she nearly whispered.

"Doctors say he's lucky. Bullet grazed the top of his head. Didn't even penetrate his skull. Some metal from the truck lodged into his calf, though. But he'll walk out of here in a few days."

"Who do you think did this?" Gloria asked.

Barbara glanced at Molly. "I can't say. You could ask James if he knows."

Molly wiped her face with a napkin and put down the last couple bites of her sandwich.

"I'll take you to him," she said.

Gloria touched her arm. "Thank you. Are you all right?"

Molly nodded, and Gloria gave her a genuine smile. Maybe Molly was being petty. Maybe Gloria *was* on their side.

She and Gloria stood, but Barbara stayed where she was. "I'll keep an eye on this sandwich," she said, winking at Molly.

When they got to James's room, Gloria waited politely in the hallway. James had drifted off to sleep sitting up but opened his eyes as soon as Molly entered.

"Sorry to wake you up," she said.

"Just resting my eyes."

"Gloria is here."

James opened his eyes real wide and then closed them again. He did it a few more times.

"Can I stay?" Molly asked.

He nodded. "Yes. Make sure I don't forget anything."

Molly grinned. "You got it." She went back out to find Gloria pacing, staring at her fingernails.

"You can come in," she said.

Gloria swept into the room, her hand on her chest.

"James," she said. "Are you all right?"

"I've felt better, but I'll live."

She nodded and, for the first time since Molly had met her, seemed at a loss for words. Molly wondered if she would start crying.

"Why don't you sit?" James asked. Gloria took the chair next to him, and Molly took the one on the other side of the room. She pulled her knees up and watched Gloria over top of them.

"Tell me what happened," Gloria said.

"Well, I was shot. While sitting on the side of the road, waiting for Molly to . . . uh . . . use the restroom."

Gloria glanced over at her. "Oh, baby. You must have been so afraid."

Molly collapsed her knees next to her so she was sitting like a mermaid. She blushed. "It was pretty scary."

"Who did this?" Gloria asked.

Molly and James shared a look. *Not yet.*

"Someone driving by. They were gone before anyone could identify them," James said.

"Couldn't have been Dale. He's in jail."

"Right," James said.

"Unless Shonto PD released him."

"Why would they do that?"

"Who else is trying to kill you?" Gloria asked.

"I've got a few ideas. But there's something else we need to talk about first. It's urgent."

Gloria watched him intently, waiting for more.

"You got a recording device in there?" he asked, looking at her purse. "Or a pen and paper?"

"What is it, James?" She rummaged through her burgundy leather purse.

"I've got some information that I need you to report on."

She pulled out a small notepad and a pen and raised her eyebrows.

"Must be pretty important."

"It is."

She flipped to a blank sheet and poised her pen, ready to write.

"There's about to be a toxic waste spill right off the reservation," James said. "The United Nuclear Corporation's dam can't hold all the radioactive waste. It's about to spill into the creeks and river. If it hasn't already. That's the company Linda worked for. The United Nuclear Corporation."

Gloria wrote with a hardened face. "According to whom?" she asked, quietly.

"Don't worry about that part," James said. "A trusted source."

Gloria looked up at him. "This is a serious accusation. I need to know who told you, so I can talk to them."

"Like I said, I can't tell you that part. They've already told me they won't go on record."

Gloria put her notepad down on the bedside table and crossed her arms. "What am I supposed to do with this, then?"

"I don't know. Your job? Go dig around in their files. Ask people what they know."

"Ha," Gloria huffed indignantly. "No one at that company is going to tell me anything. If this is even true."

Molly was surprised by Gloria's skepticism, but James didn't look it at all. If anything, he looked alert, though maybe a bit disappointed.

"There has to be some disgruntled employee or ex-employee out there somewhere. Find them."

"James," Gloria started. She took a deep breath and uncrossed her arms, sitting forward a bit. "Why are you sending me on some wild goose chase about an unconfirmed rumor when I ought to be interviewing Dale? Getting a confession. I have to admit, this feels highly suspicious."

Now, James looked a little frustrated. Like maybe he wanted to laugh at Gloria or shake her.

"Suspicious?" he asked. "Of me?"

She just shrugged.

"What if this is what *really* killed Linda, Gloria?" James asked. "What if she . . . knew? Somehow. Told someone?"

"How would she know? No offense to Linda, but she wasn't exactly sitting in on important meetings."

Molly and James glanced at one another again, and this time, Gloria turned to stare at Molly, too. She looked annoyed. Maybe she had forgotten Molly was still there.

"We think she knew," James said.

"Listen, it is very difficult for me to work with anonymous sources," Gloria said, putting her pad and pen away. "Find out if this person . . . whoever they are . . . would be willing to talk to me. Until then, I'll be in Shonto, obtaining a confession from Dale. Linda's murderer." She stood, slinging her purse over her shoulder.

"And you'll try to find some dirt on the company?" James asked.

"Sure," Gloria said. "Say, James. Why are you set on Dale being innocent? Is this some sort of Army thing? I thought you were an old pro at putting away Army killers."

"I didn't say he was innocent," James said, not at all rattled. "Dale's a bad dude. Guilty of plenty of things. But he didn't kill Linda."

"You're so sure."

"This wasn't the work of a madman. A man half out of his mind all the time. It might be the work of an amateur.

And Dale's not that, either. Dale would've shot Linda. He would've taken the kid."

Gloria shook her head. "I don't see how you can be so certain. Perhaps he was having a day of clarity. Dale has plenty of drugs at his disposal. He could have injected something into her. It *was* an old pastime of theirs. He could have tried to take Adriel, but Adriel ran or hid. The cuts on her arm . . . I think you're dismissing him too easily."

Molly could see James's Adam's apple move as he swallowed. What was that look in his eye? Uncertainty? Apprehension? Calculation?

"I think it's worth following this uranium spill lead. But even more importantly, I think we've gotta do everything we can to stop the spill from happening."

Gloria glanced at the door. "Yeah," she said. "You're right. I'll look for something more. Because I can't go with what you've given me. Talk to your source again."

"Gloria?" James asked. She crossed her arms but didn't respond. "Did you find the rest of the names of Charlie Company?"

Charlie Company? Molly wondered. *What was that?*

"I don't have the names with me," Gloria said.

"But somewhere?"

"I've found around forty of them."

"Will you fax them to me?"

Gloria sighed. "Yes. I will fax them to me when I get back to the office."

"Good luck with Dale," James said.

56

DALE

THE JAIL STANK WORSE than his apartment. Worse than when he had to hose off the sticky mat he stood on all day at the pizza place.

For the first two days, Dale had puked and shook and saw visions of Indians and gooks and people he'd killed. He laughed and cried and occasionally was yelled at to shut the fuck up. Once, someone tossed a bucket of water on him.

But today, he had a visitor. He wondered if it was that stupid cop. He hoped it was. He couldn't wait to spit in his face.

He hadn't been this sober in a long time, and he hated it. He wasn't puking or shaking anymore, but his bones still felt like they were on fire. Every movement hurt.

The guard slapped handcuffs on his wrists and yanked him out of his cell.

"Fuck you," Dale mumbled.

"Yeah, yeah," the guard said. "I'm dumb as bricks. Lazy. I eat scalps. You told me all this already."

Dale wanted to reach out and claw the man. But the

guard was big. Had a tattoo that wrapped around his neck. People with neck tattoos were not to be messed with.

He had been ready to flip over a table or some shit as soon as he saw the cop, so when it was actually a beautiful woman sitting there, he stopped walking.

He glanced over his shoulder. "She's here to see me? You sure?"

"I'm sure." The guard smirked. "Reporter."

Fuck, Dale thought. He hadn't realized his little trip to find Adriel had turned into such a big deal. He sat across from the woman, his handcuffed wrists in his lap. He didn't take his eyes off her.

"Dale, isn't it?" She flashed him a smile and flipped her hair over her shoulder. "I'm Gloria." She held out a hand, and he stared stupidly at it.

She was older but hot. Dale would definitely fuck her. He nodded and held up his hands to show her his problem with the hand shaking.

"Right," she said. "Well, I'm here, Dale, because I got a tip that you confessed to killing Linda Morris."

Dale ground teeth his together. "Who told you that?" he spat. "That cop?"

"No," she said. "A roommate of yours."

Dale scoffed. "I don't have any roommates."

He watched one of her pretty little eyebrows go up.

"Well," she went on. "Someone was claiming to be. I thought maybe you'd want to tell me your story. Tell me yourself what happened."

The woman knew she was sexy. She thought Dale was just going to admit to something. *Even journalists can be real dumb*, he thought. But he smiled at her. He'd do what he could to keep her there. Better than sitting in that piss-and-shit jail cell.

"What do you want to know?" he asked.

"Did you kill Linda?"

Dale snorted. "No. I didn't kill Linda."

The reporter's face fell.

"But," he went on, "I know if that cop is a friend of Kay's, you shouldn't trust him."

"Why is that?"

"Kay always thought they were best friends, but really Kay bullied Linda."

Gloria looked unimpressed. "Big sisters sometimes do that."

"And the last time I saw Linda, she was tellin' me about something George did. She was real upset about it. Wouldn't tell me what it was exactly, but she kept saying, 'I can't believe he did that.' Or some shit like that. I bet Kay knows. I bet that bitch is involved somehow."

Gloria's eyes narrowed into slits. "Upset?" she asked.

Dale's mouth twisted into a half grin. She believed him.

"Real upset. Maybe even scared," he said.

Gloria tapped her pen on the table like she was waiting for something else.

"Look." Dale shifted in his chair. Adjusted himself. Put his cuffed hands on the table. "I saw an opportunity to get my son back. I know no one thinks I'm a good dad. But I could be if they let me. Vietnam, man. That shit fucked me up. And I've got nothing to look forward to in my shitty little life. Nothing. When she brought Adriel back into it, I had hope. Now that she's dead? I'm never gonna see him. You think that's what I wanted?"

Gloria nodded. "I believe you, Dale," she said. She glanced quickly at the door. Making sure the guard was still there. "I was there, too. Reporting. It was hell there. It turned everyone into monsters. You couldn't avoid it."

Dale had seen a few hot reporters out there, and he wondered if any of them had been her. If he'd fantasized about her later while alone in the jungle, trying to think about anything other than stepping on a mine and getting blown to pieces.

"And now, no one cares, do they?" she went on. "They just want to act like the whole war never happened."

Dale couldn't tell if she actually believed what she was saying or if she only wanted him to think she did, but he didn't care. Hearing someone else say it out loud brought tears to his eyes. He didn't want to cry right now, but he couldn't stop it. It was like, without the drugs, he didn't have control over himself.

"Sorry," Dale sobbed. "I look like a dickhead."

Gloria reached over and touched his hands on the table between them. "It's all right," she said. "You have every right to be upset. Someone ought to care more. About all of you. It isn't right."

He turned his head and wiped his nose on his shoulder.

"Maybe . . ." She waited until he looked her in the eye. "Maybe I could help with Adriel. See if we can't get you some visitation rights."

Dale felt hot anger rise in his chest. He pulled his hands away.

"You messin' with me right now?"

She put her hands up. "No, I swear I'm not. I bet I could

talk to the judge. Maybe with some rehab, they would let you."

"And what would I have to do for you?"

"Just help me, that's all. Tell me more about Kay and George. What Linda told you the last time you saw her."

Dale's mind reeled, grasping for anything like a memory of that day. Any detail. Gloria must have seen his panic.

"Take your time, Dale. I've got time. You know what?" She stood. "Let me get us some coffee."

57

JAMES

IT TOOK James a week to get back to work after he was released from the hospital. He had received a defeated phone call from Gloria. Dale had not confessed. She wasn't able to track down the roommate. She was going to look for anything she could find on United. She faxed him a list of forty-four names from Charlie Company, so at least he had that.

At first, James had protested against staying with Wayne again. Cecil Cody's message had come through loud and clear. But Wayne argued the reservation was the safest place for him, because clearly the Codys would go after him as soon as he left it.

Finally, James relented. More for Molly's sake than his own.

He was still popping Tylenol when his daily headache hit around noon. But he couldn't sit down or lie around anymore. He had healed enough.

Wayne looked surprised when James limped into his office that afternoon. James sat, took his hat off, and rested it on his knee. The station was hot as hell today. Everywhere was.

"Gloria's half-assing this uranium thing, and I don't know why."

"Her heart's not in it," Wayne said. "She was really after Dale."

"Why?"

"Maybe she's got a thing against Vietnam vets."

James grunted. "I just thought she really cared about you people." Wayne raised his eyebrows. "You know what I mean," he added quickly.

"Then you don't know *your* people as well as I thought you did."

James scratched his prickly face. "She only cares when it's convenient for her?"

"Or beneficial."

"This *is* beneficial!" James cried, getting animated. "This is a huge story!"

"A huge story for some people. Her editors won't care. A poison is too slow a massacre to capture their attention. It isn't sexy."

"A massacre . . ." James murmured.

Wayne's face reddened a little. "Not exactly a massacre."

"Close, though," James said. His thoughts were churning slower than he was used to, and it frustrated him. "Anyway, I'm thinkin' we need to look into Jackson's men. See if any of his advisors or other cronies are Vietnam vets."

"I'll get some names from Barbara," Wayne said. "See what I can find on them."

"I'm sorry, Wayne," James said. He looked again at the photo of Wayne and Barbara on the desk. But this time, he saw a little sadness behind their smiles. Like something was missing. "I'm sorry those state police don't give a damn. The governor either."

"Yeah, me too," Wayne said. "You'd think I'd be used to it, but it still disappoints."

"Well, in . . . uh . . . two nights from now, around midnight, I might take a little ride off the reservation. Thought I'd give you a heads-up."

Wayne raised his eyebrows. "You're going to United?"

"I had a little chat on the phone this week. Figured if our friend Carl didn't want to come out with it himself, he could at least tell me where to find it."

"And did he?" Wayne asked.

"Sure did."

Wayne nodded. "I'll keep an eye on the Codys."

James stood, and the room seemed to wobble a bit. He still wasn't strong enough to be creeping around in the middle of the night. But he didn't have time to waste, either. He needed to go scope out the place, at least. This damn bullet to his head had taken too much time away already.

He put his hat back on. "Got someone else I gotta pay a visit to."

"Checked on her yesterday. George is back at his place. I think those two have had enough of each other," Wayne chuckled. "It always was a relationship of tolerance, I think."

"How's she feelin'?"

"Better than you."

"I would hope so. All right, then. I'll be back later about Jackson's men. Or you can put me to work doin' something else. Anything other than sittin' in bed smellin' my own farts."

"You have to slow down when you eat Barb's cooking. It's so good, it'll give you gas."

James nodded. "Right. I'll blame Barb."

"So long," Wayne called after him.

James stopped in the break room and poured himself a coffee. Water would probably have been better, but he wanted that jolt before going to Kay's. Besides, he couldn't stop thinking about the waste that might be in the water already, and it made him nervous. Coffee was better, he decided.

58

KAY

KAY'S ARM still ached when she did some things, and riding was one of them. But she didn't care today. She needed the ride. She took Niyol west, toward Arizona. A little south, too, toward the canyon, though they wouldn't go that far. Her arm wouldn't allow it. She had let Niyol run for a bit, Kay crouched down over her back, letting that hot air run down her spine. Now, Niyol was taking her time. Stopping to pull at some grass. Kay slid to the ground.

When Kay thought of Linda at her happiest, she thought of her out here. The two of them with their father. A horse for each of them. Spirit and Beauty. Her father had hated those names, but they had read them in books in school and their hearts were set, so he allowed it. He wanted them to connect with the horses. They were the girls' horses to take care of, after all. He knew responsibility went hand in hand with love.

The horses had taken quickly to Linda's gentle ways. It didn't come naturally to Kay, though. She learned over the years to absorb their calm energy. To follow their lead. But

Linda didn't need any practice. As a child, Linda was easy. Sweet. Shy.

Whenever Kay and Spirit got trapped in a battle of wills, Linda would put her hand on the horse and tell Kay, "The horse knows better. Listen to Spirit."

It never made Kay angry, because it worked. She would take a few deep breaths, silently apologize, and when she would start again, it was easier.

She kept Niyol from the running water, tumbling away from them, away from the canyon, toward the San Juan River.

She let herself cry as she watched it flow. The river water might not be safe for Niyol anymore. And there was nothing Kay could do about it. Nowhere to take her to protect her. Now, she would only let her animals drink from the water that came in the jugs Wayne brought her. She thought about what Niyol would do if Kay let her go to the creek. Would the horse somehow know better? Would she die of thirst before she poisoned herself?

Kay let Niyol finish grazing, then she wiped her eyes with her sleeve and headed home.

James was waiting for Kay. She hadn't seen him since he left the hospital. She was curious about his head injury, but he'd covered it with a hat. He smiled and she smiled back. That smile of his was so warm. Familiar now.

"Can't kill us, huh?" she asked, walking toward him from the stable.

"I've got more lives than a cat," he said.

He was leaning on Wayne's truck and stood up straight as she neared. He stepped forward.

"How's that arm?"

Kay held it out in front of her and spun it first one way and then the other.

"It'll do," she said. James looked at his gold-faced wristwatch.

"Want to grab lunch? My treat."

She cocked her head. "You don't want to eat my famous fried bologna and cheese sandwich with tomato soup for dunking?"

"You know what? That sounds delicious," James said. "If you don't mind. I'd be honored."

Kay snorted. "It's just tomato soup. Come inside."

She held the door open while James limped into the house.

"Your leg, too?" she asked.

"Some shrapnel got jammed in there."

"Damn, Ronnie," Kay said.

"Wayne told you, then."

"He said your rig looked like the target at a shooting range."

Kay suddenly noticed how dark the inside of her house must look to James with the windows still boarded up. She hadn't fixed it yet and had gotten used to it.

"Sit down, hobbles," she said. She squatted down at the kitchen counter, looking for her pan.

"Did you file a police report or anything?" she called over the clinking of pots and lids as she rooted out her cast iron.

"Hospital did. The state police came to talk. I think they're getting suspicious of seeing my face so much."

Kay put the pan on the stove. Opened the refrigerator.

"Well, you are bad news. Did you tell them who you suspect?"

She put the cheese and butter and bologna on the counter.

"No," James said.

"Why not?"

"They'd have asked me why and I couldn't get into all that."

She turned the stove on and turned to look at him through the cutout in the wall.

"You could've kept it vague. You could've said 'personal vendetta' or something."

"I don't think having Ronnie Cody arrested right now is in my favor. Besides, the Codys will pay for their crimes soon enough."

Kay could feel her features lift. Her heart patter faster. "You think it was the Codys?"

James took his hat off then, and Kay could see a chunk of his hair had been shaved off.

"I don't think the Codys killed Linda. But they're helping to cover it up."

Kay tapped her lip.

"So, someone from the company?"

"Maybe. I've got to find out who else she told. I'm thinkin' you're probably right."

"Jackson?"

He nodded.

Kay turned back around and hovered her hand over the pan to see if it was hot yet. "I'm listening," she called over her shoulder.

"From there, I don't know. Maybe Jackson had one of his men kill her. If he has men like that. And if he's the sort to have a woman killed and to poison his people in order to protect the uranium company."

Kay dropped a piece of bread into the pan and listened to the butter sizzle.

"What else?" she asked.

"Or maybe Jackson went to the company and someone there did it. But Jackson still would have had to be in their corner. They would have had to believe he was, too."

Kay thought about the mystery books she'd loved to read as a teenager, and an idea came to her.

"Or maybe the company killed her to scare Jackson! Maybe they were sending him a message to keep his mouth shut."

She quickly shoved the spatula under the sandwich.

"Hmm," James said, and she could tell he was impressed. She smiled to herself. "You think that would've worked?" he asked. "Is he that sort of man? To be frightened off in that way?"

"Wouldn't you be?" she asked.

"No."

Kay flipped the sandwich. It only shifted a little. The gooey cheese held the top piece of bread on, and she nudged it back to center.

"I need to meet with him," James said.

"The fair's this weekend," Kay said. "He'll be there."

She turned and stole a glance at James. He looked intrigued.

"And you'll be going?" he asked.

"Of course."

"It's a date, then."

Kay blushed. She stood on her tiptoes to reach the can of tomato soup. Then, she rummaged through the drawer second to the top for the can opener and opened it. She poured the soup in the pot that she'd set on the stove to dry overnight and turned the burner up.

James was quiet while she finished making lunch. She set his soup and sandwich in front of him and then went back to get her own. When she sat down, James was making a face of exaggerated satisfaction. His eyebrows furrowed. His lips pursed. He shook his head and said, "Mmmm, mmm! Best damn bologna and cheese sandwich I ever had."

Kay burst out laughing and smacked him on the arm. "Smartass."

He laughed, too. Then he set his spoon down, and his face grew serious. "I told Gloria," he said.

Kay lowered her sandwich without taking a bite.

"Told her what?"

"About the uranium. She came to visit me in the hospital. I'd been on my way to meet her."

Kay's heartbeat sped up again. James ran a hand through his hair, stopping at the wound.

"It wasn't enough. She won't run a story without talking to the source. She said rumors aren't enough."

Blood rushed to Kay's cheeks. She slipped her hands under her thighs to stop them from shaking.

"Did you know," she asked James, "that there is no Navajo word for journalist or reporter? We call them 'gossips.'"

James was quiet. She stared at her sandwich. The brown swirls of burnt butter.

"They'll report on rumors if it's something they care about. If someone other than just us Indians is affected," she went on.

"I know," he said. "It's not the right rumor. But you know why. These men are powerful. Hell, even the state police won't do anything. Wayne and I went to have a chat. Just to make sure Mr. Assman really did go to them like he said he did. They knew, all right."

Kay felt the rage boiling inside of her. She stood up. Almost grabbed her hair. Wanted to pull it out. Instead, she clenched her hands into fists and released them.

"So . . . so . . ."

"So, what I'm gonna do," James finished for her, "is find those original documents. What Linda had were only copies."

"How are you going to do that?"

"Don't worry about that."

59

WAYNE

THE ROAD WAS empty and the sky clear on the night Wayne went with James to check the United Nuclear Corporation's offices.

At first, James had thought Wayne ought to stay on the reservation and keep an eye on the Codys. But Wayne pointed out that he'd have no reason to detain them if they wanted to leave. This way, James and Wayne could bring radios. Wayne could keep an eye out, while James poked around the place. Did it make Wayne an accessory to a B and E? Sure. But if the Codys did show up, they might be more hesitant to try something with Wayne there. Maybe.

James relented, but they told no one where they were going. Not Barbara. Not Molly. The story would always be that James had gone alone.

They passed an owl perched on top of a pole on the side of the road, and Wayne said, "Owl." The hairs on his arms stood on end, the superstitious part of him—which he tried to always suppress—prickling his insides. He turned the radio on, turned the volume down.

"I found a Vietnam veteran on Jackson's staff," Wayne said.

"Oh yeah? What do you know about him?"

"His name is Raymond Nez. Former medic. He oversees the Department of Health."

"So, someone who would know what to use to kill someone quietly and efficiently and make it look like an overdose?"

"Exactly," Wayne said.

"What else?"

"Nez is of the same maternal clan as Jackson."

"Which means?"

"They're like family."

"Interesting," James said. "Does Nez have any connection to Cecil Cody?"

"Not at first glance, but I'll keep looking."

James pulled out a cigarette and rolled down the window. There were no streetlights. Just Wayne's headlights and the moon and, every so often, the headlights of a passing car or truck.

They drove past some neighborhoods and then took a right. After the tire shop, the big metal mill building was on their left, a sprawling parking lot beside it.

James pointed up ahead. "Pull off there. Turn around and shut your headlights off."

Wayne pulled off into the dirt and looked in both directions before slowly driving back out into the opposite lane. He pulled off again behind a large bush and shut the lights off. They could see the doors perfectly, illuminated by lights shining from the roof of the rusty building.

Wayne fiddled with the radios. He switched them on,

and there was loud static. He turned the volume down and spoke into one.

"Officer James Pinter, can you hear me? Over."

The other radio squeaked and squawked, but sure enough, Wayne's voice echoed and bounced through the truck.

"Lima Charlie, over," James said. Then he opened the door. "I'm gonna go check the doors. See if they're locked. I assume so, but you never know."

Wayne tossed him a radio. He caught it. He shut the door behind him, and Wayne watched him move slowly but deliberately toward the building.

Just then, a car pulled into the parking lot, and James crouched down behind some tall grass. A man emerged quickly from the car, ran to the front door, and unlocked it. He disappeared inside.

They waited. Two minutes, four minutes, five minutes. Finally, the same man came back out, carrying a small bag—a lunch box, maybe. He got back in his car and drove off. Wayne sat in silence. The man had not locked the door behind him.

"You see that?" he asked over the radio. It crackled.

"Sure did," James replied. "See anything around the perimeter?"

Wayne grabbed the flashlight from his center console and shone it at the back of the building. Everything was still. No wind. No movement. He clicked the flashlight off.

"Nothing on this side," he said.

"I'm gonna check the other side and then I'm going in."

"Wait," Wayne said. "You're going in now?"

"I gotta, Wayne," James said. "Watch my back."

"Damn it," Wayne muttered off the radio. He looked up and down the road. Nothing. "Copy," he finally replied.

He put the radio down, put the truck into gear, and eased out onto the road. He didn't put his headlights back on, but he did pull into the parking lot. He hadn't seen the Codys tailing them, but he had to consider the possibility.

Wayne found a spot at the edge of the parking lot and waited.

60

JAMES

THERE WAS ONLY a single light on inside the office building, and it shone on James as he entered. He walked quickly on, into the dark.

He was back in the large room, desks and cubicles scattered around in a maze. He stuck his arms out and felt around as he walked, occasionally tripping on a chair leg or running his hip into the corner of a divider or stubbing his fingers against desktops.

"What the hell?" he would mumble. Or, "Shit, that hurt."

He looked for a hallway or the closed door of an office. He imagined they'd all be locked. Still, when he found a door, he tried it anyway. Locked. He tried a few more beside the first. All locked. But then he fingered a light switch. He hoped it was just for the hallway and not for the whole room with all its windows. He flipped it on, and it illuminated a few bulbs right above his head.

According to Carl Assman, James was looking for a Henry Fields, senior manager of operations at the Church Rock Mill, or Robert Feeney, engineering director.

James found Fields's office right away. He spun around and scanned the desks behind him for a paper clip. He found a couple of heavy-duty ones in a top drawer and fashioned them into a pick. It had been a while, he thought, as he jammed it into the lock of Mr. Fields's office door. He twisted and turned and made sure he didn't push too hard, which would bend the pick.

Finally, he heard a click, turned the handle and pushed the door open.

He stood in darkness for a moment, letting the light behind him spill into the room. Desk. Coffee mug. Framed photos. Chairs. Filing cabinets. A small, high window.

James thought about how important this whole leaking dam problem would be to Mr. Fields. Had he moved the documents since Carl had been there? Carl didn't think anyone at the company knew he had gone to the police, but he wasn't sure. If Fields did know, would that make the issue more sensitive or no longer a concern? Was this a desk drawer, hidden under a false bottom, locked away sort of problem? Or just a regular sort of problem, in a folder in a regular filing cabinet, like it had been when Carl was still at the company?

James didn't know, but he started with what Carl had told him. One of the top three filing cabinets should hold the papers. He opened the first drawer and stared at the over-stuffed folders nearly toppling out onto the floor. He unhooked his radio from his belt. "Stay awake out there," he said into it. "It's going to be a long night. Over."

The radio crackled. "Copy," Wayne said.

James found some files on employees. Then financials. He ached for a coffee. He sat on the ground, his back up against the cabinets, his eyes glazing over as he flipped through. He wondered how the man got through his day without ripping his eyes out. He thought of Charles at the FBI; he had started in financial crimes. *No, sir,* James thought. *Not for me.* No wonder it was so easy for people to get away with this stuff. No one wanted to read this.

James chuckled, thinking of his younger self, who'd wanted to head an oil company. He didn't think it often, but he was grateful for the Army just then.

He put the folder back and rubbed his eyes. He stood and stretched his back. Leaned to one side, then the other.

He wasn't getting anywhere. He'd have to find Feeney's office. He crept back into the hallway and read each office door as he walked by. Duncan. Dorsey. Craig. Feeney. *Bingo.* James picked the lock.

Feeney's files were much more organized, and James was delighted to see actual tabs—including one that was labeled *Inspections.* He thumbed through the folder for 1977, the year this location had opened. He stopped when he found the inspections labeled *Waste Tailings Dam.* His heart started to beat quicker. According to what was in his hand, three cracks had been identified in the dam wall not even a year after it was built. Without further action, it said, the cracks would open up, and the holding area would fail. James put the folder aside and grabbed the next year, 1978. Further cracks had been identified then. He took that folder, too.

James also took the initial plans for the dam and a copy of a memorandum from Feeney informing Fields of the passage of the Uranium Mill Tailings Radiation Control Act of 1978, where Feeney clearly admitted that their dam was in violation. He'd read more of it all later. He had what he needed.

He spoke into the radio. "Wake up, Wayne. I've got 'em. Over."

"Back left parking lot. Over."

James locked and shut Feeney's office door behind him and then did the same to Fields's. He turned the lights off and bumped his way back to the front door, the papers gripped under his arm.

He slipped into the night, thinking about the poor bastard who was going get an earful in the morning about leaving the door unlocked. Then, he thought about Feeney. How long would it him to realize the papers were missing? Long enough. Not that he'd know who'd taken them.

James spotted Wayne's truck and made his way over.

"You really found them?" Wayne asked as James climbed in.

"Oh, I found 'em." He set the papers on his lap and looked at his watch: 1 a.m. "I don't think we'll be gettin' much sleep tonight."

"No?"

James held up the giant stack of papers. It barely fit in his hand. "We've got some reading to do."

Wayne put the truck into gear and turned the headlights back on. "Just remember," he said. "I was never here."

———————

At seven in the morning, Wayne and James went to get breakfast.

"So, it was the fact that the dam wasn't lined," James said as they sat down. "That's what's in violation of that act, and that's why the walls cracked. It wasn't lined properly."

He was talking more to himself than to Wayne. It helped to make things stick in his brain when he was overtired like this. Wayne nodded as a waitress brought them menus.

"So, they not only knew about the cracks and did nothing, but they also knew they were in violation of the law with the design of the thing," James said. "Assman was tellin' the truth."

The waitress came back with two black coffees and a bowl of sugar and half-and-half packets.

"I'll be callin' my buddy at the FBI today," James said.

"You think the FBI's going to care about this?" Wayne asked.

"He can report it to the EPA. Or tell me how to do that."

Wayne closed his eyes. "The cracks have been there for two years," he said. He opened his eyes again and looked right at James. "How much longer will they hold?"

James knew it was rhetorical, but he answered anyway. "The good news is, I don't think those cracks have opened up yet. If they had, I think I would've found somethin' about that, too. I'm gettin' Gloria on the phone today. I have her proof."

Wayne nodded and stared into his coffee. "Why do I feel like it's still not enough? With all this?"

"For a story? We've got plenty for a story!" James cried.

"No," Wayne said. "Still not enough for anything to change."

61

KAY

KAY WATCHED Molly look around self-consciously before biting into her cotton candy. Kay held back a laugh. There was no "cool" way to eat cotton candy. She nudged Molly with her elbow to get her attention and then took a giant bite of her own, feeling the sticky sugar coat her mouth.

Molly giggled. They were walking back to where James had saved them all bleacher seats to watch the hoop dance.

This was probably the first time Molly had been around kids her own age in months, and she grew shy whenever one of Kay's students bounded over and wrapped Kay in a hug.

"Ms. Benally!" the girls would screech. The boys would give her a quick nod or a half wave as they passed. Molly was so full of both longing and discomfort that it seemed to radiate from her. She missed her own friends, Kay understood. These were different kids. Strangers. But still kids. They still giggled together behind their hands. Or eyed each other with judgment or hormonal teenage attraction. And Molly was outside of it all.

Still, she was being good-natured about it. Smiling at everyone. Saying a friendly "hello" when Kay introduced her.

By the time they settled back into their seats, the arena had turned into a sea of bright colors—feathered headdresses, intricate clothing, large jewelry that hung from necks and ears and wrists.

James pointed. "Is that Wayne?"

"And Barbara," Kay said.

"They're going to dance?" he asked.

"By the looks of them, I'd say so."

James smiled. The announcer got on the loudspeaker to introduce the dancers, and the crowd quieted. Then, the drum started up. The first dancer began the dance. He jumped into a hoop, pulled it up his body and ducked his head into it. Then it went down his arm. He seamlessly picked up another and then another, weaving them in and out of his limbs as he danced.

James leaned closer to Kay. He smelled like birchwood. Aftershave, maybe.

"So, what's this dance all about?" he asked, real quiet.

"Well," she began, taking a deep breath. "Hoop dancing is about honoring all life forms. The hoop is a circle. Like the circle of life. Young to old, and then the next generation, and then over and over again. Sometimes the dancer makes shapes with the hoop and his body. They'll look like animals. Snakes, eagles, hummingbirds."

"Huh!" James exclaimed. "Well, that's neat. I like that."

"Glad to have your approval." Kay smirked. "*Bilagáana*."

"Hey!" he said. "Don't pick on me! I'm learning something *and* being respectful. Aren't I?"

"I said that with *love*," she replied.

James smiled. "I'll take it, then. Love from Kay. I'll take it."

Kay blushed. "Anyway," she went on. "The hoop dance was traditionally used in healing ceremonies."

She watched James slowly nod.

"To balance things?" he guessed. "Put things right, so to speak?"

"Sort of," she agreed.

She watched James watch the dancers. His eyebrows were furrowed, his mouth slightly turned down. He was concentrating. Kay felt a little flutter in her chest and forced herself to watch the dancers, too.

"That one looks like a giraffe," he whispered.

Kay burst out laughing. "I don't think so."

When the dancers were done, Kay, Molly, and James went down to see Wayne and Barbara.

"Well, don't you two look sharp?" James said, offering Wayne his hand.

"Thank you," Barbara said.

"That was some fancy footwork, my friend," James said to Wayne.

"You know how good I am at jumping through hoops." Wayne winked, and James laughed heartily.

"Ain't that the truth?"

"Wayne!" Molly cried. "That was *such* a dad joke!"

Wayne shrugged apologetically, and Barbara pulled Molly into a hug. When she let go, she left her arm draped around Molly, a hand gripping her shoulder.

"Are you having fun?" she asked.

Molly smiled and nodded. "Kay bought me cotton candy.

I haven't had cotton candy in, like, forever! Probably since I was, like, eight or something."

Barbara gave her a sideways smile. "That *is* forever."

"Is that George over there?" James asked Kay, gesturing with his head.

"Yep."

"A little surprised to see him here," James said.

"Everyone comes to this," Barbara said.

"He just seemed a little . . . modern? Is that the word? To be into this. When I talked to him."

Wayne's eyebrows went up, and for the first time since Kay had known James, she saw him get embarrassed.

"I don't know how else to say it . . ." he mumbled.

"I *would* be offended," Kay said, "if I didn't know exactly what you mean. And no, 'modern' is not the right word. George is here for the fry bread. He's a judge of the fry bread contest. Don't ask how me how he got that gig. But when it comes to food, George's Navajo comes out."

"You cookin', Barb?" James asked. "Or are you gonna let some other people win for a change?"

Barbara rolled her eyes. "Don't make me gag. If I weren't an old, married woman, I'd say your intentions were less than pure." James laughed and put his hands up in the air, surrendering. "But yes," Barbara went on. "I graduated from competing a while ago. I get to judge now. With George."

"How many judges they got?" James asked. "Maybe they could use one more?"

Kay shoved James gently. "Not a bilagáana like yourself."

"Come on! I'm the least biased!"

Kay scrunched up her nose. "With the least taste."

"But I loved your bologna sandwich."

"Exactly," Kay laughed. They were flirting, she realized a moment too late. In front of everyone. She took a step away and looked elsewhere. But not before catching Molly's eye. To Kay's surprise, Molly didn't seem to mind. She looked content, even.

62

JAMES

JAMES HAD to remind himself multiple times that he was not there to spend time with Kay. No matter how good it felt. No matter how much he wanted to spend his day doing just that. He was there to meet Jackson.

He scanned the crowds, the tents, the tables, looking for anyone who seemed important. Anyone who had a gaggle of aggrieved constituents or supporters trailing them.

Kay must've noticed. "You're looking for Jackson," she said.

He nodded. They were sitting under a tent having some drinks while the Miss Northern Navajo competition went ahead on their left. Kay stood up.

"Let's go find him."

"You know where he is?" James asked.

"I have an idea."

He followed her past the pageant stage and across an open, dusty expanse.

"Get ready to see your greatest admirer, too," she said.

When they rounded a corner, behind another row of

tents, James understood. Ronnie Cody looked like he'd seen a ghost. But Cecil Cody didn't look surprised one bit. Standing with his sons, wearing a denim shirt with tassels, Cecil looked almost harmless. He even smiled. Tipped his hat.

There was something there behind his eyes. A knowing. A promise. But so calm and assured. It drew James to the man.

But Kay was still moving, and so James hurried after her.

"Just standing there," Kay said. "Like he didn't try and kill us both."

"Well, I'm not sure you were a target, exactly," James said.

"No," she agreed. "Just collateral damage."

She slowly stopped walking. "There."

The table in front of them read *Peewee Basketball League*. The man who James immediately knew to be Jackson had his hands on the table and was leaning over slightly, listening to one of the younger boys who was manning the table speak. James couldn't hear what the boy was saying, but he could see his excitement. The way he couldn't stop moving in place, shuffling his feet beneath him.

Jackson was a strong man, James could see—his three-piece suit not only incredibly out of place here but also stretched to the limit across his chest. He had a sharp chin. He smiled warmly at the boy, looking him right in the eye. He was clearly a charming man, or at least an impressive one, and everyone around him thought so, too.

"See?" Kay said, crossing her arms. "There's your man. The person Linda trusted so much."

James stood silently, watching Jackson carefully. After a

minute, Jackson stood up straight and clasped his hands together in front of him.

"That sounds like one exciting game," he said to the boy. His voice was loud and deep.

"You want to talk to him?" Kay asked.

"Suppose so," James said.

Kay stepped forward into Jackson's field of vision, James right on her heels. She did a little wave.

"Mr. Jackson?" she asked.

"That's me," he said. "What can I help you with?"

"Just wanted to say hello. To meet you in person. My sister was a big fan."

"Was?" he asked.

"She passed on a couple months ago," Kay said.

"I'm sorry to hear that. She was young?"

"Three years younger than me," Kay said. "It was tragic. She battled with addiction, you know? We thought she had finally beat it but . . ."

She looked down at her boots, and James saw how raw and painful it all still was for her. How much guilt she still carried.

Jackson shook his head. "A terrible thing," he said. "A terrible thing. I can promise you that keeping hard drugs off the reservation is a priority of mine. And finding funding for additional treatment centers, too. For drugs *and* alcohol."

Jackson's gaze finally wandered to James. "And you are?" he asked.

"Friend of Kay's here."

Jackson held out his hand. "Welcome to Navajo Nation," he said.

"Thank you. Yeah, everyone's been very welcoming.

You've got an awfully good police lieutenant in Sanostee, by the way. I used to be police myself. Wayne Tully's the real deal. And a great guy all around."

James searched Jackson's face for some sort of recognition. White man. Police. Sanostee. But all he could read was masked boredom. He had better things to do.

"Glad to hear it," Jackson said.

"Say, can I ask you a question?" James asked.

"Sure, you can."

"I heard a rumor, I guess you could call it, about the uranium mill in Church Rock. The United Nuclear Corporation. Know of it?"

Now he had Jackson's attention. Sharp eyes, thin mouth.

"We've got quite a few of those uranium companies around the reservation. Oil and coal, too. We've been blessed with an abundance of natural resources here. Individuals and the council chairman before me decided to lease some land. Can't say the companies do their part in return, though."

"Why do you say that?" James asked.

Jackson crossed his arms and spread his legs a little. The man was getting ready to do some talking. It was as if James had given him a pulpit.

"I say that because they believe we ought to be satisfied with the jobs they provide. Low-paying jobs for Indians. Bottom rung. They underpay for the land, then they underpay their workers. And they get filthy rich. Does it look like Diné are benefitting from the very elements these companies pull from our own land?"

Jackson held his arms out as if to show James the poverty. The struggle.

"I'm guessing no," James said.

"My job is to get more from these companies. Make sure the opportunities they speak of when they come traipsing onto *our* land are Navajo opportunities. Not more white man opportunities."

"The rumor I heard," James said, plowing ahead despite Jackson's political sidetrack, "is that United's holding dams are cracking. That they could fail and toxic waste could leak into the Puerco River. Think there's any truth to that?"

Jackson's eyes narrowed, and he took a half step forward.

"United," he said in a voice so low only James could hear. "I do remember them now. Surrounding my tribal lands but not on them. So, James, say this rumor is true, what ought I to do about it? Hmm?"

James shook his head. "Just thought it might be something you'd like to know about."

Jackson's face softened. He nodded.

"It is," he said. "Thank you for sharing. I'll have my people look into it."

"Certainly a pleasure to meet you, councilman," James said.

Jackson smiled. "Enjoy your visit."

63

KAY

"So, is Jackson the type to have my sister killed?" Kay asked James as they stood outside the Tully residence that night, leaning against her truck.

James had been distracted ever since speaking with Jackson. He seemed only partially there when the five of them—Molly, James, Kay, Wayne, and Barbara—stumbled into Wayne's living room and drank coffee and talked about the day, laughing at the way the kids had held tight to the sheep they rode during the "woolly rodeo." The way they bounced from side to side as the sheep scurried around.

James, though, had only smiled about it before going back to staring into his coffee. Kay was leaving now, going home, and James had walked her out.

"It could have just been a reaction similar to Wayne's. 'What is it this time,' you know?"

Kay didn't respond. She wanted to hear the "or" she knew was coming.

"Or you might be dead on with your theory that Linda's

murder was a warning. He's clearly angry with those companies, even if they are paying him. But how much would they
have to pay a man to keep quiet about a thing like this? More
than it's worth, I would guess. A threat would be more
effective."

"But why do you think a threat would work?" Kay asked.
"Why wouldn't Jackson want to be a hero? Speak up no
matter the cost?"

"Because," James answered, "if what Barbara says about
the man is true, he's proved he isn't a hero. He's proved he's a
man like the rest of us. Swayed by simple desires."

"Which means he could've been bribed to stay quiet."

"I don't think so. Think how much he's probably
getting paid for simply allowing these companies to
continue to use the land. For being a friend to their business interests, so to speak. It's possible Jackson has
convinced himself that the bribes and kickbacks are a good
thing. That maybe he's the only one who will use that
money properly. He might even think himself essential to
the Navajo Nation. But it's much harder to justify
poisoning his own people. That's something that'll keep a
man awake at night."

"You got all of that from a short conversation?" Kay
asked.

James shrugged. "It ain't my first rodeo. Jackson probably
would've made a fine Army officer. But you're right. It's just
speculation, not fact."

"Okay. So, let's assume it was a message. How would
Jackson even know about this message? I hate to say it, but an
overdose isn't exactly breaking news out here."

James squinted at the sky in front of him. It was almost

completely black now, the soft hue of dusk gone. Kay couldn't see what, if anything, he was looking at.

"They could've just told him," he said. "Taken photos if they needed to."

"And the carving on her arm? The overdose cover-up?"

"Maybe it means something to Jackson. Something we don't understand."

"Why leave her at all? Why not . . . dump her in a river or bury her or—I don't know—whatever killers do with dead bodies?" Kay's stomach churned. This wasn't just a body. This was her sister, and she still wasn't used to speaking about her that way.

"I don't know. It doesn't feel like a professional job, which is a little strange. You would think the company would've hired someone instead of calling their cousin Billy or whoever. But maybe that's all they thought they needed to do. They didn't want another added expense. They must've been thinkin' by then that if they were gonna spend all that money, they might as well just fix the dam."

It hit Kay like a brick, square in the chest, and James must have realized it.

"I'm sorry," he said. "I'm talkin' to you like you're Wayne. I shouldn't have said that."

Kay forced herself to take a deep breath. To suck in the air no matter how much it hurt.

"You're right, though," she whispered. She shook her head, trying to keep in the tears. "Such a waste. Killing her."

James gently touched her shoulder and stepped closer. Kay took the invitation and buried herself in his arms, sobbing into his chest. He covered the back of her head with his hand and stroked her hair.

"Now we know," he whispered into her ear. "Jackson wasn't a hero, but your sister was. That kind of courage is special. It's rare. Standin' up to men like that. Speakin' out when it would've been so much easier to stay quiet about the whole thing."

Kay sobbed some more. Linda had been brave. Linda *was* a hero.

"I haven't told you yet," James said. She pulled away just enough to look at him. Only inches from his face.

"What?"

"I've got the proof," he said. "The original documents. I talked to Gloria and a friend at the FBI yesterday. Not only do people know, but now I can prove it."

Kay's hand shot to her mouth.

"You're serious? How?"

"Yes, I'm serious. And don't worry about that. Gloria is coming to the reservation tomorrow. And my buddy is makin' some calls right now."

Kay started crying again, but this time, she laughed, too. James kept hold of her shoulders and smiled at her.

"So, we're going to catch them?"

He nodded. "We already did."

Now that Kay was off the pain medication, she went back to her occasional Jack Daniel's on the rocks at night. On nights she really wanted to unwind.

Tonight was one of those nights. She still hadn't forgiven herself and would never know if Linda had, either. But she felt like Linda was content. She hadn't felt her ghost in weeks. So, perhaps Kay was being too hard on herself. Still. She wanted absolution, and she had no idea who could give it to her.

Kay sighed and sipped her whiskey. "Forgive me," she whispered into the empty room. But she knew Linda was gone. Kay was speaking to no one, now. Not even a ghost.

She must have fallen asleep right there in the recliner, because she woke up to dawn leaking in through the windows and a strong, loud knock at the front door.

She sat up quickly and wiped the drool from her chin. *Gross*, she thought.

"Coming!" she called. She stood and hiked up her pants. Straightened her shirt. Who was here this early? James? Wayne?

But it was neither. Strangers in brown suits stood outside her door, clipboards in hand. They looked nervous. Ashamed.

"Can I help you?" she asked.

"Ma'am." One took off his hat. "We're here from the United Nuclear Corporation."

Kay's mind went blank. She started to feel dizzy. Why were they here? Did they know she knew something? She reached out to grab something. A chair.

"You all right, ma'am?" the same man said. He looked concerned. "You're awfully pale. Do you need to sit down?"

Why are they concerned about me? Kay thought. This didn't make sense.

"What do you want from me?" Her voice was deep and raspy. It seemed to come from somewhere else.

"We . . . uh . . . we have to tell you all that there's been an accident. A problem at the mill. Something messy. We're working on cleaning it up. But for now, don't drink your tap water. And don't go into any rivers or creeks. Don't let any of your animals do it, either."

Kay understood now. James had been too late. They were both too late. She started to cry.

[64]

MOLLY

SANOSTEE WAS AWAKE NOW. The early-morning door
knocks had brought everyone outside, looking around,
confused. As if they could see the toxic waste for themselves.
James and Wayne stood feet apart, grim-faced, staring at one
another, staring at nothing.

Molly could see groups of people huddled together in the
distance where three or four trailers gathered at the end of a
road.

The men from the uranium company hadn't said much.
The neighbors probably didn't understand the deep tragedy
of what Molly knew must have unfolded that morning.

Finally, Wayne said, "We've got to do better than this.
We've got to tell people exactly what happened. Why they're
in danger."

Without another word, all four of them piled into the
Oldsmobile.

On their way to the station, they passed some more white
men in suits. They were nailing papers onto telephone poles.
Wayne slowed down and Molly read it. More warnings.

"All the good that will do . . ." Barbara muttered. "Don't they know how many Navajo can't read English?" She shook her head. "Of course they don't."

Molly grabbed her hand, and Barbara gave her a sad smile.

"What're you gonna do?" Molly asked Wayne.

"Call Jackson in Window Rock. Make sure they know. Then I'll draft something for the radio station to read in English *and* in Navajo."

They remained quiet, and when they reached the station, they all listened to Wayne's phone call.

"This is Chief Tully at Sanostee PD. I'm calling because we have some more information regarding the uranium spill last night."

Wayne listened for a moment and then started to rub his forehead.

"Then, I suppose I have some information about the uranium spill that happened a few days ago. I just want to make sure Chairman Jackson has all the facts. A . . . um . . . an anonymous source dropped off some documents. It's something we should all take very seriously."

A pause. "Yes, I'll hold."

"Chairman Jackson? It's Lieutenant Tully over in Sanostee."

A pause again. Then, Wayne looked up at James with a smirk and a shake of his head.

"A white man told you that yesterday at the fair, did he?"

James shrugged apologetically.

"No, I don't believe he was the one who left the documents, but I suppose it's possible. Either way, I can tell you this is a big deal. And I have a feeling United will make it seem like it isn't."

Wayne listened. "Uh huh. Sure. Yes, I can do that. I'll see you later today. All right."

He hung up.

"So, you and Jackson had a little chat yesterday," Wayne said.

James smiled. "Told him you were the best damn lawman this reservation's ever seen."

"Uh huh," Wayne said. "Well, Jackson wants to see these documents, but you better believe we're not bringing the originals."

Molly hopped up. "I'll make copies!" she volunteered.

"Thank you, Molly," Wayne said. "They're in my desk drawer. You know where to find the key."

Molly nodded and rushed off to make herself useful. She read a few sentences from each document before feeding them into the copier, listening to the loud hum of the machine scanning one after the next. "Possible contamination," it read. "Groundwater, soil, rivers, creeks, runoff." *No longer only a possibility*, Molly thought. It had happened.

She brought the papers back to Wayne. "Are we all going?" she asked, looking pleadingly at James. He nodded.

"We're all going," James said. "Wayne tells me they've got a zoo in Window Rock. The three of us can go, if you'd like, while Wayne talks to Jackson."

"I've got to stay," Barbara said. "Try to wrangle a council meeting for the Shiprock Chapter. Make sure Sanostee knows what's going on."

"Thanks, Barb," Wayne said. "Tell us how Cecil Cody takes the news."

"I will."

"Then just the two of us will go with Wayne?" James asked Molly.

"The two of us," she said.

The ride to Window Rock was quiet, and for a little while, Molly might have fallen asleep.

Window Rock looked a little like the rest of the reservation, but more important. Large, impressive buildings with lots of windows. Long, squat buildings with big, blocky letters. Statues of famous people. James took Molly close to one to read the plaque. It was a bronze code talker.

"Wayne's daddy was one of these, you know," James said.

Wayne looked surprised. "How'd you know that? You do some homework on me?"

"Kay told me."

Wayne smiled a strange, shy smile. He was proud, Molly realized.

"What's a code talker?" she asked. James looked like he was about to answer but turned to Wayne instead.

"Why don't you tell her?"

Wayne took a deep breath and leaned against the fence that surrounded the statue.

"So, in World War II, the US fought in Europe but also in the Pacific. Do you know about that? Pearl Harbor and the Japanese?"

Molly nodded. "I remember learning about the attack on Pearl Harbor."

"Yes, so after that, we were at war with the Japanese, too. We tried to create codes to communicate across radios and across the telegraph lines without the Japanese understanding what we were saying. But they kept breaking our codes."

Molly turned around to lean next to him.

"The Navajo language is a hard language to learn. And more importantly, it's only spoken by us." He pointed his finger down toward the earth. "Right here. The US Marines consulted with us and we created a whole new code off our language. Recruited Diné soldiers, taught only by Diné instructors. The Japanese never broke that code."

Molly grinned. "That's so cool! Your dad did that?"

"Yep. And boy did he have stories. They had to be right there, you know? In the middle of the action."

"A hero," Molly said.

"Yeah," Wayne said. "A hero." He glanced at his watch. "Time to go see Jackson."

James and Molly walked with him, as the zoo was only a few blocks from Jackson's office. There were a lot of cars, a lot of people.

"Is it always this crowded here?" Molly asked.

"Well, it is the Navajo Nation's capital. But no." Wayne frowned.

"Guess we aren't the only ones here for some guidance today," James said.

Just then, Molly spotted Gloria. She was squatting in front of a bench, a little kid sitting before her with bandages wrapped around his feet. As they got closer, Molly could see that Gloria was holding a tape recorder.

"Well, look who it is," James muttered.

"Can't have a tragedy without her," Wayne said. "I'll see you two later."

"Meet us at the zoo," James called as Wayne walked into

the crowd that had gathered outside the chairman's office building.

James approached Gloria but stopped far enough away to observe without intruding.

After a minute, Gloria stood up and tucked her tape recorder into her bag. She said something to the boy's mom, standing beside the bench, then spun around to look right at Molly and James.

"Oh, James," Gloria said, getting entirely too close to him, in Molly's opinion. "What a terrible thing. You were right. Your . . . source was right all along. I should have done something. How horrible."

"What could you have done?" James asked. "I think we all tried our best, didn't we?"

He eyed her intently.

"I suppose you're right," she said. "Those documents you told me about, you'll show them to me, won't you? We're going to get United. We're gonna make those assholes pay."

"Of course," James said.

"What's wrong with that boy?" Molly asked.

"Oh, it's awful," Gloria said. "He was playing in the river yesterday. He has burns up to his knees. The hospital mistook it for sun poisoning. But it's got to be the uranium, doesn't it?"

"Probably," James said.

Molly stared at Gloria. At her perfect hair. Her perfect makeup. Her perfect outfit. In the midst of all this confusion and pain and frustration.

WAYNE

WAYNE HAD NEVER BEEN inside Jackson's office before. Never sat across from the man face-to-face, one-on-one. When Wayne entered, Jackson was staring out the window with a grimace, seated in a high-back leather chair. Wayne couldn't help but be surprised by just how fragile and expensive everything in the office seemed. He shouldn't have been. He'd seen the suits and the watches and the cars.

"So, Lieutenant Wayne Tully from Sanostee. How did you get so involved with this mess?" Jackson asked, finally turning to look at Wayne.

Wayne reached for the copies of the documents. They could do the talking for him.

Jackson put up a hand to stop him. "Before we look at those, tell me about your white man."

"He's a friend of—"

"Kay Benally. I know that much."

"You know Kay?" Wayne asked.

Jackson shook his head. "Didn't have any idea who she was until yesterday. But after her *friend* spoke to me, I asked around. Cecil Cody told me that she's Ned Benally's daughter. That the man, a James Pinter, has been hanging around ever since her sister, Linda, died. Which, Kay told me at the fair, was due to an overdose. Cecil says this Pinter is starting trouble. Saying that Linda's death *wasn't* an overdose. You allowing that sort of thing in Sanostee, Lieutenant Tully? You allowing some outsider to come in and do your police work for you?"

Wayne's teeth clenched tighter and tighter as Jackson spoke. This was an ambush.

"Linda was found off the reservation," Wayne answered. "Off an exit on 40 behind a gas station. James was the one who found her. So, as you know, Chairman Jackson, a death off the reservation isn't mine to investigate. It's the state police's. They are the ones who reported her death as an overdose."

Jackson folded his hands together on top of his desk.

"And so that ought to have been the end of that. Why are you wasting your time—time that ought to be spent serving and protecting Diné, enforcing law and order, you know, your job—on the theory of an outsider who knows nothing about us?"

Wayne steadied himself. Focused on the crumb that had fallen onto Jackson's tie from his breakfast.

"Something had been carved into Linda's arm after she died. James found this suspicious, as did I. We both know how low a priority we are to the state police. They barely glanced at her before deciding what had happened."

Jackson shook his head, but Wayne plowed ahead anyway.

"Linda worked for United, and she knew *this* was going

to happen." He gestured toward the window. "She knew, because they knew."

Jackson was still shaking his head.

"Did you hear me, Chairman?" Wayne could feel his face getting hot now. He couldn't remember the last time he had outwardly challenged a person of authority. "They knew this would happen, and they did nothing. They knew the way they'd built their dam was in violation of the law and they did nothing!"

Jackson's eyebrows scrunched together, and he looked at Wayne intently.

"Are you saying Linda Benally's death was related to this spill?"

"Morris," Wayne said. "She was Linda Morris. Married. And yes, it's a possibility."

Jackson looked like he'd been slapped. He gave a strange little laugh.

"How did Linda know about this? I'll be shocked if you say that she was in charge over there. Is she the one who left you the documents? Did she bring them back from the next world?"

Wayne's mind reeled. He had not been expecting Jackson to be so aggressive.

"Chairman," he said after a moment, taking a deep breath. "I didn't come to talk about Linda. I came to show you these documents. Please, take a look at them."

Jackson gave a curt nod, and Wayne spread the documents across his desk. Jackson opened his eyeglass case, put his glasses on, and began to read.

Wayne watched his expression morph from one of indignation to resignation.

"This is certainly . . ." Jackson began. Then he sighed and took his glasses off again. He rubbed his eyes. "I do apologize, Lieutenant. I'm overwhelmed at the moment, as you can imagine. You're doing what any officer of the law would feel compelled to do."

He opened his eyes again and looked at Wayne. "To be completely honest, I don't know how you do it. I don't know how *I* do it. Some days I'm so tired. Tired of having to get up every single day and fight. When will the day come when we can simply live? And prosper? Without being poisoned." His voice grew quieter. "Without getting killed."

"I don't know, Chairman," Wayne said. "I'm tired, too. Which is why we must hold United accountable."

Jackson gazed out the window again. "Their mill isn't even on the reservation." He sounded far away now.

"Still," Wayne said. "We have to make a statement. We have to let them know that we know what they did. These companies must understand that we won't let them use our land if this is the consequence. All the money in the world isn't enough to allow them to knowingly poison us."

"You don't understand," Jackson said, still quiet. "You can't. These men will have their way, no matter what. They *will* get what they want."

"Still," Wayne said. "We have to try."

"Try?" Jackson's gaze snapped to Wayne. He slammed his hand down onto the desk. "I do try! Every waking moment! If it weren't for me, they'd wipe this whole reservation off the map. I'm the last thing standing in their way. You understand that?"

Wayne breathed deeply. What could he say to that? He stared into Jackson's eyes and, a moment later, saw the anger disappear from them. There was nothing in its place. No sadness. A blank slate.

"Thank you for your input, Lieutenant Tully." Jackson looked down at his desk. "And for these. I have plenty to do today. You can go now."

———

Wayne found James and Molly at the black bear exhibit.

"That's what started this whole zoo, you know," he said, and they both turned to look at him. "A rescued orphan black bear cub. Dropped off at the fairgrounds here in Window Rock."

Molly grinned. "He must have been so cute!"

"Probably pretty cute," Wayne agreed.

"So how'd it go with Jackson?" James asked.

Wayne took a deep breath and chuckled. "Not great. But I'll tell you what I learned. Jackson knows about Linda's death. He claims he asked someone about Kay yesterday. And that someone happened to be Cecil Cody, who told him all about you and about Linda."

They walked slowly down the path, birds in cages squawking at them as they passed.

"Do you believe him? That he only just found out about Linda's death yesterday?" James asked.

"I don't know what to believe. It's clear that he's angry. But angry about what? Angry about the uranium spilled onto our land? Is everything else just piling on and he doesn't want to deal with it anymore?"

"Or is he angry that he's been intimidated by these people? That he's kept quiet?" James asked.

"Or," Wayne went on, "is he angry because we know that Linda knew and are investigating it and are going to find blood on his hands?"

"Plenty to be angry about," James said. "So, here's the scenario. Walk through it with me. Linda comes to Window Rock. Maybe she sits on a bench right outside the building until Jackson comes out. She tells him what she knows. Shows him the documents. Jackson seems appalled. He takes the documents. Tells her he will most certainly look into it. Not to worry. He'll handle it."

Wayne nodded and watched a family walk by. A little girl with a missing front tooth and a purple pleated dress smiled at him.

"Then Jackson goes to United. First option is that he says, 'What is this, you bastards? You've gone too far, about to poison my people. You better fix this.' UNC says, 'Sure, we'll fix it all right.' Then they kill Linda? But how do they know it's her? Why would Jackson give her name?"

They had reached the zoo gates. They stood in a small circle, thinking.

"I don't know," Wayne finally said.

"Second option is that Jackson says to United, 'This is a problem. Y'all should've told me. But don't worry. I'll handle it.' Then Jackson has Raymond Nez—or maybe someone else —kill Linda."

"What's in it for him?" Wayne asked.

"Maybe an ungodly amount of money."

"Okay, but let's think about option one first. Is there any way they coerce the name from Jackson? Or maybe they check their employee payroll list. Figure out it's Linda. Somehow."

Wayne knew he was grasping at straws. The obvious answer was that Jackson had had her killed. That Jackson was angry now because even after going through all that trouble to hide the evidence, to have Linda killed, still, Wayne and James had found out.

"I suppose there's a way they forced the name out of him. But I don't see how or why. At that point, Linda is irrelevant as far as Jackson is concerned. And even to United, Linda doesn't matter as much because now Jackson knows. And Jackson's angry, and Jackson is the problem."

"So, they find out some other way. And only for the purpose of scaring Jackson," Wayne countered. "That's what Linda was to them. A message. Because they can't go after Jackson directly. They can't kill the chairman of the Navajo Nation."

"So how do they find out?" James pressed.

"Maybe this is where the Codys come in," Wayne said, his voice getting stronger. "United goes to Cecil's brother. He looks into it and figures out it was Linda."

"But how?" James asked. Molly was clearly interested but also getting tired. She shifted her weight. Leaned over slightly for a moment.

"Think about how many Navajo work at the mill itself," James said. "They were probably dumping the waste into the dams themselves. You think they didn't see how weak it was? It's very likely one of them could have told."

"But they wouldn't have known that United knew about it. Or that United knew they were breaking the law. Especially if Jackson brought the documents to United. Showed them, maybe. Those documents would have confirmed that it *wasn't* a mill worker."

"But we can't know if he did. We don't know what he said to them."

"Why wouldn't he have mentioned the papers? That's the part that would have angered him the most. Otherwise, it's just a mistake to be rectified—and quick. But that's not what Linda would have told him or shown him. She would have shown him that they knew."

"Maybe," James conceded. "It seems like an awful lot of work for the Codys to accomplish in a week. First being asked to find the person and then to kill them. And what's the Codys' motivation to get involved in this? If anything, they have more stock in the health of the land than Jackson. They own sheep. They rely on the water supply. I would bet the Codys knew nothing about the uranium until yesterday, just like the rest of the reservation. They were asked to help cover up the death. Or at least get me off the trail. But they were on a need-to-know basis, and they sure as hell didn't know United was poisoning *their* land."

Wayne sighed. Why couldn't he accept that Jackson had ordered Linda killed? Why was it so hard for him to believe that money alone would motivate the man?

"What else could United have given Jackson, assuming it was scenario two, aside from money?" Wayne asked.

"Information?" James guessed.

"Votes?" Molly said in a quiet voice. James and Wayne regarded her curiously.

"Votes," James repeated. "Do you think Jackson needed votes?"

"The next election isn't for another two and a half years," Wayne said. "But that's a great guess, Molly."

"Do you know who his opponent will be?" James asked.

"I could take a pretty good guess. Timothy Emerson. Well-liked, funny, smart, college-educated just like Jackson. I would be very surprised if he didn't run."

Molly plopped on the ground right there, legs crossed, neck craned up toward them, the flat of her hand covering her eyes.

"So, maybe it is information if it's too early for votes. Information on Emerson. To help Jackson in the next election," James said.

"How would United's management know anything about Emerson that Jackson himself wouldn't already know? Unless . . ."

A new thought occurred to Wayne, apparently at the same time as it occurred to James.

"Unless it was *actually* information on Jackson," James said.

"Right," Wayne said. "Instead of threatening Jackson with his life . . ."

"They threatened to reveal his secrets," James finished. "That's a fate worse than death to a man like Jackson."

They stared at one another in new understanding.

"So it *was* Jackson," James said.

Wayne crossed his arms and shook his head. "It was Jackson."

[66]

JAMES

NO ONE LIKED ADMITTING DEFEAT, but James hated it more than most. He stood in front of Kay's front door and thought about how he had told her that they'd already won. That they had caught United. That they were going to fix things. But instead, they had been spending the last few days standing in line to drink bottled office water at the community center. At least he could deliver the news about Linda's suspected killer. He knocked. He expected Kay to be angry. He expected her to blame him. But when she came to the door, she hugged him tight.

James didn't know what to say. That he had moved too slow this whole time? That he was out of practice? But as much as James loved to blame himself, it wasn't really his fault. Jackson was, most likely, entirely to blame for Linda's death and a little at fault for the spill. But mostly, the spill was Henry Fields's fault. And whoever else knew and didn't do a damn thing. The governor. The state police.

He held Kay and neither spoke. He smelled her hair. It was floral and earthy. Like she had shampooed it and then worked outside in the sun, which was probably exactly what she had done.

"I'm sorry," he finally said. Kay only nodded, and he wondered if she was crying silently into his chest. He waited another minute before saying, "Wayne and I are pretty sure it was Jackson who killed your sister."

Kay breathed deeply and then pulled away.

"How are you sure?" she asked.

"At first we ran with your idea. That Jackson went to the mill and demanded they do something about it. But we don't think he would've given up Linda. Why would he?"

Kay bit her lip and looked just past him. He could tell she was thinking but continued anyway.

"We think that Jackson probably did go to the mill angry. And we're guessing that the mill management did threaten him, but not by killing your sister. They know that Jackson takes money from them—and from those other companies. They threatened to expose him, and so Jackson needed to silence your sister."

Kay searched his eyes for something, though he didn't know what.

"And we found a friend of Jackson's. Someone of the same clan who heads the Department of Health. He served in Vietnam as a medic, so that could explain the carving."

"And the overdose. Or whatever it was," Kay said.

"That too." James nodded. "I still can't explain the lack of bruising. I can't remember any signs of a struggle. But then again, I never examined her body. I don't know what shape the back of her head was in or her ribs. I didn't look under her fingernails. There are plenty of ways he could've overtaken her and covered it up well enough."

"And he would know us—Diné—well enough to know we wouldn't be surprised by an overdose and that we wouldn't ask for an autopsy."

James stared at her, waiting for some sort of reaction.

Finally, she nodded. "It makes perfect sense. So, what do we do? Nothing? Just know that it happened?"

"I don't think that's why you came to me in the first place, and it's not what I want from this, either. Molly, Wayne, Barbara and I are gonna talk about what's next tonight over dinner. Will you come? I want to find justice for your sister, Kay. I want to do everything in my power to make that happen."

"How?" Kay asked. "You're not even police anymore. And Jackson is Jackson. The most powerful man in Navajo Nation."

He grinned. "I think I've got a few more tricks up my sleeve."

Kay smiled back. "You are relentless. I bet you made one hell of a cop."

"That's debatable," James said. "I'll see you at seven?"

"See you at seven."

The five of them sprawled across Wayne's living room. James on one side of the couch, Kay on the other, Barbara on the floor, Molly draped across the recliner, feet hanging off the armrest. Wayne leaned against the wall, arms crossed, and paced every so often.

"Maybe we ought to try to get Jackson's phone records. See if he made calls to the mill or to Nez around that time."

"So what if he did?" James asked. "That doesn't prove anything. We need to find those original documents that Linda gave someone. I'll bet Jackson or Nez or whoever killed her still has them. They wouldn't destroy them. They might need them at some point."

"Maybe one of you ought to see if you can find them in Jackson's office," Barbara suggested.

"You gave him a copy of ours, didn't you, Wayne?" James asked.

"Yes."

"That won't work, then," he said. "We won't know if we've found our copy or hers."

"Nez is the key to this," Wayne said. "I think I need to talk to him. Assuming Jackson hasn't already warned him away."

"Hm," James said. "It's possible that he's been too busy with the spill. But I doubt it. If I were Jackson, it's the first thing I'd've done when you walked out of my office."

"I ought to try anyway," Wayne said.

"You think you can get him to talk?"

"I doubt he'll confess. But maybe he'll slip up. Admit he has Linda's documents, at least."

"How do you think you'll go about it?" James asked.

"At first I thought I should tell him about Linda outright. Act like I was coming to him for medical expertise or something. Maybe have Molly sketch out the carving on her arm and see how he reacted."

Try to take the man by surprise, in other words, James thought.

"But I don't think I'll get much that way. I don't see him getting comfortable enough in that situation to slip up."

James nodded. "I agree."

"What if, instead, I bring up the 'anonymous documents' left to me before the spill? What if I insinuate that Jackson told me to go see him? Confuse Nez a little. Why would I know, and why would Jackson give him up like that? He might reveal something trying to defend himself."

"I like that," James said. "And make sure he knows that you understand the difficult position Jackson has put him in."

"I better go soon before Jackson gets to him," Wayne said.

"Barbara, what do you know about Nez?" James asked.

"He's one of three children. His mother is highly respected here on the reservation. A real bull. Gets things done for the people. Doesn't just talk, like Jackson. She and Raymond are very close. His younger brother died in Vietnam. When Raymond got back from the war, he went to college. He lives in Gallup now and just got married last year to a nice young Diné woman."

"You said he had another sibling?" James asked.

"An older sister," Barbara said. "She's off the reservation, too. All the way out in California now."

"And Raymond seemed to adjust to life after the war all right? Even with his brother killed?"

"Oh, no," Barbara said. "He drank heavily when he got home. For years. Crashed his car. The family had a rough patch, for sure. But he turned around when he went to college. Got serious. He's real put together now."

"You think you can work with that, Wayne?" James asked.

Wayne sighed. "Easy. I got this, cowboy."

67

WAYNE

RAYMOND NEZ HAD a round baby face and a warm, easy smile. His hair was cut close to his head and his figure was trim. He looked like he'd just left boot camp. He welcomed Wayne into his office with a two-hand handshake and a sincere look in his eye. It did not make Wayne feel good. Nothing about the man read "killer," and Wayne questioned everything he was about to say and do.

"So, what brings you down to Window Rock, Lieutenant?" Raymond asked as Wayne sat down.

"I'm sure you're dealing with the effects of this uranium spill right now. I appreciate you seeing me on short notice."

Raymond gave a single nod, his intense gaze trained on Wayne.

"I . . . uh . . . spoke to Chairman Jackson just a few days ago."

Another nod.

"I told him I received these documents." Wayne fished out of his bag the new copies he had made especially for this visit. "I'm not sure from whom." He placed them on the desk and watched Raymond's eyes scan over them. He saw no trace of recognition, just the widening eyes of a shocked man. Finally, Raymond shook his head.

"This is not good," Raymond said. "Not good for United either. But also, it's not surprising. None of these companies care about the health of Indians. Or the health of anyone, for that matter. Money. That's what they care about."

"It seems that way, doesn't it?" Wayne said.

"This is good to know, though. Good to know. DNA legal services might like to have a look once people start complaining of health problems. Do you mind if I keep these?"

Wayne put on his best surprised face, though he *was* more surprised than he'd expected to be. Maybe Raymond was a good liar.

"You've never seen these before?" Wayne asked.

Now, Raymond appeared truly confused. "No. Should I have?"

"Like I said, an anonymous source left them for me. When I asked Jackson about them, he told me to come to you. Like, maybe he thought you'd left them? He seemed very unhappy."

Wayne expected the man to go pale or get angry or perhaps even look sadly resigned to some fate. But Raymond's bewildered expression didn't change.

"I have no idea why Jackson would mention me. Are you sure he wasn't simply saying that you needed to tell me? Or show me?"

If this was the man Jackson had chosen to kill Linda, he had chosen wisely, Wayne thought.

"No, no," Wayne said. "He most certainly implied that

they had come from you. And he wasn't happy about it. I thought it was strange."

Raymond sat back in his chair and frowned.

"If Teddy thought they had come from me, why did he have you bring them back to me?"

"I had some more questions for whoever left them. But I suppose that wasn't you?"

"I'll have to speak with him later. Had I known, I would obviously have taken precautions."

"Right," Wayne said. "He did put you in a difficult position by implying that the head of the health department knew about this."

Raymond raised an eyebrow, and Wayne went on, "I'm not going to say anything. To anyone. I believe what you're telling me. I respect you. I respect your mom. She'd make a hell of a chairman, I tell you."

Raymond sank into his chair a little and smiled. "She would," he said. "The woman has nerves of steel. She's incorruptible. I don't think she's ever made a bad decision in her whole life."

Raymond was clearly comparing her to Jackson—not that he would ever admit it.

"Well," Wayne went on. "If you didn't give me these documents, you haven't got any idea who did, do you?"

"Like I said, I would've done something with this information. No one would have shared it with me if they wanted to keep it a secret. And no offense, Lieutenant, but I also wouldn't have quietly handed it over to the police. But there are plenty of politicians and councilmen with secrets to keep. No shortage of people to suspect. Living on the reservation, though?" Raymond looked back down at the papers and shook his head. "I don't know why any Diné would hide this."

Wayne nodded. *Give me a name*, he silently begged. The way Raymond kept opening his mouth slightly and then closing it again, he clearly had one in mind. At least one.

"I'd appreciate any help I can get. If you give me a name, it won't leave this room."

Raymond eyed him cautiously. "Why do you want to know?" he asked. "If you find out someone *did* know about this," he tapped the paper, "what will you do to them?"

Wayne thought about that. If it weren't for Linda, if someone had just had this information and didn't do anything with it, what would he do? What could he do?

"Usually," Wayne answered, "if someone is hiding something like this, it isn't the beginning or the end of their corruption. Usually there is more to uncover. More dirt to dig up. If you smell shit, there's usually shit around, right?"

Raymond studied him but didn't seem angered or hurt.

"Let me think about it, Lieutenant Tully, and I'll get back to you. I live in Gallup. You find yourself over there often?"

Wayne grinned. "Often enough."

Raymond stood and shook Wayne's hand. "You'll stay by your phone, won't you?"

"Yes, sir," Wayne said.

Raymond walked him to the door and patted his back. "I'll be seeing you soon," he said.

When Wayne stepped into the sunlight, he chuckled to himself. He had either just made an incredibly helpful friend or an extremely dangerous enemy.

68

JAMES

LINDA AND GEORGE's home phone bill for May had been left in the station mailbox, but it had clearly been tampered with. The last phone call listed had been on May 15, but when James measured the bill against another sheet of paper, he could see the bottom had obviously been cut off. Just enough that there was no way to tell how many sheets the bill had originally been.

"We need a warrant," James said to Wayne. "For the original phone bill."

Wayne held up the bill and closed one eye. "You think George did this?"

"I don't know," James said. "It was probably sittin' in the mailbox for a few hours. George told me his shift starts at 3 a.m. Could've been him. Could've been someone else. Either way, we need those original records. Someone is tryin' to hide something."

Once the warrant was obtained the phone company needed a few hours to get the information he requested. So,

James made his way through the numbers on the tampered phone bill, finding out which person belonged to each number, and asking if they remembered Linda going to Window Rock in May. None of them did.

James went to the fax machine. Those records were coming any minute now. He paced. He left the room only to pour himself another coffee. Finally, the fax machine started to dial and beep. Something was coming in. He scanned it quickly. There was a new number there that hadn't appeared on George's copy. One he had seen before. It showed up twice. His heart beat quickly, but his mind worked even faster. Could there be an explanation? There could always be an explanation. But the more he thought about it, the more it made sense.

Damn. He had been wrong, then, about Cecil Cody. Completely wrong. He shook his head at himself. It made perfect sense. He picked up the phone one last time.

"Hello, this is Gloria."

"Can you come by?" James asked. "I've got some information."

He heard her moving some things around.

"I'd love to," she said. "Tomorrow? I've got some things to tell you, too. I was so distracted by this awful spill the last time I saw you, I completely forgot."

"Tomorrow sounds good," he said. "I'll see you then."

James hung up and gathered his things. His hat. His thermos. His pack of cigarettes. He would speak with Wayne later. He needed to go find Molly.

The next day around noon, Gloria pulled up in front of Wayne's porch, where James was waiting. Her smile was tight. Her hair and outfit flawless. *Damn, she looks like a movie star*, he thought.

"I'm sorry I haven't been in touch as much as I should have been," she said.

James leaned against the railing. "Lots going on around here," he said. "We've both been busy. But I wanted to tell you about a lead. Hear your thoughts."

She nodded. She was still standing next to her Barracuda. "Of course. Should we go get some lunch?"

"Sure," James said. "Why don't you come in for a minute first. I've just got a few more things to do before I'm ready. Some dishes to wash real quick." He gave her a crooked smile. "Be a good houseguest, ya know?"

Gloria smiled, too, and walked up the porch steps.

Just then, Molly came bounding through the front door, a grin plastered across her face.

"Gloria!" she gushed.

Gloria gave her a hug. "You look stunning today," she said, and Molly actually blushed.

"Oh my gosh, you're driving that car again!" Molly squealed.

Gloria laughed. "I always do. It's my only one."

"Can I look inside? I've never been in one before!"

Gloria tossed her the keys. "Take it for a spin if you want." She winked. "But not off the reservation! No major highways!"

Giggling, Molly gave her a little salute before hopping down the stairs.

James held the front door open for Gloria.

"Well, aren't you sweet?" she said. He offered her a seat at the table, but she shook her head. "I'll talk while you scrub. I have something I think you should know about."

She glanced over her shoulder.

"It's just us here," James said, and she leaned against the doorframe.

"You know I went to the Shonto jail and spoke with Dale."

James turned the faucet on. "Uh huh."

"Well, he told me that when he last saw Linda, she was talking about George. She was upset about something he did. She wouldn't tell Dale what it was. This was probably only a week before she died, although I'm not sure how much we can trust Dale's timeline."

"Or version of events," James added. Gloria swatted the thought away and crossed her arms.

"I confirmed it with George," she said. He looked at her, eyebrows raised. "I mean, George wouldn't tell me what it was, either. But he got very serious and told me he didn't want to discuss it, so clearly it was something."

James picked up a plate. "Hmmm."

"Dale was rambling about how we shouldn't trust Kay, that she probably knew or had been in on it with him or something, but again, we need to consider the source. Still, I think it's worth pursuing. If it happened right before Linda was killed, it might be important."

"Maybe," James said. He turned off the water and dried the plate with a towel.

"I was thinking you could talk to Kay. You two seem awfully . . . close." She said it with just a hint of bitterness.

James grunted. "We're friends, yes. So, you want me to take advantage of her trust?"

"If it helps us learn what happened to Linda, then yes."

He turned the water back on and rinsed his coffee mug.

"Will you?" Gloria asked.

"All right."

"So. What did you want to talk to me about?"

"Do you know Raymond Nez? He's the head of the Department of Health for the Navajo Nation."

Gloria chewed her lip before shaking her head.

"I'm sure I've spoken to him before for stories, but I can't remember."

"Not for this one?"

"I haven't spoken to anyone about this one. Other than Dale."

"I meant the uranium story."

"Oh." Gloria's face reddened. "Well, not yet. But I probably will. Why?"

"He's a Vietnam vet, too," James said. "Former medic."

He watched her. She tried to stay impassive, but he could tell she was intrigued.

"I was hoping you could help me look into him. I don't know. See what you can dig up on the guy. If it's worth pursuing, maybe we can interview him."

He turned the faucet off again and towel-dried the mug.

"You see, Wayne and I think that Linda went to someone in the government. Maybe Jackson, maybe not. Anyway, Raymond Nez looks suspicious to me, wouldn't you say?"

Gloria nodded. "He's definitely a possibility."

James smirked. "Glad you agree. So, I help you by talking to Kay and you help me by looking into Raymond Nez?"

"Deal."

She didn't even asked why he didn't want to do it himself.

MOLLY

MOLLY'S DAD had told her exactly what to do. Showed her, even. And so, while James spoke with Gloria, Molly got to work.

She felt shaky and nervous but excited, too, and she knew she wouldn't let him down. She felt the weight of her revolver in her purse against her hip. She didn't exactly know why she had brought it, but James had been right. It made her feel just a little safer. A little more in control.

She had also brought her Polaroid camera. She worked fast, her heart drumming in her ears. Once she was done, she felt relief. And pride. And fear.

This changed everything.

ADRIEL

ADRIEL WAS OUT OF BREATH. He had just finished a basketball game with his cousins and their neighbor and a few of their friends from school. He liked it there in Shonto. His oldest cousin, Nolan, always stood up for him. So even if these kids thought Adriel was a freak—and he assumed they did—Nolan wouldn't let them say it. And Nolan was a big kid. He didn't seem to be afraid of anything. Adriel wished Nolan could be his big brother instead of just a cousin.

Adriel wiped his sweaty forehead with the bottom of his shirt.

"Bye, Adriel!" one of the friends shouted as Adriel veered off the road toward his aunt and uncle's house. He turned and waved. Nolan and Zonnie, his cousins, were still a little ways down the road.

He took the porch steps two at a time like always but stopped short when he saw something lying on the doormat.

He stood over it for a moment and then crouched down to pick it up. But when he saw what it was, his chest tightened. His hands began to shake.

RAYMOND

RAYMOND HAD ALWAYS KNOWN this day would come but not how or why or when. The day when Raymond Nez stopped simply surviving and started to live a life he was proud of. To do the right thing. The thing he should've done years ago.

When Raymond came home from Vietnam, he'd felt like his life was already over. He hated himself for failing so many dying soldiers and innocent civilians, and he hated the Vietcong who'd killed his little brother. He hated most people back here, back home, who kept living their lives as if hell hadn't erupted from the core of the earth and threatened to suck every person on the planet back down with it.

He hated waking up in the morning. He hated looking at his mother's face. He hated going to the store for a gallon of milk. And so he drank with the sole purpose of hating everything just a little bit less, even if it meant the death of him. He wasn't a particular man in most things, but he found vodka and whiskey went down the easiest and never left the house without a bottle of one or the other.

Every day he woke up again, he was surprised. But the day he woke up in a hospital bed, his mother's tears hitting his forehead, was the day he realized just how selfish he had been. His mother—his good and strong and compassionate mother—had lost one son already. How could he cause her more pain? And so, that day he made a promise to himself. It wasn't anything crazy. He wasn't one for grand gestures. It was simple. Survive the next day without alcohol. And then the day after that. One day at a time.

It was how anyone did anything, and yet, Raymond found it to be one of the hardest things he'd ever done. To wake up every day, to look at himself in the mirror, to remember what had happened in Vietnam, and then, to simply go about his day with no crutch, no Band-Aid. To feel the pain and guilt and hatred, raw as it was, and to move through it anyway.

But he had. He had done it, and now, he rarely thought about drinking. Even on his bad days. But he knew part of the reason he had been so successful was that he had kept his head down. He worried about those things that were within his control. And when he heard things about other people— things that would make him angry, things that would require him to get involved in another's business—he shut down. He didn't want to get involved. Didn't need to. He put those things out of his mind and went about his day. Still, he heard about them and knew what was happening, and more and more, he'd started to become uncomfortable with this policy of his.

And then, Wayne Tully walked into his office and offered him a hand. After Wayne left, Raymond thought about all the things he had tried—and failed—to forget. The corruption, the secrets, the lies piling up all around him.

Now, here were these documents that might or might not prove that someone in this government was dirty.

Raymond reminded himself of all the shit he'd been through. Of how hard and long he had worked with wailing, dying men all around him. Sweat dripping into his eyes. The blood of soldiers staining his fingernail beds so bad that it took months to scrub out. This would be nothing.

Raymond knew what he *couldn't* tell Wayne Tully. He couldn't tell him that the chairman of the Navajo Nation—Raymond's own blood—was the dirtiest of all. But he could tell him other things. And he would.

———

Wayne pulled up to Raymond's house five minutes after their agreed-upon meeting time. He climbed out of his truck, put his hat on, and went up to Raymond, who was already waiting and who opened the glass door and shook Wayne's hand.

"Thank you for welcoming me into your home," Wayne said.

"Of course. Please, come in. Make yourself comfortable."

Wayne seemed like an easygoing guy. Easy to talk to. It must have been an important trait to have in his line of work.

After Raymond made some tea, he and Wayne sat across from each other in the living room, Raymond on the couch, Wayne on the loveseat.

"So those documents," Raymond started. "They just appeared on your desk?"

"At the station, yes."

"And who do you think left them?"

"I haven't got a clue," Wayne said.

"But Jackson said to talk to me?"

"That's right," Wayne said.

Why? Raymond thought. Did Jackson want Raymond to rat on the government officials Raymond had suspected of corruption? To what end? Was Jackson using Raymond to clear away his own dirt? He wasn't sure any of them were involved in this particular thing. But they very well could be. They were involved in enough.

"I've got a few names for you," Raymond said. "I didn't know about this—this uranium business—and so I don't know who's involved. But I do know the old heads on the council get their kickbacks from any corporate dealings on rez land. Unfortunately, they're very good at hiding it. I don't have any proof to offer you other than my word."

"Your word is enough for me," Wayne said. "It'll get me started."

"You don't seem surprised," Raymond said.

"My wife is on the council," Wayne said. "She's had her suspicions. She's not very popular, though, so she's not even allowed in the meetings where they would admit such things. They're very careful about what they say around her. But she's noticed."

"A woman council member. Like my mother was."

"Like your mother was. So you know it's not an easy job."

Raymond chuckled. "No. No, it's not easy."

Wayne sipped his tea. He was more relaxed this time. Not rushing Raymond at all.

"They aren't the most open with me, either," Raymond

said. "But they also aren't the most careful. I've got a reputation for being quiet at work, someone who's not going to rock the boat."

Wayne nodded, listening intently.

"I've heard Cecil Cody a few times. I think he's involved in drugs. He's always talking about funding rehab programs, and every now and then, he'll throw his money at one. I think it's funneled through the church. The drugs and the dirty money. But I'm not sure."

"Cecil is from Sanostee, so it doesn't surprise me. Everyone sort of knows what the Codys are about. But for the most part, they do a good job of staying off my radar."

"Another one is Aaron Hunt," Raymond went on. "He's from Tsegi. He's involved with the coal mining company over there. Lots of dough right in his pocket to look the other way when it comes to regulations and safety. Again, he's never said it outright. But he sure makes a lot of effort to keep everyone away from that company. Makes sure no one questions what they're doing. Or makes a fuss. Just leaves them be."

"Hmmm," Wayne said. "Sounds like something similar could be happening with United."

"I wouldn't be surprised," Raymond said. "If that's the case, my suspicion would be Cecil Cody. I believe his brother works for them."

"Well, if he's involved, he didn't leave those documents for me to catch him. Someone was ratting him out."

"Someone close to him who knows about it but thinks it's wrong?" Raymond guessed.

"Maybe one of Cecil's sons," Wayne said. "Anyone else you can think of who's involved in dirty politics?"

"Jonah Dennison," Raymond said. "From Many Farms. He has a history of helping . . . officials." He paused and swallowed. "Helping officials acquire land for the Nation. He's a lawyer. He makes sure all of it is done legally. But there are lots of personal payments right after these dealings. Somehow, the Nation is paying for the land, but councilmen are getting paid, too."

"So, more kickbacks," Wayne said. "More loopholes."

"Exactly."

"A lawyer, huh?" Wayne said, almost to himself.

"Do you think he could've been the one to leave those documents?" Raymond asked.

"I suppose anyone could be," Wayne said. "This is a safe way to clear someone's conscience without admitting to anything."

"Or someone could be informing on someone else," Raymond said.

"Without context, it's hard to say."

Wayne looked distracted now, his thoughts elsewhere. "Well, Raymond," he finally said. "This was helpful." He stood up and brought his teacup to the kitchen. He shook Raymond's hand.

"Can I call you with more questions if something else comes up?"

Raymond smiled. He opened the door for Wayne.

"Please do."

CECIL

IF THERE WAS one thing Cecil Cody respected, it was a brave man. That was why when James Pinter strolled up to Cecil's front door all by himself, Cecil let him in. James was armed, sure. If he hadn't been, Cecil would have known that he was a stupid man, and Cecil had no time for stupid men.

He listened as James Pinter sat at his kitchen table and spun tales of secrets and lies and murder. Cecil wished he could say he'd known about it all already. But he couldn't. It was one thing to play the fool, but to be played a fool made Cecil furious. And so, when James asked him outright, he told him. He told him every little bit of it.

And when James walked back out Cecil's door, he left promising he wouldn't go after any of the Codys for what they had done to him. It was as good as forgotten. James Pinter shook Cecil's hand. Looked him right in the eye. "It's been a pleasure," he said.

That man, Cecil thought, must have been one hell of a cop.

GLORIA

GLORIA HAD BEEN to the courthouse, the DMV, the University of New Mexico, and the veterans hospital searching desperately for something, anything, on Raymond Nez. She even called the military personnel records center to request his records. Now, she sat with all of it on her desk.

She found the car accident first. Nez was an alcoholic. She stored that away.

She hadn't wanted to investigate any Navajo, but at this point, she had no other choice. Because Dale was out of the picture. Because of the carving. Nez made sense. She had to make it fit. She just needed to find enough to convince James.

She had been stupid to put so much confidence into the Dale theory. What had she expected James to do? Force a confession? She supposed she had expected Dale to say or do something outrageous, unpredictable as he was. She had also, probably, underestimated James. She had made a lot of mistakes, actually.

She read Raymond Nez's service record. It seemed to Gloria that he had been a perfect combat medic. There was no evidence of a man who'd shirked his duties—no reprimands, no cowardice.

But then, Gloria found it. A passionate letter from Raymond to President Johnson about the atrocities he'd witnessed at the hands of the US troops. Rapes. Torture. It read like some of the others she had dug up for My Lai years ago.

It was the closest Gloria was going to get to any kind of link between this man and what had happened to Linda. She picked up the phone and dialed the number for Sanostee PD.

"Hello. It's Gloria Fenwick. I'm looking for James Pinter. Is he there today?"

"I haven't seen him," the man said. "Better call him at Wayne's home number."

"Thanks." Gloria hung up. She ran over what she would say to him before picking up the phone again.

Raymond Nez had been angry about Vietnam for a while now. The carving was a message. But what message? A message to Jackson for making Raymond do his dirty work? That was good, Gloria thought. A message to Jackson. She dialed Wayne's number.

"This is the Tully residence," James answered.

"Hi, James. It's Gloria."

"Hi, Gloria. What'd you find out?"

She took a deep breath.

"Raymond was clearly upset about what was happening in Vietnam. He wrote a letter to the president. He was one of those soldiers who was unable to live with what he'd seen. The letter detailed some of it. He wasn't at My Lai, but he was shaken by witnessing similar things."

"So you think that makes him the likely carver?" James asked.

Gloria chose her words carefully. "Maybe Raymond wasn't too happy about doing Jackson's dirty work. But he couldn't say no for whatever reason. This is his silent protest. He was forced to kill his own—an innocent woman. Just like the soldiers in Vietnam were forced to take innocent lives."

Gloria didn't think it was a bad theory, but James was quiet on the other end.

"I think it was him," she said.

"Wayne's been workin' on getting Raymond to turn on Jackson. Maybe with this letter, we can pressure him to confess. Convince him not to take the fall for Jackson. So many like him took the fall for LBJ. He doesn't need to do it again here."

Gloria smiled. James believed her. This was messier than Dale, but it was something.

"I'll meet you in Window Rock with the letter," she said. "I think you'll be better at getting the confession out of him. But I'll be there."

"I'll call Wayne," James said. "They've built a relationship. He can set up the meeting."

"Perfect," she said. "How much time do y'all need?"

"Tomorrow is good," James said. "We'll meet you tomorrow."

Gloria hung up. She gathered her documents into a nice, neat pile and carefully slid them into a folder.

until Officer Sanchez pulled up.

[74]

JAMES

As MUCH AS James would have liked Molly to witness the
results of what she had done, he also knew how these things
usually went. They weren't pretty or easy, and a guilty
person could be unpredictable when they were cornered.

"You did good," he told Molly that morning before
leaving for Window Rock. He gave her a Queen album called
Jazz he had picked out at the store a few days before.

"Your bonus," he said. "For finding Carl Assman."

Molly grinned and hugged him. "Be safe, Dad."

He hugged her back. "That's 'Captain Daddy' to you."

She giggled. James was a lucky man. He knew that now.
If only he could get those years back.

He climbed into Wayne's truck with everything he
needed. Linda's phone calls, Molly's Polaroids, Cecil Cody's
recording. They would meet Officer Sanchez there. He might
not have been able to do anything about a uranium spill, but
he could do something about a homicide.

When Wayne and James pulled up outside of Raymond
Nez's office building, they could see Sanchez's patrol car

parked a few blocks away. They waited in their parked truck until Gloria's Barracuda pulled up.

James and Wayne got out and walked over. She flashed a smile.

"Good to see you, Wayne," she said. "You boys ready for this?"

"You bet," James answered.

They took the elevator to the fourth floor. Wayne knocked on Raymond's office door.

"Come in," he called.

James opened the door. "After you," he said to Gloria. She walked in, head held high.

When he closed the door, he glanced behind him at Sanchez, who was already in the room, leaning against the wall and grinning. Gloria hadn't noticed him yet. She stuck her hand out for Raymond to shake.

"Mr. Nez. Thank you for meeting with us," she said.

"Of course. Please sit."

That was when Gloria saw Officer Sanchez. She froze.

"What's he doing here?" she asked. "We haven't even gotten a confession yet."

"Sure we have," Wayne said. James pulled the recording device out of his satchel and pressed play. His voice filled the small office.

"So, Mr. Cody, if you could repeat what you just told me, I'd be grateful. Who was it that asked you to run me out of town?"

Then, Cecil Cody's voice. "Miss Gloria Fenwick, the reporter."

Gloria gasped. She went ghost white. "I don't know what he's talking about."

"Shhhh," James hushed her. "There's more."

"Did she tell you why or how Linda Morris was murdered?"

"No, she did not. She told me that you, Mr. Pinter, were investigating a suspicious death and that it was in my best interest to keep you away from it. That you would be poking around in things that weren't your business."

"And you didn't question her? You just . . . did her bidding?" James asked on the recording.

"Well, you see, Miss Fenwick has some information about me. About some of my not-so-pleasant extralegal activities. She threatened me. Told me she'd write a story about me unless I did everything in my power to keep you away."

"So she blackmailed you?"

"That's correct," Cecil said. James stopped the recording.

"That's just . . . that's not . . ." Gloria spluttered. James had yet to see the woman flustered like this. "I mean, that's ridiculous! Why? Why would I do that?" she finally managed.

"We were hoping you could tell us that," Wayne said.

"Y'all don't believe him, do you? He's clearly lying. Trying to get immunity for his own crimes."

"Maybe I'd think that," James said, "except for a few other things. The reason I visited Cecil Cody in the first place was because I received a copy of Linda's phone records. And guess whose phone number she called not once, but twice in the week before she died?"

Gloria was speechless.

"And then I've got these Polaroid photos here. The documents given to Linda by a United employee, found in the trunk of your car. Hidden in the spare tire compartment."

"What?" Gloria's face reddened. "You set that up! Or someone did. For a photo! I've never seen those before in my life. You told me about them. And that was the first time I knew they existed!"

"Don't you worry," James said. "Officer Sanchez here has got a warrant to search your car right now, so we'll know for sure if they're there. You know how we know they're Linda's? She took notes. Right in the margins. In Navajo, mind you. Identified as Linda's handwriting by her own sister."

"You . . . you . . . you set me up! You put those documents there!"

"Now why would I do that?" James asked.

"This whole time you've hated me. You've hated that I've been suspicious of Dale and of every soldier involved. It doesn't make any sense, because you of all people should know what they're capable of. You know what they did, in gory detail. And you've hindered this investigation every step of the way because you won't admit how dangerous they all are!"

James chuckled. "Frankly, I'm a little embarrassed it took me this long. And then I had to get hit in the face with it. I suppose I'm a little rusty. I was distracted by the idea that Linda must have gone to Jackson with this information. But Linda never went to Jackson. She remembered that white woman who was always hanging around. The journalist who'd reported on the high school opening. She went to her instead. She went to you."

"This is ridiculous." Gloria tried to stand up, but Officer Sanchez held up a hand to stop her.

"You aren't going anywhere, ma'am," he said.

"Am I under arrest, then?"

"You're being detained until I can execute this search warrant on your car."

Gloria glared at James. "I'll sue you for this, you asshole."

"You can try. I don't think you'll be very successful."

She threw her arms up.

"Why would I kill Linda Morris? I've done nothing but help the Navajo people!"

James nodded. "I was a little confused about that at first, too. But then I thought about it. You learned a lot in Vietnam. You went there ready to expose the US government, ready to expose the military. And you tried. But your stories got buried, cut, sometimes outright censored. Your publisher refused to run them. I talked to some people back at your office. You sent the stories back, sure. But you got reprimanded. Told this wasn't the kind of the thing you'd been asked to report on. Until My Lai happened. Until the military was already caught. It just had to be a big enough story, you learned. You couldn't let United bury this one. You couldn't let your publisher warn them first. You had to let the tragedy happen. And for that, you had to silence Linda. Your reporting here, on the reservation, it was never about the Navajo people. It was always about *you* being the hero. The hero you so badly wanted to be in Vietnam."

Gloria's stare was icy, but a tear rolled down her cheek.

"You don't have proof," she whispered.

"Officer Sanchez is gonna help us with that. Oh, and one other thing, you probably assumed the BIA would dispose of the needle. Or maybe you didn't. Maybe you didn't think that far ahead. Lord knows only a stupid person would have kept Linda's documents. So, maybe you didn't even think about what would happen to the needle. The BIA didn't dispose of it. Molly and I found it. Had it sent off to the lab. Turns out, there's absolutely no evidence that the syringe contained any narcotic. No residue at all. So then I made some calls. According to your pharmacy, you ordered almost twice the insulin you normally do for the month of May. You don't need me to tell you that insulin is an incredibly effective poison."

Gloria's one tear turned into an angry sob. "How dare you? My health concerns are none of your fucking business! Fuck you, James Pinter!"

"Can you handle this, gentlemen, while I search Miss Fenwick's car? It might be just about time to read her her Miranda rights," Officer Sanchez said.

"We've got this, Trooper," Wayne said. "Please proceed with the search."

Gloria crossed her legs and sank into her chair. Her jaw clenched. Her hands formed into fists in her lap. She was shaking.

"I understand," James said to her after a minute. "The desperation. The feeling like nothing you do makes any bit of a difference. Why pursue truth if justice doesn't follow?"

No one said anything.

"And you're probably right in thinking that story wouldn't have done much. Even if your publisher had allowed it to go to print. Maybe United would have fixed their dam. Maybe they would have slapped a Band-Aid on it. A half-assed, temporary solution. That's more likely. But it wouldn't have been much of a story."

"The thing is," Wayne jumped in, "I don't think this story will do much, either. It was awfully bold of you to assume that anyone would care about Indians either way. Even with burns on our children's skin and poison coursing through our veins."

"But it *is* a story now," Gloria finally said. "It was on the front page. People couldn't ignore it."

"At first, I thought that when Linda met with you to talk and hand over the papers, you must have snuck up behind her and knocked her unconscious. On the head. But no. She would've met you in the parking lot at the gas station. And then there was all that extra insulin."

"I did not hurt Linda. I would never have . . ." Gloria started.

"You killed her, though."

"Stop," she said. "Just stop."

"If you didn't knock her out, how did you inject her in a way that she didn't see it coming? That's what my buddy Raymond and I talked about. You know his medical background, don't you? Well, anyway. He told me a thing or two about insulin. Why don't you tell her what you told me?" James asked Raymond.

"The thing about insulin," Raymond began, "is that if you were trying to kill someone with it, you wouldn't want to just jam it in. If you hit muscle, the effects of the insulin wouldn't be as great. Ideally, you'd want to hit a vein. That would cause the victim to lose consciousness almost immediately."

"And where might there be a good vein for that?"

"There's a big ole one right here on your chest." Raymond showed them. "The biggest one in your body, in fact. It's called the superior vena cava, and if you can get the needle to the right of the sternum, in between the ribs, you'll hit it. Straight shot to the heart at that point."

"Right where that stain was. That stain I thought was a coffee spill. It was actually blood."

Gloria's lip started to quiver. She took a loud, sobbing breath.

"The real fuckup, though," James went on, "were the carvings. Hell, if you hadn't had done that, I might have just let all this go. That right there was the fuckup. And it's also how I knew—how I was *sure* even before I spoke to Cecil Cody—that it was you. Because you're the only one who still fucking cares about My Lai, Gloria. Everyone else has moved on. No one even remembers. Except for you and me and those people whose family members were slaughtered. That's it."

"You're wrong, James Pinter!" Gloria shouted. "I *made* people care! I seared that shit into their memories! When I went to those My Lai trials day after day and I listened to what those boys had done, even though it made me nauseous, even though it made me remember all the shit I would've rather forgotten, I reported on it. *You* sure as hell didn't do shit during those trials! Do you think regular people would have put themselves through what I did? In Vietnam first, and then that? Everyone was horrified by what I told them! And they'll be horrified by this, too. People are soft and selfish. They don't want to hear about these terrible things, and they don't want to pick up one finger to do what's best for other people. I tried to talk her out of it. But she just wouldn't keep quiet. A lesser journalist would've run with the story then. But *I* was willing to do what needed to be done. To make a damn difference for the rest of us!"

James raised his eyebrows at Wayne. There would be more, he knew.

"Now these companies will *have* to pay. There will be *actual* damages now. United will feel the pain. And people will see them for what they really are. Crooks. But if Linda had told, they would've gotten away with their bullshit. *Again!* I'm done with doing exactly what these assholes want. They'll make people suffer as long as it fills their bank accounts. *I* didn't make anyone suffer. I doubt Linda felt any pain at all." Now she had a wild look in her eyes. A desperate look. "I told her I had to hook her up to a microphone. She unbuttoned her top just enough. She . . . she trusted me. It was quick. I swear."

The room was silent, then, other than Gloria's heavy breathing. James thought she was about to burst into tears again, but he didn't care. He would talk. There was no more spell to break.

"And Adriel?" he asked.

"He wasn't part of the plan," Gloria muttered. "I didn't know she was bringing him."

"And it was fine because he doesn't speak, but you threatened him anyway."

"I didn't know! Maybe he could write."

"He's a damn kid!" James shouted.

Gloria finally began to cry again.

"Shit," Wayne hissed. "And I sent that poor boy your postcard."

"You're telling us this because Officer Sanchez is gonna find those documents, isn't he?" James asked.

Gloria nodded. Just then, Officer Sanchez returned.

"I think we've got enough to arrest her," he said.

James sighed. "I'd say so."

[75]
WAYNE

OFFICER SANCHEZ HAD ARRESTED Gloria with little problem, and James accompanied them to the station for questioning and evidence documentation. Wayne was confident that Gloria would sign a confession.

Wayne and Raymond now sat in Raymond's office. Raymond had suggested grabbing some lunch or coffee, but first Wayne had a proposition.

"I have to be honest with you," he said. "I know this morning James and I only told you what you needed to know."

"Bombarded me with it, more like." Raymond grinned.

"James and I have been investigating this homicide for a few months now. Recently, you became a suspect."

Raymond smile faded quickly. He sat back in his chair, arms crossed. "Wow," he said.

"You weren't a suspect for very long. Shortly after I first came and met with you, James figured out it was really the reporter. But I had to keep up the ruse so she wouldn't feel the heat."

Raymond nodded. He forced a tight smile. "And here I went blabbing about all those people to you."

"The documents were not left at the station anonymously. James obtained them. But we knew the woman who was killed—Linda—had a copy. And we knew they were out there somewhere."

"Find the papers, find the killer," Raymond said.

"We were hoping," Wayne said.

"So maybe we can forget all that I told you about the councilmembers and the lawyer?" Raymond suggested.

"I don't think we should," Wayne said. "I wasn't lying about my wife and her suspicions. I've been wanting to do something about these dirty politicians for a while, but I always had an excuse. Too much else to do. Too small of a force. Both of those things are still true. But I want to make this a priority."

Wayne folded his hands in his lap. "The last time we spoke, you said you didn't have any proof other than your word."

"That's right," Raymond said.

"How would you feel about helping me find some proof?" Raymond sighed. He was quiet.

"We're up against some major forces here," he said at last.

Wayne raised both of his hands to stop him.

"I know," Wayne said. "And I have a hunch that this goes further. All the way to the top. I won't ask you to implicate your own kin. But Jackson might get caught up in our investigation eventually. It could destroy him. I want you to think about that before giving me your answer. But think about this, too."

He leaned forward, forearms rested on his legs. "You and

I believe in the same kind of future for Diné. Prosperous, yes. Of course. But true and honest. No cutting corners. No making deals with men who would rather see us disappear. Would rather push us away for good, to take care of us once and for all."

Wayne paused, choosing his next words carefully.

"We've been promised leadership who will stand up to these giants. But instead, they've given in. They've proved that everyone has a price. Including them. But us? Me and you? We believe in accountability. I know this about you because that reporter, Gloria? She found the letter you wrote to the president while you were over in Vietnam. And you know what that tells me? That you aren't afraid to fight for what's right. Even if that means standing up to your own people. Whether it's a fellow soldier or fellow Diné."

Wayne watched Raymond lift his head a little higher. Watched his breath quicken. Wayne stood up.

"Think about it," he said. "Don't say anything now. Just think about it."

Raymond nodded but remained seated, so Wayne walked around the desk to shake the man's hand. He patted his shoulder. And then Wayne left.

[76]

KAY

WHEN KAY SAW JAMES APPROACH, a cloud of dust in his wake, she knew why he'd come. She didn't know how she knew, but she did. Her heart began to thud in her chest, but she forced a smile. Leaned against the corral. James helped himself through the gate.

"You've got some news for me," she said. It wasn't a question.

"We've arrested Linda's killer," he said.

Though Kay had known it was coming, her knees still went weak. James caught her before she could fall. He scooped her up and held her.

She had no words. Only relief. Relief that was so strong that at first she laughed. It felt so freeing. But then, it turned into a sob, and she felt the pain of her sister's death crash over her again.

Finally, she pulled away. "Was it Nez?" she asked.

"No," James said. "It was Gloria Fenwick."

Kay gasped. "The reporter?" she asked, stupidly. "How? Why?"

"She injected your sister with insulin. Gloria's a diabetic and a morality warrior. Thought your sister's life was a small price to pay to write a grand story that would punish United."

"What do you mean?" Kay asked. James led her to the stable, where they sat on some wooden crates.

"Linda went to the press. Not to Jackson. Gloria understood that if she reported it, United would pivot and the contamination would get swept under the rug. She wanted a bigger story. She knows that only the most grotesque acts of apathy move the needle. Death and destruction change things. She tried to convince Linda to keep the documents to herself at first—or so she claims. But Linda was persistent."

Kay could feel herself trembling now. "That stupid bitch," she said through clenched teeth. "I trusted her!"

"I know," James said. "But she confessed. She's going to prison."

Kay stood and walked away from him. Her sister had died. Her people were being poisoned. All for a story. She sobbed violently. She kicked a bale of hay. Over and over. James didn't go to her. When she felt the energy draining from her body, the sorrow taking over instead, she stopped kicking. She stood with her back to him, breathing in and out until her heartbeat slowed. At least she had answers now. Useless though they were.

She sat down beside James again. "Thank you," she said.

"I'm sorry I didn't figure it out sooner," he said. "I ought to have."

"You didn't have much to go on. To be honest, I didn't think you'd ever get a confession or an arrest. This is . . . I'm grateful."

"Can I ask you something?" he asked.

"Maybe."

"Dale said Linda was upset about something regarding George. To be honest, the man has been pretty strange this whole time. Do you know what was going on between them?"

"No," Kay said. "Maybe that's what she was trying to tell me when I blew up at her. I don't know what's going to happen to Adriel now. I don't know if I can trust George. I've never really trusted him. Maybe, if you stick around, you can help me figure it all out."

James raised his eyebrows. "You want me to stick around?"

"I wouldn't object, but the Codys might," Kay said.

"Nah," James said. "Cecil and I made nice. Turns out Gloria was playing him, too. He went on record with that."

Kay's mouth fell open. "How did you get him to do that?"

"I'm just *that* charming." He grinned.

Kay toed a weed growing from under the stable's wall. "So . . . will you stick around?"

He took a second to answer. "I'd like to," he said. "But I have to ask Molly. I have to leave it up to her. The kid's been through a lot these past few months."

"Yes," Kay said. "She has. You think she'll want to live in Oklahoma with you?"

James shook his head. "I'm thinking she might want to move back to Texas. She probably misses her friends."

Kay tried to hide her disappointment. "And your rig?" she asked.

"Gotta fix it up first. But I imagine I'll sell that, too. Time to be a dad. Maybe try out the old nine to five."

"It would be a shame for a man like you to waste his talents."

"What talents are those?"

"Finding the truth."

"Ah," James said. "If anything, I think I proved just how out of practice I am."

Kay shook her head. "I don't think anyone else could've done it."

"Well, thank you," he said. "I do love a compliment from a beautiful woman."

Kay's skin got hot all over. She stared hard at James. Silently willed him to acknowledge this thing between them. Finally, he looked up into her eyes. Then, he looked at her lips. Kay moved first. The kiss was warm and soft and perfect. She forced herself to pull away after a minute, but she didn't want to. She was already out of breath.

"If I stay," he whispered, "do I get more of those?"

"I'm not getting between a man and his daughter," Kay said, their foreheads still touching. "Find out what Molly wants. Then we'll talk."

77

JAMES

JAMES WAS NURSING a beer at the closest bar to Sanostee—
an hour's drive away. He wanted Wayne to enjoy himself.
They had both had quite the summer.

"I wonder how long I'll be hauling water onto the reservation," Wayne said.

"Wish I could tell ya," James said. "The bastards."

"Jackson's asked the governor to have the president
declare the site a federal disaster area."

"What'd the governor say?" James asked.

"What do you think?"

"Told Jackson to go kick rocks?" James guessed.

"You know it."

James shook his head. "We sure made an enemy out of
Jackson, didn't we?"

"Suppose so," Wayne said.

"Guess we never even needed to involve him."

Wayne threw back the rest of his beer. "It's all right," he
said. "Jackson's no friend of mine anymore, anyway."

"You'll have your hands full with that case."

Wayne grinned. "I could always use some help."

James stared into his beer. "I've got to talk to Molly."

"You're actually considering staying?" Wayne asked.

"Kay asked me to," he said.

"Ah. That'll do it. Won't stay for old Wayne, though."

James laughed. "All right, wise guy. So what if I do stay? Then what?"

"Then you can help me with these damn restrictions they put on me. You know help from Sanchez and the state only goes so far. On their terms. When it's convenient."

"What would I do? I can't join your force, can I?"

"You could, but I'd rather you didn't. You'd be much more helpful on your own."

"Some kind of private eye?" James laughed a big laugh. He remembered Kay calling him that.

"That's right, cowboy. I'd refer folks to you. They'd trust my judgment. They'd pay you. And if it involved Diné but was off the reservation, we could work together."

"Huh," James said. He sat up straighter on his barstool. The big, dirty mirror behind the bar made them look like mirages. "There seems to be enough trouble around here."

"Be an investigator again," Wayne urged him. "You know you'd enjoy it. Better than bumping down Route 40 every day and sleeping in that cramped cab."

"That life's behind me anyway with Molly here. But if she wants to move back to Dallas, I've got to do that."

"You know Barb and I love having her. She's a good kid. We'd help out anytime. You've got some support here. People who care about her. Care about you both."

"I appreciate that, Wayne. I've grown to love you all, too.

Hell, I might even be kinda sad if you put Cecil Cody behind bars."

Wayne chuckled. "His boy did more damage to your head than I thought."

James took off his hat and touched the top of his head. "I like it this way," he said.

78

MOLLY

ONE DAY, Molly had asked Barbara if people were allowed to climb the rocks.

"Of course you can!" Barbara said. "Just not with those shoes."

"What shoes would I need?"

"Boots. Good boots. Don't want to step on a snake out there."

So Molly asked James, and James took her boot shopping, asking her to walk from one end of the store to the other in each pair.

"How's that feel?" he'd ask her.

He was very pleased with the pair she chose, and now, as they stood atop one of the rock formations that Molly had been staring at for months, he admired them again.

"Those are some good boots. You could do anything in those boots. How do they feel?"

Molly smiled. He sounded like her friends' dads back in Dallas. Corny. Practical. It was strange finally having a dad. She hugged his waist with one arm.

"Thanks for coming up here with me, Dad. The boots feel great."

He wrapped his arm around her shoulder and squeezed.

"I'm sellin' the rig. And the house in Oklahoma."

"You are? Why?"

"Because I've got you now. I don't need a rig."

"But you need a job! And where are we gonna live?"

"Where do you wanna live?" he asked her.

Molly gazed out at the land below them. Green bushes and trees dotted the valley. Swirling paths of white and gray and pink and orange lined the rocks as if they'd been painted on. Everything around her was hard and soft, sharp and smooth, all at the same time. It felt like a dream.

"Here," she said.

"Here?" James asked, dropping his arm. "You're sure you don't wanna go back to Dallas?"

"Can you get *this* in Dallas?" she asked.

"You're not a city girl anymore, then?"

Molly shrugged. "I didn't know what I was until I came out here. I've only ever lived in the city. But I really like it out here."

"What about your friends?"

"We can visit, right?" she asked. "You don't mind driving." She nudged him, and he smiled.

"Of course we can visit," he said.

"That school was the worst sometimes," Molly went on. "Everyone was trying to win. Have a nicer house. A nicer car. I like how it's slower out here. It fits me."

"I can understand that," James said. "So you wanna live here? Right here? On the reservation?"

"Can we?" Molly asked. "I don't want to be too far from Wayne and Barbara."

"I guess we can find out."

"Maybe Kay can be my teacher." Molly smirked at James and raised an eyebrow.

James laughed now. "Would you like that?" he asked.

She nodded. She would like that. She was fine with James and Kay together. She liked Kay, too.

"Well, then, that settles that," James said.

"What will you do now?" Molly asked.

"Wayne's asked me to open up my own private investigation practice. And I just might do it. I didn't realize how much I'd missed it."

Molly's eyes widened, and a big grin spread across her face.

"Can I help sometimes?" she asked.

"Where else am I gonna find a sketch artist as good as you?"

Molly beamed. She rubbed her palm across the rock they sat on. Felt the silky sand and jagged pebbles on her skin.

"What will you call it?" Molly asked.

James looked at her for a moment. Rubbed his chin.

"How about you decide?"

Molly leaned back on her elbows. Closed her eyes and pointed her face up at the sun.

"Pinter PI," she finally said. "That includes me. Molly Pinter."

"I like that," James said. "I like that a lot."

AUTHOR'S NOTE

On July 16, 1979, more than 1,100 tons of uranium mining waste burst through a ruptured dam into the Puerco River in Church Rock, New Mexico. It is still the largest nuclear accident in the history of the United States. The people affected by this massive spill were those living on the Navajo reservation, and therefore, the incident has gotten much less attention than other nuclear spills (for example, the Three Mile Island spill near Middletown, PA, that happened only months before Church Rock).

As explained in this story, the United Nuclear Corporation was aware of the weak spots in the dam and made little effort to reinforce it. They were also aware that they were in violation of the Uranium Mill Tailings Radiation Control Act of 1978 by failing to line the dam. The waste was full of both radioactive material and hard metals such as cadmium, aluminum, magnesium, manganese, molybdenum, nickel, selenium, sodium, vanadium, zinc, iron, and lead, as well as sulfates.

US Representative Morris K. Udall testified before

Congress that at least three state and federal agencies had had "ample opportunity" to predict the spill. This served as inspiration for the United Nuclear Corporation ex-employee's report to state police in the story, though there is no evidence that anyone from the company reported the impending spill.

The effects of the spill were numerous, including documented cases of burns on the skin of Navajo children and adults—some of which required amputation—and the deaths of herds of sheep and cattle. An estimated 1,700 people lost access to clean water, and just two years later, the state of New Mexico and the federal government stopped providing drinking water to the reservation. The Navajo Nation spent a total of $100,000 on clean drinking water. The three community wells that served Church Rock had been closed prior to the incident, due to high levels of iron and bacteria. As referenced in the story, the governor of New Mexico refused to have the president declare the site a federal disaster area, which would have provided many more resources to the Navajo people.

There have been no ongoing epidemiological studies done at Church Rock, though studies have shown that some cancer rates among the Navajo population are significantly higher than the national average.

While Linda Morris is a fictional character, there are thousands like her on or near reservations across the country. Because of jurisdiction, communication, and reporting issues, missing and murdered indigenous women receive far less attention and resources than their non-native counterparts. According to the Urban Indian Health Institute, the murder rate for native women living on reservations is ten times higher than the national average. If you are interested in donating your time or money to this crucial issue, please check out The National Indigenous Women's Resource Center or the Coalition to Stop Violence Against Native Women.

The sale of the Big Buck Boleman Ranch in this story was loosely based on the real life Big Boquillas Ranch sale of 1987. Elements of the 1991 US District Court for the District of Arizona case *United States v. Brown* also inspired parts of the book.

Though I researched reservation life and Diné history thoroughly, this story is not meant to be a comprehensive account of life as a Native American or life on a reservation. As a white American of European descent, I couldn't possibly provide the authenticity that a native writer can. I encourage readers to seek out these stories, as well. Some of my favorite Indigenous authors are: Louise Erdrich, Tommy Orange, Diane Wilson, Arlene L. Walker, and Morgan Talty, though there are countless others.

The horrific massacre at My Lai, which is mentioned at various points throughout this book, was a real event, occurring on March 16, 1968. An estimated four hundred Vietnamese citizens—mainly old men, women, children, and babies—were raped, tortured, and killed by United States troops. Soldiers of Charlie Company testified to these horrific acts, including the CC and ace of spades carvings on the bodies of the victims. The only person who served any time for their crimes was a Lieutenant William Calley, who was imprisoned for a total of three weeks at Fort Leavenworth and then for just over two years in an apartment at Fort Benning, where he was allowed frequent visits from his girlfriend and to keep three different pets. Calley not only participated in the massacre but also forced at gunpoint reluctant members of his company to participate as well.

While researching for this story, I read the following books: *Four Hours in My Lai* by Michael Bilton and Kevin Sim; *Diné: A History of the Navajos* by Peter Iverson; *The Official US Army Law Enforcement Investigations Handbook Updated Edition: The Manual of the Military Police Investigator and CID Agent*; *CID: Army Detectives in Peace and War* by Hubert Marlow; and *Covert Ops: Those Were the Days My Friends; The Lives and Times of Covert US Army CID Agents* by Bill Ivory.

Thank you to my wonderful beta readers: my husband, Tim Boyle, who is always the first to read and the first to help me reconstruct my messy first drafts; Latia Sanders, my honest and dedicated friend and supporter; my brother-in-law, Joe Boyle, who is one hell of an Army investigator; and my colleague, Arlene L. Walker, who is a fantastic writer and who reads with a critical eye. I am so grateful to you all for being such an excellent team.

And of course, last but not least, the Bookstagram community! You all continue to amaze me with your dedication and support. Thank you so much for your lovely reviews and shares. It means the world to me.

COMING SOON: BOOK [2] IN THE PINTER
P.I. SERIES

GEORGE NEVER THOUGHT they'd come for him. It was all part of the arrangement. But now, here he is, running again. He feels a little foolish.

One week into the search for George and Adriel, James Pinter gets a call to help with a new case. A judge and his wife are found dead. The bodies are found in two separate locations, but the deaths are assumed to be connected.

When James finds evidence linking the victims and George Morris, he realizes that Adriel is in even more danger than James could've possibly imagined.

ABOUT THE AUTHOR

Born and raised in Finksburg, Maryland, Lisa Boyle received bachelor's degrees in journalism and international affairs from Northeastern University in Boston, Massachusetts. Lisa has held many different jobs over the years from cheesemonger, to educator at the U.S.S. Constitution Museum. Lisa lives in South Carolina with her husband and daughter. Her debut historical fiction book, *Signed, A Paddy,* was the recipient of the 2022 Eric Hoffer First Horizon Book Award, the 2022 Eric Hoffer Historical Fiction Book Award, and the 2022 IPPY Best Regional Fiction, U.S. Northeast, Bronze Medal. *In the Silence of Decay* is Lisa's first crime fiction novel.

Sign up for Lisa Boyle's newsletter, and be the first to know when the sequel to *In the Silence of Decay* will be released.

Did you love this book? Don't forget to leave a review!

Printed in the USA
CPSIA information can be obtained
at www.ICGtesting.com
JSHW030722241023
50728JS00008B/25

9 781736 607763